Praise for Den

"A tragic accident gives a divorced couple a second chance at love in the warmhearted third installment of Hunter's Riverbend Romance series (after *Mulberry Hollow*) . . . Readers looking for an uplifting Christian romance will appreciate how Laurel and Gavin's faith helps dispel their deep-rooted fears so they can find a way to love again. Inspirational fans will find this hard to resist."

—*Publishers Weekly* on *Harvest Moon*

"Denise Hunter has a way of bringing depth and an aching beauty into her stories, and *Harvest Moon* is no different. *Harvest Moon* is a beautiful tale of second chances, self-sacrifice, and renewed romance that addresses hard topics such as child death and dissolved marriages. In a beautiful turn of events, Hunter brings unexpected healing out of a devastating situation, subtly reminding the reader that God can create beauty out of the most painful of circumstances and love from the most broken stories."

—Pepper Basham, author of *The Heart of the Mountains* and *Authentically, Izzy*

"A poignant romance that's perfect for fans of emotional love stories that capture your heart from the very first page. With her signature style, Denise Hunter whisks readers into a world where broken hearts are mended, lives are changed, and love really does conquer all!"

—Courtney Walsh, *New York Times* bestselling author, on *Mulberry Hollow*

"Hunter delivers a touching story of how family dynamics and personal priorities shift when love takes precedence. Hunter's fans will love this."

—*Publishers Weekly* on *Riverbend Gap*

"Denise Hunter has never failed to pen a novel that whispers messages of hope and brings a smile to my face. *Bookshop by the Sea* is no different! With a warmhearted community, a small beachside town, a second-chance romance worth rooting for, and cozy bookshop vibes, this is a story you'll want to snuggle into like a warm blanket."

—Melissa Ferguson, author of *Meet Me in the Margins*

"Sophie and Aiden had me hooked from page one, and I was holding my breath until the very end. Denise nails second-chance romance in *Bookshop by the Sea*. I adored this story! Five giant stars!"

—Jenny Hale, *USA TODAY* bestselling author

"*Autumn Skies* is the perfect roundup to the Bluebell Inn series. The tension and attraction between Grace and Wyatt is done so well, and the mystery kept me wondering what was going to happen next. Prepare to be swept away to the beautiful Blue Ridge Mountains in a flurry of turning pages."

—Nancy Naigle, *USA TODAY* bestselling author of *Christmas Angels*

"*Carolina Breeze* is filled with surprises, enchantment, and a wonderful depth of romance. Denise Hunter gets better with every novel she writes, and that trend has hit a high point with this wonderful story."

—Hannah Alexander, author of *The Wedding Kiss*

"A breeze of brilliance! Denise Hunter's *Carolina Breeze* will blow you away with a masterful merge of mystery, chemistry, and memories restored in this lakeside love story of faith, family, and fortune."

—Julie Lessman, award-winning author

"*Summer by the Tides* is a perfect blend of romance and women's fiction."

—Sherryl Woods, #1 *New York Times* bestselling author

"Denise Hunter once again proves she's the queen of romantic drama. *Summer by the Tides* is both a perfect beach romance and a dramatic story of second chances. If you like Robyn Carr, you'll love Denise Hunter."

—Colleen Coble, *USA TODAY* bestselling author of *One Little Lie*

"I have never read a romance by Denise Hunter that didn't sweep me away into a happily ever after. Treat yourself!"

—Robin Lee Hatcher, bestselling author of *Cross My Heart*, for *On Magnolia Lane*

"*Sweetbriar Cottage* is a story to fall in love with. True-to-life characters, high stakes, and powerful chemistry blend to tell an emotional story of reconciliation."

—Brenda Novak, *New York Times* bestselling author

"*Sweetbriar Cottage* is a wonderful story, full of emotional tension and evocative prose. You'll feel involved in these characters' lives and carried along by their story as tension ratchets up to a climactic and satisfying conclusion. Terrific read. I thoroughly enjoyed it."

—Francine Rivers, *New York Times* bestselling author

"*Falling Like Snowflakes* is charming and fun with a twist of mystery and intrigue. A story that's sure to endure as a classic reader favorite."

—Rachel Hauck, *New York Times* bestselling author of *The Fifth Avenue Story Society*

"*Barefoot Summer* is a satisfying tale of hope, healing, and a love that's meant to be."

—Lisa Wingate, national bestselling author of *Before We Were Yours*

A Novel Proposal

Also by Denise Hunter

Stand-Alone Novels

Bookshop by the Sea

Summer by the Tides

Sweetbriar Cottage

Sweetwater Gap

The Riverbend Romance Novels

Riverbend Gap

Mulberry Hollow

Harvest Moon

Wildflower Falls (available September 2023)

The Bluebell Inn Novels

Lake Season

Carolina Breeze

Autumn Skies

The Blue Ridge Novels

Blue Ridge Sunrise

Honeysuckle Dreams

On Magnolia Lane

The Summer Harbor Novels

Falling Like Snowflakes

The Goodbye Bride

Just a Kiss

The Chapel Springs Romance Series

Barefoot Summer

A December Bride (novella)

Dancing with Fireflies

The Wishing Season

Married 'til Monday

The Big Sky Romance Series

A Cowboy's Touch

The Accidental Bride

The Trouble with Cowboys

Nantucket Love Stories

Surrender Bay

The Convenient Groom

Seaside Letters

Driftwood Lane

Novellas Included in

This Time Around, *Smitten*, *Secretly Smitten*, and *Smitten Book Club*

A *Novel* Proposal

DENISE HUNTER

A Novel Proposal

Published in Nashville, Tennessee, by Thomas Nelson. Thomas Nelson is a registered trademark of HarperCollins Christian Publishing, Inc.

Library of Congress Cataloging-in-Publication Data

Names: Hunter, Denise, 1968- author.
Title: A novel proposal / Denise Hunter.
Description: Nashville, Tennessee : Thomas Nelson, [2023] | Summary: "From
the bestselling author of The Convenient Groom (now a beloved Hallmark Original movie) comes a sweet and sizzling story of a romance writer surprised by her own happily ever after"-- Provided by publisher.
Identifiers: LCCN 2022040203 (print) | LCCN 2022040204 (ebook) | ISBN 9780840716590 (paperback) | ISBN 9780840716606 (epub) | ISBN 9780840716613
Classification: LCC PS3608.U5925 N68 2023 (print) | LCC PS3608.U5925 (ebook) | DDC 813/.6--dc23
LC record available at https://lccn.loc.gov/2022040203
LC ebook record available at https://lccn.loc.gov/2022040204

Printed in the United States of America

23 24 25 26 27 LBC 5 4 3 2 1

ONE

Open your romance novel with a character who is *in medias res*—in the midst of things.

—*Romance Writing 101*

Sadie Goodwin's literary dreams came to a shuddering halt in the middle of her favorite SoHo coffee shop. She blocked out the honking traffic and the May sun streaming through the plate-glass window. Blocked out the lively chatter and cheerful tinkling of a spoon inside a coffee mug and leaned toward her agent. "I'm sorry, what did you say?"

The corners of Gillian's eyes tightened in a wince. "Rosewood House is canceling your contract."

"But . . ." Sadie's tongue froze for a long second, all the ramifications kicking in.

No more books. And she'd already turned in book three. Was halfway finished writing book four.

No more Lonesome Ridge stories.

To say nothing of more practical matters like rent and

utilities and chocolate chip cookies. Then there was that hefty book advance she'd already spent. She pushed away thoughts of money. "But I'm getting such great reviews, and *Sundown at Lonesome Ridge* was a finalist in the—"

"Those things don't matter. It's all about sales—and yours are dismal."

Gillian had never been one to soften a blow, but *yikes*. That was brutal.

"But it's a four-book series . . ."

"I know how much you love these characters. It's a terrific series—it really is. I knew it was special the moment I read book one. But your novels aren't selling and the publisher wants to cut their losses."

Sadie's lungs emptied. She couldn't go back to writing obituaries. She just couldn't. It would be the death of her. (Yes, she'd heard all the puns.) Sure, she had her job teaching art at the elementary school, but that hardly kept her in the black. She had to share a tiny Queens apartment with a roommate just to make ends meet.

And what of her family's legacy?

"I know you're disappointed."

Understatement of the century. Her friends and family were so proud of her, especially her dad's family. To them she was a star, rising from the ashes of her grandfather's literary career. Maybe she didn't see herself in quite that light, but she'd thought she was headed toward a promising career, a steady income . . . basically her dream. Now the aforementioned star seemed to fizzle across the sky as it plummeted to planet earth.

She had to regroup. There had to be something she could do. "Can you sell the rest of the series to another publisher?"

"You know it's already been rejected by everyone else.

Westerns are a tough sell in this market. Rosewood thought the granddaughter of Rex Goodwin might stand a chance. And they liked your writing so much they were willing to take a risk—but it didn't pay off."

Sadie suspected the publisher, especially the marketing team, liked her connection to Rex Goodwin the most. She took an unsteady sip of coffee, gathering the courage to ask the money question. She'd read her contract, after all. Albeit three years ago and with stars in her eyes, every sentence of legalese a pure thrill. But maybe they'd have a heart. After all, she'd done nothing wrong.

She swallowed hard. "What about the advance?"

"Unfortunately, you'll have to pay it back."

Sadie squeezed her eyes shut. Talk about adding insult to injury. Her series was discontinued and her readers (all twelve, apparently) would never know the end of the Lonesome Ridge story. And she was now up to her eyeballs in debt. Harsh. Her advance had amounted to ten thousand per book.

"But not on the last book, right, since I turned in a perfectly good—?"

"I'm afraid so."

Twenty thousand dollars. A veritable fortune.

Sadie rubbed the back of her neck where sweat had broken out. She visualized her bank statement and the $311 balance. "I don't have that kind of money, Gillian."

Her agent patted her hand. "I know you must be overwhelmed. But the good news is they offered what I feel is a fair solution and a wonderful opportunity as well."

"Okay . . ." She'd take anything at this point. What did she have to lose?

"You know Erin and the entire team love your writing. You bring such emotional depth to your stories. Your characters are nuanced and authentic, and your plot twists are compelling. You truly do have a special gift."

Why did she feel like a hog being led to slaughter? "Um, thank you . . ."

"While the team wasn't enthusiastic about your sales, they are open to the idea of seeing something else from you."

Her stomach shot upward like a helium-filled party balloon. "Oh! That's great news. It's funny you mention that because I've had this other series idea brewing for months. It features a desperado-type character who arrives in a gold-mining town along the banks of the—"

Gillian shook her head. "No, kiddo. They absolutely will not entertain the idea of another western. They were wondering if you'd be willing to . . . make a slight genre shift."

She couldn't imagine what they'd want. But the thought of paying back that advance tightened around her neck like a noose. "Oh. Well, sure, I guess so. Maybe something like a mystery? I could alter the plot a bit, advance the story a hundred years—there was already sort of a suspense thread in there, so I could just—"

"No, Sadie. I guess what they're asking for is less a shift and more of an . . . about-face. But I know you're up for the challenge. I believe in you—that hasn't changed."

Well, that was nice to hear. Sadie searched for her familiar sunny side and smiled. "Thank you. Okay, I'm all ears. What is it they'd like me to write?"

"They'd like to see"—Gillian waved a hand, voilà style—"a romance novel!"

Sadie blinked. Opened her mouth. Closed it again. "A romance novel."

"Boy meets girl, boy gets girl, boy loses girl, boy gets girl back . . . You know the kind of thing."

Yes, yes, she knew what a romance novel was. She was just . . .

"We believe you could bring something special to the genre with your emotional depth and creativity. And, Sadie, this is a genre that sells. They're offering a one-book contract, due date of September first. I know that's fast, but it's a chance to earn back that advance. You'd earn out and the royalties would eventually pay off, I'm sure of it. And I have every confidence you can write a romance novel that readers would clamor for."

Sadie had no such confidence. She'd never even read one, for crying out loud, unless you counted *El Paso*. None of her Lonesome Ridge books held even the slightest whiff of romance—despite a complaint or two about that in readers' reviews.

Romance. Her mind conjured up a dreamlike image of a couple running toward each other in a field of wildflowers, arms extended, hair flagging behind them. She envisioned the book's cover—a shirtless man and a scantily clad woman tangled in a steamy pre-kiss moment.

Her face heated. She wasn't the person to write this kind of novel. Or even read them. She'd had a poor example in the romantic love department. Her parents, though still together, were often at odds. She'd had a front-row seat to their roller-coaster relationship. Not exactly inspiring.

These were all valid reasons Sadie had no business writing a romance novel. But no reason was as compelling as this: at the ripe old age of twenty-six and a half, Sadie Goodwin had never been in love.

Sadie spotted her best friend, four dogs in tow, on the other side of the park. Caroline's brown hair fluttered in the wind, and as Sadie approached she realized it had been her friend's image she'd superimposed on that hazy romantic scene she'd envisioned earlier. No wonder. Caroline was the epitome of a romantic heroine: beautiful, smart, and personable. Basically a man-magnet.

Sadie had met Caroline their freshman year at Pace University and they immediately bonded. Caroline had been born and raised in the Big Apple, where Sadie had always dreamed of living.

Upon graduation they rented an apartment in Queens. Sadie got a job at the local elementary school and Caroline managed the corner coffee shop. It was there she met the love of her life, Carlos, whom she'd married last year about the same time she started her dog-walking business.

"Milo, stop that." Caroline tugged at the leash. "You can't eat Honey's collar. It's not nice and it doesn't taste good. Go potty, Finn. Yes, I know you haven't—" Her eyes lit up as she spotted Sadie. "Oh, hey, you made it. How'd it go with your agent? Your text was maddeningly lacking in detail."

She'd had the entire train ride from Manhattan to reflect, and there was no point beating around the bush. "They're canceling my contract and I have to pay back my advance."

"No!" Caroline enveloped her in a hug, their jackets and scarves—and four leashes with dogs attached—squished between them. "Honey, I'm so sorry. I don't understand. Your stories are so good, and you have super reviews online, and you won that contest and everything. They're crazy if they don't want to publish you."

Sadie waited for the commercial airliner to pass overhead before she tried to speak. "Apparently none of that matters."

Caroline drew back, her green eyes widening. "You know what? You should self-publish the rest of the series. You could use the profits to pay back your advance."

"If Rosewood's marketing plan couldn't sell my books to the masses, I doubt sticking them up on Amazon will do the trick. They did offer me another contract though—one book in a genre completely outside my wheelhouse. I can't even entertain the idea. It's ridiculous—they want me to write a *romance novel*."

The dachshund had wound itself around Sadie's leg, and the large black poodle was getting up close and personal with Sadie.

"Honey, no!"

"Yep. 'Fraid so."

"No, Honey's the dog." Caroline tugged the leash, forcing the poodle away from Sadie. "Can we walk? They're getting restless and I need to stimulate Finn's digestive system because—well, long story."

They started off at a stroll.

"You could totally write a romance novel, Sadie. I have every faith in you."

Sadie snorted. "Right. Like I have so much experience in that department."

"Well, have you ever been in a gunfight? Drifted down a raging river on a whiskey barrel? Have you taken down a bad guy with nothing but an empty gun and a broken leg? No? Well, you wrote about all the above in a way that was so real it had me on the edge of my seat. You are seriously gifted, girl."

Sadie waved her off. "That's different. It's . . . guy stuff. It's like the old westerns I watched with my grandpa. I could see it all in my head. You can't see romance in your head. It happens on the inside."

Two twentysomething guys passed them, practically breaking their necks for a better view of Caroline.

"Of course you can see it in your head. It's a guy giving a girl a single rose. A devastating breakup scene at a ritzy restaurant. Some grand gesture to win her back."

Sadie stabbed a finger at her friend. "See? You know all that because that's your life. *Your* life, not mine."

Caroline slid a pointed look at her. "Well, maybe it would be yours if you gave a guy half a chance."

"Can I help it if I end up with all the duds? If there's absolutely no connection? I know zip about love and romance, Caro."

"You watched *You've Got Mail* with me that one time."

"I fell asleep."

"You had a long day. Listen, westerns have a formula, right? Stop it, Milo." She petted the corgi. "Romance novels do too. You just have to follow the formula. You can totally do this. What choice do you have anyway? You have to pay back the advance, right?"

"Did I mention the September first deadline?"

"Well, you'll have the whole summer to write it. Three months is long enough, isn't it? You wrote *Lonesome Ridge* in ninety days."

"That was different. I know how to structure a western. I've read a million of them."

"Just start with an alpha male, throw in a meet-cute, and end with an HEA. You'll nail it."

"I have no idea what you just said."

"Start reading romance novels—I know all the best ones. Good boy, Milo! Watch some rom-coms. By the time school's out you'll be ready to go."

Apparently Gillian and Caroline both believed she could do this. Maybe she could. All she had to do was study the genre and follow the formula, right? She didn't have to *love* it. She just had to *do* it.

A jet went streaking over their heads, reminding her of her noisy apartment, just a stone's throw from LaGuardia, with thin walls and thinner windows. Not to mention the construction project that had been going on next door since the Revolutionary War.

"I'd really have to be homed in on this. You know how distracted I can get."

Caroline glanced up at yet another jet taking off for parts unknown. Then her gaze darted back to Sadie, her eyes widening. "I just had the best idea. What if you had a place to write—someplace quiet where there were no distractions? No people. No planes or construction. Just you and your laptop and a warm, sunny beach."

"Do you own a time-share I don't know about?"

"No, but my mom does. Well, not a time-share, but remember that beach cottage she bought last summer in South Carolina?"

"Isn't she using it?"

"Just a few weeks in the winter—she's dreaming of retirement. It's a duplex, so she's renting out one side, which basically pays the mortgage so she doesn't have to rent out her own living space. Smart, right?"

"I won't be able to afford that, Caro. I'm barely making ends meet as it is."

"Please, as if Mom would take your money. She was just saying the other day how she hated the idea of her unit sitting empty. This would be perfect. You could write on the deck! Just think—nothing but sea breezes and sunshine. That's right, Finn, buddy, go potty."

The dog led her to a nearby copse of trees, where he sniffed around.

Sadie considered her friend's suggestion. Maybe she could write this novel if she really focused and applied herself over the summer. Plus the beach was romantic, wasn't it? Inspiration at her fingertips.

She could use these last few weeks of school to bone up on romance novels. Then once school ended, she could drive to sunny South Carolina and start writing that novel.

Another jetliner screeched by, and she sent it a withering look. Her roommate had promised she wouldn't hear them after a while. She was a liar. Plus she'd failed to disclose the aforementioned construction. A least Julie was quiet—when she was even home. She toiled toward her master's degree by day and worked nights at a fancy steak house that kept her out late.

"Good dog, Finn! Mommy will be so happy." Caroline led the tangle of dogs back toward Sadie, then they headed toward the street. "So what do you think?"

"I think if by some crazy chance your mom would let me crash at her beach house for free all summer, I'd be nuts to turn it down."

Caroline beamed. "Great then! You're going."

"Um, you might want to run this plan by your mom first."

Caroline held up her phone in a fistful of leashes. "Already done. She's sending you the information now."

Sadie's phone buzzed and she checked the screen, skimming the note from Mrs. Miller as realization settled in. "She really said yes."

Caroline transferred all the leashes to one hand and gave Sadie a sideways hug. "You, my friend, are headed to Tucker Island, where you're going to write a fabulous romance novel—and I can't wait to read it."

TWO

A *meet-cute* is a charming encounter between two characters that leads to the development of a romantic relationship.

—*Romance Writing 101*

Every ounce of Sadie's travel fatigue fled at first sight of her summer digs. She pulled into the driveway on the right side of the blue beach cottage. The two-story home perched cheerfully on a mound of sandy soil, its white shutters and trim a lovely contrast to the periwinkle siding. There were two small stoops, two front doors, both crisp white and devoid of windows.

"We're here, Rio. Oh boy, are we here."

She shut off the ignition and stepped out, drawing in a lungful of salt-laden air. A sultry breeze lifted the few wisps of hair that had escaped her ponytail on the twelve-hour drive. Two seagulls soared overhead, crying out their welcome.

"Thank you, birdies." She glanced back at the house, unable to keep her smile from spreading. "Yes, I think this will do."

She leashed her Maltipoo and set her on the ground. The caramel-colored dog tugged on the leash, nose down, eager to explore her new playground. After she pottied, Sadie said, "Let's go see the house. Wanna go see the house? Yes, we do."

Leaving her things for later, Sadie unlocked the front door using the keypad. Once inside she shut the door and let Rio off the leash. The hot air that washed over her didn't even put a dent in her mood. The pictures of the place hadn't done it justice. The open floor plan led to a wall of windows at the back side of the house where a sliding door welcomed visitors onto the deck. Evening light flooded the immaculate space. Splashes of pastel blue complemented the muted tones of gray and white. The décor was simple, the furnishings lush.

"Wow, are we lucky or what?" After sharing a miniscule apartment for an outrageous sum, this place felt as big as a palace.

Rio was busy scampering around, sliding across the floor in her excitement to see it all, experience it all right now.

"Do you like it? Isn't it so beautiful?"

Sadie walked across the wooden plank floor, running her fingers across the butter-soft sofa as she went, then kicked on the air-conditioning. The unit clicked on, then began to hum quietly. The cottage still smelled of new construction—Mrs. Miller had had it completely renovated when she'd bought it last year.

Rio yapped at a floor sculpture of a pelican.

"Be nice to our new friend. She won't hurt you."

Leaving the dog to her explorations, Sadie continued her

tour upstairs where the lavish master bedroom exceeded all her expectations. She threw herself onto the king-size bed and stared up at the ceiling fan. "God, You are so, so good." While the fan whirled in slow circles, she made a snow angel on the puffy duvet, then hopped up to investigate the master bath.

The focal point of the room was a floor-to-ceiling-tiled shower featuring multiple showerheads, including a giant rain showerhead. In the corner a clawfoot tub stood, a fluffy white towel draped over its side.

She flashed the tub a wink. "See you later, big guy."

She exited the master and peeked into the tastefully appointed guest room, then headed back downstairs. It was so quiet here—no jets soaring overhead, no cars honking outside her window, no toddlers screaming through the wall, no jackhammers clanging. Just the quiet sounds of the surf. In other words, perfect for writing. Thoughts of starting the dreaded project tightened her neck muscles.

Rio approached, tiny tongue lolling, brown eyes sparkling. "We just won't think about that right now, will we?" She dug her phone from her pocket and called Caroline, who answered with, "Have you started writing yet?"

"I just got here. This place is beautiful." Sadie spun in a circle, arm flung out, head flung back.

"Glad you like it."

Sadie got dizzy and fell into the welcoming arms of a plush leather armchair.

A dog yipped in the background. "I'm at the Fraziers'. Their Chihuahua doesn't want to go out. Oh well, I'll just carry her. Did you get unpacked? Meet your new neighbor?"

Her friend knew her all too well. Mrs. Miller said the duplex neighbor would probably keep to himself. He was renting for the summer. "Not yet. Maybe I'll bake him cookies or something."

"Don't get sidetracked. You have a book to write."

"It's the weekend. I'm not writing till Monday."

"Fair enough. Trixie, no! Don't piddle on my favorite . . . Ugh. Gotta go. Have fun."

"See ya." Sadie ended the call. Time to bring in her things.

"Know what this place needs, Rio? Some happy music." She retrieved her smart speaker from her purse and started the Spotify Summer Romance playlist she'd set up during a free hour her last week of school. She'd been overdosing on romance material of all kinds. Couldn't hurt.

The happy riffs of "Summer Nights" from *Grease* began. She cranked it up, beaming broadly. "That's better. Let's go get our things. Will you help carry the bags? No? Oh, you're so useless. Why do I keep you around?"

Back at the car, Sadie loaded down: rolling suitcase, snack bag, Kate Spade laptop bag, and one heaping box of romance novels. She hadn't read them all—certainly not the more, shall we say, smutty ones with the clinch covers. She waggled her head, proud of herself for knowing the correct term. She'd come a long way in the past month. But no way was she writing *that* kind of romance. She still had no idea what the plot would be, but it would definitely qualify as a slow-burn romance that culminated in a simple kiss. She was already pushing her boundaries far enough.

It was a handful with a wriggling Rio on the end of the leash, but she made it back to the porch in one trip. She let go of the rolling bag and turned the knob . . .

It was locked.

Sam Ford glared at the wall separating his unit from the one next door. The upbeat music had started just a few minutes ago, but it was already on his last nerve. And that was before the dog started up. Some ankle-biting menace, no doubt.

So much for the nice, quiet neighbor the owner had told him was moving in for the summer. The whole summer. He put the throw pillow over his head. *A little peace and quiet, God. Someplace to lick my wounds. Is that too much to ask?*

The room went blessedly quiet.

Before he could draw a breath, another bebopping tune started up.

Growling, he got up and went out to his deck where the sounds of surf covered the music. He glanced across the house-length deck, which he would now have to share.

Well, he could do a little rearranging, couldn't he? Give himself some privacy. And he should do it before the woman came out here and noticed he'd moved things around. Wouldn't want to get off on the wrong foot. He glanced at the three planted palms. Those would suffice. He lined them up across the middle as a sort of barrier and stood back to survey the change. Better than nothing. It certainly got the point across: this side is mine; that side is yours.

That done, he took the three deck steps into the backyard and walked around his side of the house to where he'd done a little landscaping for Mrs. Miller. He'd dug up the scrubby old bushes, put down a weed barrier, and added some nice crepe myrtle. The bushes would grow well here in the sunlight, and the blooms added a splash of bright pink. He ambled toward the front of the house, his feet sinking in the sandy soil as he went.

The cottage itself was in immaculate condition—the front of it holding plenty of curb appeal. Though he couldn't have cared less about the appearance of the house when he'd rented it. Anything that got him out of Bluffton suited him just fine.

A knocking sound came from the direction of his stoop.

He stepped closer and saw a woman jabbing the doorbell, not once but three times.

"Can I help you?"

She jumped and whirled around. Stepped back. Tripped over a little dog who let out a squeak.

Sam foresaw the inevitable and darted forward. But he was too far away.

"Oh!" The woman stumbled down the steps, landing on the sandy soil on one knee as a box spilled from her arms and rained down a cache of books.

She looked behind her. "Rio!"

The dog, tail wagging furiously, jumped up on the woman and licked her chin.

"My poor baby, are you okay? I'm so sorry." The woman checked over the mutt.

"You okay?" Sam asked because that seemed the appropriate thing to say.

"Sure, sure, I'm fine." She blew a strand of short blonde hair from her face and shot a smile his way. "You scared me there. You must be my new neighbor. I expected you to show up on the other side of the door." She let out a nervous laugh. "Well, hi. Hello." She waved, too, in case the verbal greetings weren't clear enough. "I'm Sadie."

"Sam."

"Right. Nice to meet you, Sam."

He knelt to help with the books, and his gaze dropped to the cover in his hands. Wow. Those were some impressive pecs. He lifted a brow as he dropped the book into the box.

Sadie's cheeks bloomed with color. Long lashes swept down over brown eyes. "Oh, thank you, but I've got it. These are just a little bit of, uh, research. I'm a writer. Not a romance writer but . . . Well, I am now sorta, I guess. But that's a long story. We'll just put these away." She shoveled the books into the box and stood.

She came up no higher than his shoulders. Speaking of small, her dog jumped up on his leg, making it only as far as his knee.

"I locked myself out—can you believe it? Been here all of two seconds, and I left my phone in the house when I went out to unload my car and . . . Well, I don't have the code memorized yet, of course—and it's on my phone, which is in the house. This is Rio, by the way. I named her after the vivacious character of Rio McDonald from *The Outlaw*. She was played by Jane Russell."

She took a breath. "Sorry, I'm talking too much. I do that sometimes." She shifted the box to one arm and stuck out her hand. "Nice to formally meet you. We'll be neighbors all summer after all."

He had a feeling this woman sent peace and quiet running for the hills. He sighed as he took her hand. "Pleasure." Her hand was small and dainty in his. Smooth skin. And she had some kind of clean, sweet scent that teased his nose. Maybe her hair.

"Down, Rio. Get off the nice man." Sadie grabbed the dog's leash and gave a little tug. "She's harmless, I promise. And I'll keep her out of your side of the yard. I'm sorry to bother you, but can I use your phone? I need to call Mrs. Miller to get the code."

"I know it."

Her brows pulled together. "You know it?"

"The code. Had to go over and check on the hot water heater last week."

Her eyes widened. "Oh! That's great then. I was already going to bake you a cake—you know, just to be neighborly, but now I'll make you cookies too."

His head was spinning a little. He hadn't heard this many words in the two weeks he'd been here. "That's not necessary."

She waved him off. "Oh, I don't mind. I love to bake. But I'll get out of your hair if you tell me the code?"

"It's 124060. Can I carry the . . . ?"

But she was already skirting the dog and carting her box and belongings off toward her own stoop. "Thank you. Sorry to have bothered you. I'll memorize the code this time. Go on, Rio, that's a good girl." She leaned close to the keypad, pressed some buttons, straightened, and twisted the knob.

She threw him a smile over her shoulder. "Worked like a charm. 124060. See? I already have it memorized." She juggled the box, leash, and suitcase as she navigated the screen door. "Thank you again!" She gave another wave. "I'll bring those goodies over in the next day or two."

"You don't have"—he began, but she was already gone—"to do that."

THREE

Weave the threads of your characters' pasts into their present-day lives in a way that deepens the story.

—*Romance Writing 101*

Sadie woke to the bright morning sunlight puddling on the white duvet. In the distance the surf *whooshed* against the shoreline in rhythmic waves. *Aah.* She could get used to that sound. When she stirred, Rio hopped up and licked her face. "Good morning, baby. Did you sleep well? Yes, you did. Do you have to go potty?"

Rio froze, all but her fluffy tail, her brown eyes lighting.

"Let's go! Let's go potty." Sadie grabbed the dog and stopped by the restroom on her way downstairs. Wearing a pair of leggings and a tee, she deemed herself presentable enough to make an appearance outside.

She detoured to the kitchen. "Just a minute. Gotta get the

coffee going . . . Mommy needs her caffeine. There we go. See, that didn't take long. Now we're ready to go outside."

She slid open the patio door, and Rio dashed past her onto the deck and down the steps to the fenced-in yard. Sadie followed. She'd be sharing the long wooden deck, which was divided by three potted trees. She peeked around the palm branches and spied her neighbor reading the newspaper with his morning coffee. "Well, hello! Good morning."

He turned her way and muttered what she assumed was a greeting before returning to his paper.

Someone needed more coffee. Then again, he hadn't been all that friendly last night either. As she walked down the deck steps, she remembered that Mrs. Miller said he kept to himself.

Maybe she should ask the woman about changing the key code since Sam knew it. She'd thought of that about midnight when a sound awakened her. But it was only Rio, gnawing on Sadie's favorite sandals.

While the dog sniffed around in circles, Sadie took in her surroundings. The deck itself took up most of the yard. The beach began only twenty feet or so beyond the property line. There were already joggers and shell seekers at the waterline. She couldn't wait to put on her tennis shoes and hit the shore. Mrs. Miller had said it was a busy public beach—the access pathway cut through on Sadie's side of the house.

She glanced back at her neighbor, still locked in on his newspaper. His thick black hair was sleep tousled, and his facial hair hovered between five-o'clock shadow and beard. He was a handsome man, if a little on the Neanderthal side, with thick prominent brows set over amber eyes—lion eyes. And even though they were barely into June, his olive skin was already bronzed.

Well. She should probably stop staring.

Rio found an agreeable spot by some sort of palm bush. "Good job, Rio."

After a cup of coffee she'd go for a nice jog, then she'd head to the store and stock up on food—including the ingredients to make Sam's goodies. Nothing softened up a neighbor like baked goods. She'd make those today so she could focus on plotting her book tomorrow. Her publisher wanted the proposal ASAP.

The thought of that task overwhelmed her. Not to mention the large sum of money she owed. Her stomach twisted hard.

She mentally took a brush and painted a swath of black across those worries. She didn't have to think about any of that today. Today, she'd jog on the beach. She'd enjoy every last one of those shower jets. (She'd had a delightful soak in that clawfoot tub last night.) And then she'd bake a yummy cake for her neighbor.

Sam flipped the burgers, the savory aroma of grilled beef making his stomach growl. He'd been inside most of the day—hiding, let's face it. Because little Miss Chatterbox and her tiny yappy dog had taken over the deck this morning.

First she'd appeared straight out of bed to let the dog out, then she'd returned, minus the dog, in a pink leotard thing that left little to the imagination. She'd come back from her jog glowy somehow and with more energy than she'd had before.

She had left the house for a while—groceries, she'd said—but by then it was lunchtime and he decided to go to Vinnie's Diner. By the time he'd returned, so had she.

So he stayed inside for the afternoon and watched the Braves lose to the Reds. Then he fell asleep on the sofa because he'd lain awake half the night reliving that ridiculous meeting with his neighbor and wondering how he was going to avoid her the whole summer when she so clearly wanted to talk, talk, talk. He wasn't necessarily opposed to conversation in general, mind you. He chatted with clients and . . . well, family.

Okay, he wasn't the talkative sort. But he'd come here to think and take a *break*, for crying out loud. If today was any indication, he'd be tiptoeing around his neighbor all summer.

The yapping dog had woken him from his nap just after five, and he remembered the beef patties he'd bought at the Piggly Wiggly. Weighing the odds of having another encounter with Chatterbox, he grabbed the beef and slipped outside.

Now said burgers were done and—bonus—he'd managed to avoid the woman next door. Congratulating himself, he set the burgers on the loaded buns and shut off the grill.

"Hi, neighbor." Sadie slipped out onto the deck, wearing her third outfit of the day—white shorts and a blue top that bared her shoulders.

Nice shoulders, he had to admit. As far as shoulders went. Since when did he care about shoulders? "Hi."

"Wow, that smells great. Do you grill out a lot?"

He grunted and glanced back at the grill. "Came with the house. You can use it if you want."

"I didn't even think about that when I went to the grocery. But to be totally honest, I've never used a grill. My apartment doesn't have a balcony, and I wouldn't even know how to turn it on."

He grabbed his seasonings and turned for the door. "It's not difficult."

"Well, maybe you can show me sometime. I love a good grilled steak. Are they hard to cook? How do you know when they're done the way you like? I prefer medium myself, and I use a thermometer when I'm broiling, but I don't know if the house has one of those."

Mercifully his phone buzzed in his pocket. He pulled it out. "Gotta take this."

"Oh, sure. Enjoy your dinner."

He slipped back inside and checked the screen. Sighing, he set his plate on the coffee table and took the call. "Hi, Mom."

"Hi, honey. What are you doing? Is this a good time to chat?"

"Sure. What's up?"

"Well, I was just checking to see how things are going on the island. I hope you're not working too hard." Before slinking away from Bluffton, he'd committed to maintaining the yards of their island customers. Far be it from him to let down his dad and cousin.

"It's okay. I prefer to stay busy."

"I know you do. But I worry about you, honey."

"I'm fine, Mom. I just needed to . . . get away for a while. I haven't had a vacation in four years."

"This is hardly a vacation. And you can't tell me the invitation didn't have something to do with your sudden departure."

His eyes cut over to the drawer where he'd shoved the unopened envelope. "They sent it through the mail." Even though he saw Tag every darn day at work.

"I'm sorry, honey. I know this is hard. I'm not excusing what he and Amanda did, but what's done is done, and we have to figure out a way to make this work. He's family."

Sam wished his cousin had remembered that last year when

he was busy moving in on Sam's girlfriend—practically his fiancée at the time. But Tag was his mom's sister's son, practically his parents' surrogate child. Tag, a year younger than Sam, had attended the same school, played on the same baseball team. Both had started working for Sam's dad at Ford Landscaping in the summers. Both had become full-time employees upon graduation.

"I hate what happened, honey. I hate that you're hurting. But he feels just terrible, and so does Amanda."

Not bad enough to stop their wedding though.

"Are you planning to go?"

There was the question of the hour. He didn't even know the wedding date as he hadn't opened the invitation—and his family hadn't exactly included him in the planning. "I don't know, Mom. I don't really want to think about that right now."

A brief pause followed. "I understand. Is there anything I can do? You know I love you and I just hate this for you." Sadness tinged her voice. This debacle had splintered the family—but that wasn't his fault.

"I love you too, Mom. I'm fine. I just needed a breather." From that remorseful look Tag wore like a naughty puppy. From the sudden halt of conversation every time Sam walked into a room.

"All right, honey. But maybe we can meet up for lunch next week, just you and me. I could come to the island . . ."

He'd gone out of his way to refrain from mentioning exactly where he was staying. But he could meet her at a restaurant. "Sure. I'll text you."

He wrapped up the call, but the conversation was still heavy on his mind. He'd managed to go most of the day without thinking about this mess, but the call brought everything back.

He grabbed his plate where the two burgers sat cooling. His appetite was long gone, but he grabbed one of the sandwiches anyway and opened his mouth to take a big bite.

The doorbell rang. Glancing that direction, he glimpsed Sadie through the sidelight. She saw him, too, darn it. Grimacing, he set aside his cold burger and went to the door.

"Hi, sorry to bother you," she said when he opened the door. "This is for you." She shoved a huge domed container at him. "It's a Bundt cake. I couldn't believe the kitchen was equipped with a Bundt pan, but there it was. I have a thermometer too—I just checked, so I guess a grilled steak is in my future. I hope you like chocolate."

She sure did have a wide smile. And eyes that matched the cake. "Thank you."

The dog yapped through the wall.

"I should get back to Rio, but just send the container back when you're done. And thank you again for your help last night. Do you have a favorite kind of cookie? I should've asked before I went to the store, but I think I have plenty of ingredients no matter what your preference."

"I don't—you don't have to do that."

She waved him off. "Oh, I don't mind. I'll give you a few days though—the cake's kind of big for one person."

Was she hinting at an invitation? He was not inviting her in.

"Well . . ." She shrugged her bare shoulders.

His eyes caught on a faint smattering of freckles there.

"I'll let you get to it. See you around—'cause we do share a deck and all."

"Yes, we do." He tried for a smile but she was already bounding off his stoop.

"See ya."

"Bye." He shut the door and glanced down at the cake. Was there anything to that cliché about drowning your feelings in chocolate? He was about to find out.

FOUR

The best ideas often come when you least expect them.

—*Romance Writing 101*

"You can totally do this. You just need to focus."

Sadie glared at the cursor blinking on the blank document of her laptop. She sat at the counter, facing the kitchen. She had her favorite handy-dandy guide to writing romance novels. Her box of novels. A folder with a writing schedule she'd printed out at home. A pencil. A highlighter.

What she didn't have was a plausible plot. Or a plot of any kind, really.

Come on, God. I need an idea. And since there's three of You and You did create the entire universe, I'm sure it's within Your skill set to give me just one tiny idea.

It wasn't as if Sadie hadn't plotted a novel before. She had, three and a half times. This was just a different genre. Instead of a lone cowboy, a trusty steed, and shoot-outs, there would be an alpha hero (apparently the best way to go), a spunky heroine, and a happily ever after.

Some of the books recommended starting with characters. In a western the hero was focused on the antagonist. His job was to rescue the victim by defeating the villain. In a romance the plot revolved around the relationship of the hero and heroine. Very different things, though the hero of both genres might demonstrate some of the same positive traits.

She rubbed her eyes. Maybe she should just start with a good trope instead. Friends to lovers seemed to be a reader favorite. Or enemies to lovers since it came with inherent tension. Marriage of convenience also held some appeal. She rapped her fingers on the white granite countertop. Once. Twice. Three times.

Music.

"That's what's missing." She dug out her phone and started her romantic playlist. The slow melody of "Can't Help Falling in Love" came on. There. Now she was ready to write. Ready to create. Ready for an inspired light bulb of an idea to flash on above her head.

She stared at the cursor. Tapped her fingers in time with the blinking.

Her phone buzzed with an incoming text. Caroline. Sadie grabbed at the lifeline.

How's it going? Caroline asked.

Great! I love it here. Everyone's so friendly. I met three people at the grocery store alone. But don't worry, I'm already hard at work. (She was trying to think positively here.)

I'll leave you to it then. Have a productive day. Wish me luck. I have the Bernards' dog all week.

The terrier had unfortunate tummy troubles. Good luck!

"Please don't go," Sadie said to the empty house, still staring at her phone. "I need an idea. Stay and help me."

But the three dots were gone and so was Caroline.

"What kind of friend are you anyway?"

Elvis crooned on with that velvet voice. Sadie frowned at the screen and returned to her list of songs. This was very romantic but it wasn't conducive to brainstorming an idea. She needed something more up-tempo, something more exciting, and . . . She scrolled through her playlist, stopping at "Baby Love" and tapping the screen.

She nodded as the tune filled her kitchen. "Much better."

Twenty minutes later she was digging through the novels she'd enjoyed, trying to figure out which trope appealed most. She had to be invested in this story if she was going to spend all summer writing it. If she was going to put anything on paper her editor and readers would actually want to read.

She grabbed a familiar book. She'd liked the spunky heroine. She was a bit of a tomboy and ran a ranch, which made her kind of a modern-day cowgirl, didn't it? Sadie could write about a woman who owned a ranch—no, inherited a ranch. But the property was . . . in default. Because bad guys had been rustling the cattle, and the heroine could do a stakeout and catch them. A gunfight would ensue and . . .

She dropped her head to her keyboard. No, no, no. She had to stay far away from anything that smacked of westerns. She had to starve this line of thinking. "No more westerns—books or movies. You're banned for the entire summer, Sadie Goodwin!"

Come to think of it, she hadn't read a romance novel in more than a week. Probably best to keep the romantic train of thought going. Which meant she needed to find the local bookstore and purchase more.

Her soul perked up at the thought of doing something else—anything else. "No, you're working," her more mature self admonished. "Or trying to work or something."

She was going to end up with a whole library of romance novels. She turned and scanned the living room. No bookshelves. Oh well.

She picked up the pencil and tapped it.

Tapped it some more.

Tapped it in time with the blinking cursor.

Then with the beat of the song.

Picked up the highlighter and tried to tap in time to both. Nope. She was no drummer.

She heaved a sigh and slammed both writing utensils on the countertop.

Rio glanced up, startled.

"Sorry, baby. Mommy's just frustrated."

This wasn't working. She needed a change of scenery. This whole stove-top backdrop wasn't doing a thing for her. She had a beach outside. It wasn't a distraction—it was inspiration. What had she been thinking?

"We're moving this party outside, girl. You wanna go outside? Yes, you do!"

She let Rio out, then gathered her things and carried them outside, taking two trips to do so. Her neighbor was nowhere to be seen—probably a good thing since he and his biceps were a bit of a distraction.

She set herself up at the circular table, facing the ocean,

because why not? The chair was comfortable enough. The view inspiring.

"Okay, Sadie, *think*. You have a spunky heroine and an alpha hero. You need a setting." Why not the beach? Tucker Island? Or someplace more exotic. More tropical. Readers loved to travel in their minds.

"St. Lucia."

She'd been to the beautiful island two summers ago on a seven-day cruise (bon voyage, book advance!) she'd taken with Caroline and two other friends. St. Lucia had been her favorite because of the lush mountains that edged right up to the crystal-blue sea. She opened a website about the island to refresh her memory and perhaps spark an idea.

Twenty minutes later she was sold on the island but fresh out of ideas.

"Good morning!" a woman called from the public-access pathway not twenty feet from where she sat. The woman was perhaps thirty and carried a baby on her back.

"Good morning. Oh, what a cutie. How old is he?"

"Eleven months." The woman paused not far from the deck, tucking her short black curls behind her ears. "It's his first beach day. We moved to the island last week, just a few streets over."

"How wonderful. You'll love it. Everyone's so friendly here. Where are you from?"

"Oh, not far, just Savannah. My husband got transferred and we decided to move here instead of commuting."

"Not too shabby. I'm just here for the summer, visiting from New York. I'm Sadie."

"Keisha. And this is Marcel."

"Nice to meet you both." Rio barked, making Sadie chuckle. "And this is Rio, who clearly wants an introduction."

"So cute. What kind of dog is he or she?"

"She's a Maltipoo. A real sweetheart."

"Well, you'll both be seeing a lot of us this summer. I'm finally trying to lose my baby weight, and I figured taking walks on the beach would be the least painful way to accomplish that."

"You can't beat it really. But you look fabulous. I'd never have guessed you had a baby at all if he wasn't strapped to your back."

"Thanks. I'd hoped the pounds would just fall off, but not so much. Of course, I've mostly just been sitting around the house reading and nursing, so what did I expect?"

"What do you like to read?"

"Fiction mostly. Thrillers, mysteries, romance. I'm not too picky."

"Well, I've got a whole box full of romance novels here for the taking if you need reading material."

"Thanks. I might take you up on that. Well, we should get going before the crowds arrive. It was nice to meet you, Sadie."

"You too. Have a nice day."

"Thanks, you do the same."

Well, she sure was nice. And what an adorable baby with those chubby cheeks and that cap of black curls. And maybe Sadie could put all these books to good use. Of course, if she could trade them in for new ones, that would be even better. Was there a used—?

Something flashed in her mind. Not a plot idea (more's the pity), but still a good idea. She could put up one of those Little Free Libraries right here on the property. People would take a book and leave a book. She'd make use of the novels she didn't need anymore and have fresh reading material practically delivered to her doorstep. What a great idea. She loved it.

She sent Mrs. Miller a text asking if it would be okay to put up the structure—just for the summer. She could put it on the property but close to the path so beachgoers could pick up something to read on their way past. Genius!

An older couple passed on the path, wearing floppy sun hats and loaded down with beach chairs.

"Good morning!" Sadie called.

"Morning," the woman said.

"Beautiful day," her husband added.

"It sure is."

They walked on.

Her phone buzzed and Sadie reached for the welcome distraction.

Love that idea, Mrs. Miller said. Go for it!

A rush of adrenaline had her searching for *Little Free Library*. They sold kits online, but she didn't want to wait that long. She'd passed a hardware store on the way home from the grocery. She could make something as simple as a box. She knew how to use basic tools—after all, she was the son her father never had. And she'd helped her grandpa around the ranch, mending fences, fixing porch rails.

She closed the website . . . and there was her blank document.

"Back to work." When the sun popped out from behind a cloud, she brightened the screen so she could see it better in the sunlight—in case she ever had anything to write.

"This is nothing new for you, Sadie. You know how to do this."

Come to think of it, when she plotted her westerns, her best ideas hadn't come when she was sitting at her laptop. They'd come when she was busy doing something else. Like taking a walk or a shower or going for a drive or . . .

Building a Little Free Library.

FIVE

Tension between the hero and heroine will keep your reader flipping pages.

—*Romance Writing 101*

Hey, Butthead."

Sam smiled at his sister's greeting—one of the many derogatory names she'd assigned to him during her childhood. Who was he kidding? At seventeen Hayley was still a child.

"Hey, Meatball. What's up?"

"When are you coming back to Bluffton? And don't tell me you're playing it by ear."

"Miss me?" The doorbell rang and he got up to intercept the pizza.

"Mom's dragging me into all the wedding stuff, and now that she doesn't have you to fuss over, she's asking how my grades finished up."

"How *did* your grades finish up?" He opened the door and

nodded at the teenaged guy as he withdrew his wallet, phone tucked to shoulder.

"Don't change the subject. Where are you? At least let me come stay with you until this stupid wedding's over. Have a heart."

"I need a breather, Sis. I had them to myself for fourteen years before you came along. You'll survive. Also, why do you sound like you're in a hole?"

"I'm hiding in the pantry."

"Thanks," he said to the delivery guy, then took the pizza and shut the door.

"You ordered pizza, didn't you? Come on, invite me over. I'm drowning in tulle and candles, and I don't even want to go to this stupid wedding."

"You have to go. Tag's your cousin."

"So you're going too, then?"

"I don't know yet."

"Seeing them together makes me want to vomit. She's been calling me *Cuz*. Um, hello, you dumped my brother and I don't like you. How are you coping with all this?"

"By running away from home. Listen, I appreciate your allegiance, but the wedding is happening and we'll all have to adjust."

Her voice dropped to a whisper. "I have to go. Mom tracked me down—save me!"

The line went quiet and he pocketed his phone, then settled at the dining room table with his pizza. He opened the lid, drawing in the fragrant aroma of Antonio's deep-dish meat lover's pizza with extra cheese. Eating your feelings wasn't such a bad way to go.

A sudden piercing sound cut through the room.

What the . . .

He looked around, trying to detect where the shriek of death was coming from. It seemed to reverberate off the walls. Was that . . . a *saw*?

He pushed back the pizza, got up, and peered out the sliding glass doors. Movement from the corner of his eye drew his attention. Sadie was on the deck, hunched over . . . He couldn't see what she was doing as the planters were in the way.

No doubt about it though. She was using a saw. A circular saw if his ears hadn't failed him. What in the world was she doing? The ear-shattering noise stopped as she finished the cut—or sliced off a finger. He had a hard time believing a woman who couldn't navigate porch steps might be handy with tools.

But no, the screeching started up again. Okay, she was apparently fine.

Sexist pig. His sister's voice cut into his thoughts. Yeah, maybe. But it wasn't every day you saw a five-foot-nothing woman handling a circular saw.

But, hey. None of his business.

He went back to the table and tried to enjoy his pizza, but the earsplitting sound soon tweaked his last nerve. He'd been working in the hot sun all day, mowing lawns, mulching beds, trimming bushes. After a nice, long shower he just wanted to enjoy his supper in quiet. Was that too much to ask?

Apparently.

Three hours later Sam turned up the Braves game yet again and glared at the sliding glass door. It was dark now, but Sadie had turned on the porch light, which glowed amber on account of the nesting turtles. It was ten o'clock at night and some people had to work in the morning. Some people weren't on vacation for an entire summer—who did that anyway?

A text buzzed. His sister. Neck deep in burlap. Burlap!!

His lip twitched, then dropped as he thought of the upcoming wedding. The plans were going forward. What, had he thought they were going to cancel the thing? Did he want them to? That would be an unequivocal yes. Not because he wanted Amanda back. He was no slow learner. But the thought of having her in the family for the rest of his life sucked rotten eggs.

He glanced at the drawer where he'd stashed the invitation, debating whether to open the thing. On one hand, seeing the formal invite might make it more real. On the other hand, hadn't he just advised his sister to adjust to reality?

The high-pitched wail of the saw cut through the room yet again. Seriously. What was she thinking?

He cut his gaze back to the drawer. What the heck. He was already in a bad mood.

He made a beeline for the drawer and jerked it open. Grabbed the invitation and ripped the thing open. The fancy card felt like velvet, but the color resembled regurgitated peas. He steeled himself before reading the fancy script.

Mr. and Mrs. Daniels, along with Mr. and Mrs. Borden, joyfully invite you to the wedding of their children, Amanda Rose Borden and Taggart Ryan Daniels . . . He cut his gaze down to the date.

July third.

Only a month away. And really? Fourth of July weekend?

How inconsiderate. But of course, Amanda wouldn't think of other people or their holiday weekend plans.

The piercing shriek of the saw started up again. He tossed down the invitation and strode to the door.

Sadie ran the saw over the pencil line for which she'd meticulously measured. After a couple of flub-ups she had one last cut and she'd have all the pieces ready to assemble. She'd found instructions online, and the man at the hardware store had been very kind, helping her locate all the supplies.

A pair of feet appeared at her side.

She jumped, letting loose of the saw, which went silent. She pulled her safety glasses up and met Sam's gaze. The lighting wasn't very good, but she managed to make out his rigid stance, crossed arms, and dark scowl. "You scared me."

"Isn't it a little late for this?"

She glanced at her watch. "Oh goodness. How'd that happen? I'm so sorry. This is my last cut, I promise, then I'll be done making noise. I have to return the saw in the morning and I didn't want to use it at dawn. This thing is pretty powerful, huh? I'm making a library."

He rubbed his temple. "What?"

"A library. You know, one of those Little Free Libraries you see standing in neighborhoods or by a church or whatnot. I'm gonna put it up over there by the public-access path—isn't that a great idea?"

His scowl deepened.

"Well, one last cut and I'm all done. Sorry to interrupt your evening. Thirty seconds—really. I promise."

He pierced her with a lingering scowl, then turned and skirted the plant divider.

"Good night!" she called.

He slipped inside the house.

"Well. Somebody's grumpy."

SIX

An *alpha hero* is powerful, protective, and confident. Though at first glance he may appear single-minded or heartless, make no mistake—he's a complex and layered man.

—*Romance Writing 101*

The cursor blinked accusingly at Sadie.

She sat on the deck, coffee at her fingertips, listening to Rio snoring under the table. The late-afternoon sun had already dropped behind the house, and a warm breeze ruffled Sadie's hair. The surf pounded the shoreline in that soothing, rhythmic way, and her friends, the seagulls, shrieked overhead.

She glanced at her Little Free Library, which she'd painted blue and white and screwed to the fence post right at the edge of the pathway two days ago. She planned to shingle the roof as the abrasion from the wind and sand would erode the paint.

Every day people commented on it as they passed and

stopped to peruse the titles. Books came and went. Her new friend, Keisha, came by each day with her adorable baby. She'd borrowed a book and brought another back the next day. Sadie fielded questions about the books themselves and the way the library worked. She'd finally added a hand-painted sign that said *Take a book, leave a book.*

But no one was on the path now, and Sadie was sitting in front of her laptop with a still-blank document. It had been almost four full days now, and she'd made little progress. Okay, *no* progress. But now that her library project was finished, she could lock in and focus on this plot.

She glanced down the beach where a couple played in the surf. The woman dunked him under the water, and he came up under her, lifting her on his shoulders while she squealed and clung to his head.

Was he an alpha male? None of the men in her life fit the mold. The male teachers at her school were more scholarly. Her dad was definitely a beta. Her grandpa, while certainly a man's man, had been talkative and gentle.

She had a sudden vision of her neighbor storming out onto the deck a few nights ago. Definitely alpha behavior. She had no idea if he was protective, but he was certainly assertive. And he was the strong, silent type, wasn't he? Had hardly said twenty words to her in five days.

Did she dare use Sam as her alpha prototype? She glanced down at her blank document, desperation knotting her stomach. Why, yes, she would.

She jotted a few notes: *swarthy-skinned, muscular frame, black hair, rugged, facial hair.* She remembered those lion eyes and wrote that down too. Her hero would be staying at the beach too. On vacation? Could a romance develop in a week or two? That sounded challenging, not to mention unlikely.

Maybe he could be taking a leave of absence—or he could be independently wealthy. Those billionaire books appealed to some women. But not Sadie, so maybe not a billionaire romance.

Perhaps she should consider the heroine. She could be—Sadie glanced back at the house—sharing a duplex with the hero? A little familiar, yes, but everyone advised writers to "write what you know." And this she knew—she was living it after all. Maybe her living situation would even spark ideas for her story.

She read her notes. Okay, great. She was getting somewhere. At least the page wasn't blank anymore.

The slide of a door alerted her to Sam's presence. He stepped out onto the deck, still wearing his work uniform. The pale gray tee sported the same logo as the truck and trailer in his driveway. The shirt was paired with khaki shorts and dirty tennis shoes.

"Howdy, neighbor." When he glanced over she gave him a big smile and a wave.

"Hi."

"Finished working for the day?" She glanced at her watch. "Oh goodness, it's dinnertime already." She'd wasted almost the entire day.

She hadn't seen much of him lately. He'd been gone—working, she presumed—from dawn to dusk. And he tended to stay inside once he returned home.

He lowered himself into a chair and pulled off his shoes and socks. At least, that's what she thought he was doing. It was hard to see around those trees. And more was the pity, because she could get ideas just by observing him. (Not exactly a burdensome proposition.)

He cupped the back of his neck—was he stressed, or were his muscles strained from work? She'd also seen him rub his temples a time or two. Did he have chronic headaches? And then there was that low, throaty voice of his. And let's not forget the biceps. She wasn't likely to.

"Did you see my library?" She pointed toward her masterpiece. "People have been checking out books already."

He grunted and settled back in his chair.

Hmm. The alpha male grunts. She noted that in her document. Then she got up, wandered over to her library, and took a peek inside. She straightened the books. Someone had placed a newer beach book inside. Looked like her next romance read. She pulled it out and shoved the door closed. Time to think about dinner.

Dinner took longer than expected. She decided on spaghetti and Caesar salad, which required a quick grocery run. Once home, she washed and chopped the romaine, shredded a block of parmesan, and whipped up a dressing with a recipe she found online. She browned the beef, boiled the pasta, and cheated on the sauce with a jar of Prego, which she spiced up with fresh herbs.

By the time she finished eating, the sun was setting. "Wanna go outside, Rio? Gotta go potty? Mommy's favorite girl, aren't you? Yes, you are." Sadie rubbed her ears affectionately, then slipped outside and set her down.

The dog took off, nose sniffing the air.

Surprisingly, Sam was still reclining in the same chair, feet propped on the railing, eyes closed. Sleeping, perhaps.

Sadie followed Rio into the yard. The beach had emptied while she'd been inside, everyone going home for their own meals.

Leaving Rio to do her business, she wandered over to the library and checked inside again. She felt quite possessive of the structure, like an actual librarian.

"I'm a little librarian." She snorted.

Ah, a new book. She pulled out the title—a hardcover edition of *Christy,* which sported a nice burgundy cover featuring nothing but the title and author's name, Catherine Marshall. The book was either old or made to appear old, she couldn't tell which.

She'd never actually read the novel, but she'd heard of it. She was tempted to give it a read, but no. She needed to stick to contemporary romance if she was ever going to get this book finished.

Still, curious, she opened the cover, taking a moment to smell the pages, because why not? She flipped through and frowned. Something was wrong. The middle pages were cut out and something was . . .

Something nested inside of a hidden compartment.

A black velvet box.

SEVEN

Telling the story from the hero's and heroine's points of view allows the reader to view the story through two pairs of eyes.

—*Romance Writing 101*

Sadie gaped at what appeared to be a jeweler's box. What was inside it? Almost before finishing the thought, she reached for the container. Her fingers trembled as she grasped and tugged—the thing was in there tight. Finally she pried it free and snapped open the lid.

And gasped again.

A gorgeous solitaire diamond gleamed back at her. An engagement ring! Her heart threatened to pound right out of her chest. Who would put a ring inside a—?

Her mind flashed back to a Facebook post she'd come across recently in one of her book club groups. A member's fiancé had proposed by hiding an engagement ring inside her favorite novel.

She glanced down at the ring. But how had it ended up here, in her Little Library? Someone must've made a terrible mistake. She scanned the beach. Maybe whoever had left the book was still on the beach. She jogged a few steps before remembering to close the yard gate, ran back and shut it, then took off again. A middle-aged woman sat in a beach chair not far from the waterline.

As Sadie approached the woman, she snapped the jewelry box closed and tucked it back into the book. "Excuse me!"

The woman looked up from her phone.

"Did you leave a book in the Little Library over there?" She held up the novel.

"No, sure didn't."

"Did you see anyone go over that way?"

"No, but I've only been here a few minutes."

Sadie's spirits sank. "Okay, thank you." She was already scanning the beach for other occupants. A male jogger had recently passed by on his way south. An older couple strolled the waterline, heading north. No one else was sitting on the beach as far as she could see.

Sometime in the past hour and a half, someone had left this book in the library. If only someone had seen—

Sam. He'd been sitting on the deck all this time. Surely he'd seen who'd placed the book in the library.

She struggled through the deep sand and back up the pathway. Rio met her at the gate, but Sadie was in a rush to reach the deck. She barreled around the tree divider. "Sam! Sam, did you see someone stop at the—?"

His dark brows furrowed over narrowed eyes. She'd obviously awakened him from a nap.

"Sorry," Sadie said. "I'm sorry to disturb you, but did you see who put this book in my Little Library?"

What bee was in her bonnet now? He'd been in the middle of a nice nap wherein he hadn't been dreaming or thinking about or cursing his cousin and ex-girlfriend. "I was sleeping."

"Right, right. I'm sorry to wake you, but before that did you happen to see anyone on the pathway? Anyone coming or going at all? It's really important."

His gaze focused on the book she waved around like a maniac. Seemed like everything was really important to her. The dog, Fifi or whatever, jumped into his lap and licked his face. Blech.

"Sorry." Sadie lifted the dog from his lap and set her on the deck. "Go play, Rio, that's a good girl. So did you see anyone? Just someone passing by maybe, in the past hour and a half since I went inside?"

He blinked the sleep away and tried to think. "I don't know. Maybe there was someone. I wasn't really paying attention."

"Male? Female? Old? Young?"

"I don't know. I can hardly see out that way." He gestured toward the trees. "What's the big deal? It's just a book."

She cracked open the spine and extended it dramatically, pages up.

He blinked at the unexpected interior. What the—?

"There's a ring inside that box—an engagement ring! This"—she shook the book—"was supposed to be somebody's proposal."

"Proposal?"

She rolled her eyes. The golden hour made them a pretty

caramel color. "A man tucks an engagement ring into a hidden compartment inside a woman's favorite novel and presents it to her, then gets down on bended knee and asks her to marry him—a *proposal*."

"That's a thing?" Her dog squatted on his side of the yard. Perfect.

"Look it up. But whoever left the book couldn't have possibly known the ring was in it. And now some poor guy's proposal is ruined!" She removed the box from the compartment and opened the lid. "Look."

He hitched his eyebrows. Nice. Solitaire diamond, at least a carat and a half. White-gold band. Yeah, he'd done some ring shopping with Amanda.

"We have to find the person who put it there or this guy's proposal will be ruined."

There was no "we" about it. This whole engagement business put him in mind of Tag and Amanda, and that was the last thing he wanted to think about. "Well, I didn't see anybody, so I don't know how you're going to find them."

She plopped down on a chair—on his side of the deck—and began flipping through the pages. "Maybe there's some clue inside. Or maybe I can visit the jeweler. They keep records, right?"

"No idea."

"Ooh, it's got a stamp inside the back cover. Moss Creek Community Church."

"What?" That was his church—at least, his parents' church. He and Amanda had attended someplace else, when they attended at all. But now Tag and Amanda attended there with his family.

"You know of it?"

"It's off island, between here and Bluffton."

She fiddled with her phone. "There probably wouldn't be anyone there this late on a Thursday. Here's the number." She tapped her screen and put the phone to her ear. Half a minute later she sighed. "It went to voice mail, darn it. Why would someone leave a library book in my box? Wouldn't they have to return it?"

"I guess you'll find out soon enough. Call tomorrow and ask for Ms. Stapleton's number. She runs the church library."

"Wait, you know her? This is your church?"

"Used to be. But I don't think you'll have much luck finding the owner of that book through her."

"Why not?" She tilted her head, seeming so innocent with those wide brown eyes blinking back at him.

"She's a stickler for the rules." Once, she'd gotten him out of Sunday school to interrogate him about the whereabouts of a book he'd checked out and lost. He wasn't allowed to borrow books from her library again—not even once he'd become an adult.

"A stickler for the . . ." Sadie beamed at him and waved his words away. "You only think that because you haven't seen me at my best. I can be quite charming when I want to be. By the time I finish with Ms. Stapleton, I'll have her eating out of my hand. You'll see."

He almost wished he could be there to see it. "Well, good luck with that."

EIGHT

> The hero and heroine must spend time together in order for their relationship to develop. Devise a valid reason for their togetherness rather than relying on a number of chance meetings.
>
> —*Romance Writing 101*

It had been all Sadie could do to wait for Sam to return home from work the next evening. She'd even given him twenty minutes before she knocked on his sliding glass door. And now he stood there, hair still wet, frown tugging a pair of perfectly nice lips.

"I need your help," she said.

He crossed his arms, eyes narrowing with suspicion. "Is that so?"

"I talked to Ms. Stapleton today. She purged the library and is having a book sale this week—that explains why the person left it in my library instead of returning it—so I caught her at the church this morning."

He quirked a brow.

"She was heartless! Imagine not even trying to return a missing engagement ring to the man who'd bought it. The poor guy could be planning to propose this weekend. He could have made a restaurant reservation weeks ago. They could be here on vacation and leaving soon."

"Those charms failed you, did they?"

She notched her chin upward. "And not very gentlemanly of you to point it out. Are you going to help me or not?"

"Not." He started to slide the door closed.

She stuck her foot in the door before it shut. "Wait! Seriously?"

"It's been a long day. I'm tired and hungry."

"But you have to help me. You know the woman. Surely she'll shoot straight with you."

"She won't even let me check out a library book. Listen. Maybe you're better off working the jewelry store angle."

"I already tried that. Our guy didn't buy the ring at the local store, and they have no way of tracking jewelry bought elsewhere. Ms. Stapleton is the key to this whole thing, and I could just tell she knows where that book came from."

"Maybe she'll inform the book's owner herself."

"I did leave her my number just in case, but I can't count on that. Time is of the essence. Just go with me to the church and have a word with her."

Sadie did her best to appear helpless and hopeful, adding an eyelash flutter for good measure.

His gaze roved over her features. Then his lips pressed together and his jaw hardened. "I'm not attending church there, if that's what you're asking."

"You don't have to. The last day of the library sale is tomorrow from nine till one. Just come with me and have a chat with her. Please?"

"I work tomorrow."

She huffed. "Don't you take a lunch break?" She didn't know what the big deal was. The church was just twenty-five minutes away and only required basic conversational skills. Then again . . .

"I'll think about it."

He had to *think* about it? She kept herself, just barely, from stamping her foot. "Fine. But just remember, some man went to a lot of trouble to make his woman happy, and your friend, the librarian, is the only thing standing in the way of their happily ever after."

"Well, as long as it's no big deal."

She rolled her eyes.

"I'll let you know later tonight. After I've had some food." And then he slid the door closed.

Sam did not want to go to that church. He headed straight into the kitchen and went to work making a deli-meat sandwich.

First of all, there was a chance he'd run into people he knew. They'd tilt their heads and give him those pitying looks he'd really come to hate. Then word would undoubtedly spread to his family that he'd been back to Bluffton. The distance between there and Tucker Island wasn't much, but he wanted to keep that barrier in place for now. He wasn't ready to face all the wedding stuff or commit to the wedding itself. That's why he'd come here to begin with.

That new neighbor of his couldn't seem to help but disturb his peace with her ridiculous noise and imposing requests. Plus there were those sun-kissed shoulders.

He toyed with the idea of calling Ms. Stapleton. But no, he wouldn't get anywhere with her on the phone. He'd be lucky to get through to her in person. He'd always suspected she wasn't a fan of little boys. Maybe she wasn't too fond of men either, as she'd never married.

He finished stacking the turkey, drizzled on some mustard, then topped the sandwich with a bun and added chips to the plate. He carried it along with a bottled water to the dining room table. After working in the heat all day, the air-conditioning felt good. Plus Sadie was probably outside with her yappy dog, just waiting to pressure him about Ms. Stapleton.

He understood. The lost ring was a big deal to the poor chump who was about to turn over his life to some woman who'd probably break his heart somewhere down the line.

Yeah, he was a little jaded.

He picked up his sandwich and was about to take a big bite when his phone vibrated with a phone call. He checked the screen.

Mom.

He was starving and really wanted to forget about his life back in Bluffton for the rest of the day. But that old familiar son-guilt kicked in, reminding him of all the laundry, dishes, and home-cooked meals. Of all the baseball games attended, homework assisted, and prayers sent up. Not to mention the not-so-small matter of the long labor and delivery of his nine-pound-two-ounce body that she brought up on occasion.

He heaved a sigh and accepted the call. "Hey, Mom."

"Hi, honey. Hope I'm not interrupting anything."

"Just got home from work and will be settling in to watch the game here soon."

"Braves are having a good season so far."

"They are."

"Dad said you've had a full week."

He communicated with his dad frequently via text and calls about the business. "We have a lot of customers on the island, and I did a few bids this week too."

"That's good. The business is having a good year. Dad was talking about hiring more help—nothing to do with your leave of absence, just steady business growth. Have you talked to Hayley lately? I think she misses you."

"She called earlier this week and we text here and there."

"By any chance, did she say anything about a boy?"

A *boy*? "No, why? Is some guy sniffing around?" Hayley was a very pretty girl but a bit of a late bloomer. She'd been more interested in sports than boys so far, and that was just fine by Sam.

"No, but she's hiding away in her room a lot. A few days ago I caught her on the phone in the pantry of all places."

No boy then. Just avoiding wedding hoopla, but Sam wouldn't out his sister. "Hmm."

"Listen, honey, I hate to bring up the wedding again, and I'm not calling to pressure you. I just wanted to let you know that we've booked two rooms in your name just in case—just to hold them—for you and a plus one. The hotel block closed yesterday, so I went ahead and did it. If you don't go, Dad and I will cover the rooms."

Yeah, the affair was to be a destination wedding—Anna Maria Island, Florida. A whole weekend event for close family and friends. Wasn't enough that he'd just have to endure a three-hour affair. "You didn't have to do that, Mom."

"We don't mind. Needless to say the airline prices are going to go up the closer we get, but you could always drive instead. Anyway, I didn't call to pressure you."

Of course not. "Thanks for letting me know. I'm still thinking about it."

"And that's just fine. We understand. But if you need someone to take along, Marcee's granddaughter would be more than—"

"No, Mom. Thanks, but no." Marcee's granddaughter had all but humped his leg the last time he'd seen her. She was an attractive woman in her midtwenties, but her aggressive manner put him off, if her nasal voice and banal conversation hadn't already done the job.

"Well, all right then. I guess I should go get some work done on the books."

His mom handled the accounting and billing part of the business. "Sure, Mom. I'll call Hayley soon. Talk to you later."

"Bye, honey."

He set his phone down and tucked into his sandwich, his mind on the upcoming wedding and his mom's efforts to get him there.

Oh, sure, he would go. He'd come to that decision slowly and painfully over the past several weeks. He just wasn't quite ready to admit it out loud. That and having no date. He hadn't been out with anyone since Amanda, despite his sister's efforts to get him onto a dating site. She'd even offered to set up his profile—God forbid—but he just wasn't ready to dip his toe back into those waters.

He didn't have a close female friend who'd help him out, and the only women his business put him in touch with were married or too old for him.

He took another bite. He didn't want to think about the wedding anymore. It would be here soon enough. He'd rather think about anything else—including his pesky neighbor and this quest she'd taken up.

Much as he didn't want to go to the church, he'd probably end up saying yes to that too. She was a little hard to turn down, to be honest, with her genuine delight and hopeful attitude. She had a sweet innocence about her that appealed to him. Maybe because it offset his new cynical nature.

A chair scraped on the back deck and music poured through the thin glass of the sliding door. Something peppy and loud. Her dog emitted a high-pitched bark. She was certainly distracting.

He had a thought.

It was a crazy one really, but . . . what if he asked her to the wedding? True, he hardly knew the woman. Maybe she was a little excitable and talkative, but she might be fun at a wedding. And there was that distraction factor she had going on—he'd need plenty of that for the event.

No reason she'd say yes though, considering he was practically a stranger.

Unless . . . he leveraged this ring quest she was so hot on.

He took a long sip of his water, the idea settling in, feeling not so terrible. Pretty good, really. Having a date for the wedding would make him feel—and look—a little less pathetic. Might stave off some of those sympathetic glances, not to mention all the setups his aunts would no doubt attempt. That Sadie was a knockout wouldn't hurt one bit.

NINE

You might choose to have your hero and heroine working together on a project or working at odds.

—*Romance Writing 101*

Sadie could not focus on this romance novel. She set down the book, turned off the music, and stared off into the distance. The vast blue ocean met the ridge of clouds set low on the horizon. At the shoreline the waves rolled in undisturbed by sunbathers, and closer to the house the palm trees whispered in the wind.

The setting couldn't be more restful, but she was anything but at peace. She couldn't get that beautiful ring off her mind. It was Friday, and what if the proposal had been planned for tonight? What was this poor guy going through? He'd probably turned his house upside down searching for that book. Had he spent his entire savings on the ring? He must be devastated.

She got up and stepped down into the yard, Rio on her heels. "Just checking the box, girl. Stay in the yard."

She didn't know what she was looking for, but the library offered her peace and a connection to other people, and she needed both in equal measures.

She opened the Little Library and perked up at the yellow sticky note with scrawled handwriting hanging from the top shelf. She grabbed the note, hoping it had something to do with that ring.

Thank you for putting up this Little Library! It's so convenient. I took a book today, and I will bring another one back tomorrow to replace it.

Well, that was nice, even if it didn't help solve the mystery. She was glad people were enjoying the library. She took a minute to straighten the contents. Someone had brought a few kids' books, so she put them on the lower shelf with the others. There was nothing new in adult fiction, but a couple books seemed to be missing.

She went back into the yard and played with Rio for a while, laughing when the dog bowed down in her playful pose. She let out a high-pitched bark, then pounced on Sadie's sandaled feet as if they were the enemy. "You leave my good sandals alone now. These are Mommy's favorites. Where's Mr. Mouse, huh? Where's he at? There he is!"

Rio scanned the yard, then dashed toward the pink squeaky toy by the fence. "Bring him here, baby. Let's go inside."

Sadie turned and found Sam on the deck watching her.

She pressed a hand to her chest where her heart threatened to pop from it. "You scared me. I didn't hear you come out." Sadie stepped up onto the deck. *Please, God, let him decide to go with me to see that stubborn librarian.*

The wind ruffled his hair, and the evening light made those

eyes seem like liquid gold. His facial hair had officially reached beard phase over the past week. It suited him quite nicely.

He straightened from the rail and crossed his arms, pinning her with an unswerving look. "I have a deal for you."

"Yes, I'll do it." Had she agreed so readily because she was desperate to find the ring's owner or because of the way he was staring at her, all hot and scowly?

He quirked a brow. "Don't you want to know the deal first?"

"If it has to do with you getting Ms. Stapleton to talk, my answer is yes. What do you want? I already promised no more power tools. Turn down my music? Let you have the deck? Clean up the little gift Rio left in your yard? Okay, I was going to do that anyway."

Thought lines furrowed his forehead. "Maybe I should've leveraged this a bit more."

"Out with it. You already know I'm desperate to get to the bottom of this, so there's no need to play coy. What do you want?"

His gaze flicked over her face, making prickles of heat flare beneath her skin. Awareness zinged between them. Or maybe it was just her. Was it hot out here?

"Go to a wedding with me and I'll talk to Ms. Stapleton."

She blinked. "A *wedding*? Is this a random wedding or a particular wedding?"

"Particular."

"So you're asking me to be your plus one at a particular wedding."

"My cousin's."

"Ah, a family wedding. Interesting. And when will these happy nuptials occur?"

"July third."

"Are you in the wedding party?"

He sighed. "No. Do we have a deal or what?"

"Wait, I have to know more."

"You said yes before I even stated the terms."

"But now I have more information and therefore more questions. For instance, what exactly would my role be as your wedding date? Are you trying to stave off all the aunties' fix-ups? Or would I be pretending to be your girlfriend to make someone jealous with displays of affection? Would we make up a fake backstory of our dating history and—"

"No, you won't be—no. No girlfriend. Just a plus one." A flustered flush crawled up his neck as he muttered something. Kinda cute.

"So I'd just be your date then."

"A friendly date. No displays of affection necessary."

Pity. She pretended to think about that for a beat. "It so happens I'm a very fun wedding date. I don't think you'll be disappointed. Okay, now that we've covered my role in this family wedding, what exactly will your role be in this search for the ring's owner?"

"I told you, I'd talk to Ms. Stapleton."

She pursed her lips. "Hmm. But what if you can't get an answer from her? Then I have nothing and you have a wedding date."

He glowered. "You already said yes."

"I'm just trying to clarify the deal, and I'm thinking if I agree to definitely attend a wedding, I should have some kind of guarantee."

"I can't guarantee Ms. Stapleton will be forthcoming."

"No, I guess not. But you could promise to stick with it and help me figure it out even if we can't pry it out of Ms. Stapleton."

"Why would you want *my* help?"

"I saw how stubborn that librarian is, and I'm not confident she'll spill, even for you. So we may end up having to put our heads together, and two heads are better than one. Plus everything is more fun when someone else is along for the ride." She smiled widely.

He seemed skeptical about that last one. "Fine. Whatever you say. I'm in it for the long haul."

She stuck out her hand before he could change his mind. He took her hand in his big one. His palm was rough and warm against hers. And something about his direct stare made her pulse flutter.

"Then we have a deal," she said.

TEN

When a hero and heroine work toward a common goal, it gives them a shared bond.

—*Romance Writing 101*

Sam's truck pulled into Sadie's driveway at twelve fifteen on the dot. She was wearing her favorite baby-blue shorts, a breezy white top that showed off her newly acquired tan, and wedge sandals.

Sadie grabbed her purse, which held the book, and stuck her sunglasses on top of her head. "I'll be back, girl. Be good. Don't chew on Mommy's things. And be nice to Mr. Pelican."

Rio cocked her head, brown eyes turned down at the corners, tail low.

Sadie reached down and gave her a quick rub. "Don't be sad. I'll be back soon. Go get Mr. Mouse! That's it. Oh, you got him. That a girl. Wish me luck."

She locked up and headed toward Sam's truck. She hadn't made any more headway on her plotting since she'd found the ring two days ago. But she was about to spend time with the inspiration for her hero, so she'd just make some mental notes. That was progress, wasn't it?

She stepped up into the cab, which was a bit of a climb, and closed the door. "Right on time. Let's go find this man."

He put the truck in Reverse and pulled out onto the road. The cab smelled faintly of cut grass and gasoline, but she didn't find the scent offensive. Rather than having the air-conditioning on, he had his window down, allowing the warm breeze to flutter through the cab. He wore his usual work uniform—tee with a logo, cargo shorts, and boots—with a pair of sunglasses that made him seem even more enigmatic than usual.

Her hero would wear sunglasses the way her usual protagonist wore a cowboy hat. Pleased with that small detail, she turned to Sam. "So, you own a landscaping business."

"It's a family business."

"You didn't start it yourself then?"

"My dad did."

"Right. That's cool, working together and all. So I guess it's something you must really enjoy doing then? Mowing grass and, uh, mulching and stuff?"

He spared her a look.

"Well, I mean, some parents push their children into the family business because they want them to carry it on or because they enjoy the idea of working together as a family—or so I hear."

"I like it just fine."

He liked it. Swell. "Do any other family members work in the business?"

"My cousin and my mom."

"The cousin whose wedding we're attending?"

A slight pause. "Yes."

"Do you have any siblings?"

"A sister."

"There's no ration on words, you know. You can use as many as you like. For free even. So . . . how old is your sister? And what does she do if she's not working in the family business?"

"She's seventeen and she does school."

A whole sentence. That was okay. She could carry a conversation quite well. Otherwise it would be a long twenty-five-minute ride. Also, there was that research.

"That's quite an age gap. You must be . . . what, thirty-four, thirty-five?"

"Thirty-one."

Whoops. "The beard makes you seem more mature, I think. And since you didn't ask, I'm twenty-six and an only child and I live in Queens, but I'm originally from Scranton, Pennsylvania. I'm just on the island for the summer. I'm an elementary school art teacher, and I chose that field because I love kids and never want to stop coloring. Also, I love the expression a child gets when she creates something from the heart. I'm a firm believer that anyone can make art, and there's no such thing as a mess-up."

He only grunted, so she continued. "I also write novels on the side—that's a fairly new development but a lifelong dream. My grandpa was the illustrious novelist Rex Goodwin, so I'm trying to carry on the family legacy. Plus I always thought it would be nice to teach kiddos during the school year and write novels during the summer. So that's what I'm doing. Or trying to do. Westerns are my preferred genre, but—"

"Westerns?"

He speaks. She glanced at him. "Yeah, you know, Louis L'Amour, Zane Grey . . . *Rex Goodwin*?"

"I know, I just . . . westerns, huh?"

"I know, most people are surprised by that. But my grandpa had a horse ranch in northern Pennsylvania, and I spent a lot of time there when I was growing up. I loved the way he and my grandma lived off the land. I helped my grandma with the garden. I loved the horses, not to mention the foals. When we weren't working on the ranch, Grandpa and I used to watch westerns together—*Stagecoach, Red River, Butch Cassidy and the Sundance Kid*—so many good ones." He'd been such an influence. Her only regret was that he'd passed before she'd gotten her first contract. But at least he hadn't seen the failure of her first novels.

"I didn't realize they were still publishing westerns."

She snorted. "They're not. Or not hardly anyway, which is why my first two novels sold about three copies each—too bad I don't have a bigger family, huh? So my publishing contract was canceled—midseries—and I'd already written and turned in my third book. Brutal. They did invite me to try my hand at a romance novel, though, so that's my summer project. And when my best friend, Caroline, suggested I write it at her mom's beach cottage, I could hardly refuse. So that's enough about me. How'd you end up at the beach house?"

"Maybe I live there."

"The address of your business is on your trailer—Bluffton—and Mrs. Miller mentioned you were only staying for the summer. So are you having your home remodeled, or are you in between places?"

"None of the above."

She waited, but he didn't add anything. "Okay, I guess you

don't want to talk about that. But as your future wedding date, is that something I should know? If not, that's fine. I'm not one to pry."

He grunted, or maybe it was a huff. "I just needed a little distance from home."

"Because . . ."

"There's some . . . tension."

"Like in the family?"

"In the business. In the family."

"All of the above, huh? I guess they sort of go together, don't they? That's gotta be hard. So you moved out to the island to get away a bit, but you can still get your work done. That's handy. And you can't really beat the view. So this tension . . ."

"Oh my gosh," he muttered.

"I'm just wondering if I should have a little prepping on all this. Will it come up at the wedding? I shouldn't be caught off guard. I want to be a good date."

"If there's something you need to know, I'll tell you. What did Ms. Stapleton say when you asked her about the book?"

She decided to let him change the subject but tucked away that information to use later—maybe even in her book. "Well, at first I approached her and just told her I'd found the book in my Little Library—thought she'd recognize our common bond, you know—and told her I'd like to return it to its original owner. I wasn't going to give her more information than she needed to know. I mean, what if she claimed it was her book and her diamond? So I asked if she might remember who'd donated the book and then she asked why. I told her there was something in the book that made me think the owner had donated it on accident."

"And she asked what that was."

"I see you know Ms. Stapleton pretty well. So I went ahead and told her about finding an engagement ring. I didn't show it to her—it's a big diamond—but she just made a prune face and said she didn't 'rightly recall,' and I could tell she was holding out on me, but accusing her of lying wasn't going to help. So I just told her how sad it was, how some wonderful guy must be so distraught over losing that ring, and how his girl would be deprived of the romantic proposal he'd planned."

"She didn't care."

"She didn't care! I mean, really. How bitter can you be?"

"She's not a trusting woman and she doesn't know you."

"Exactly! But she knows you, so what's your game plan?"

"I gotta stop by my apartment, then we'll head over to the church."

"That doesn't sound like a game plan."

He raised a brow. "Trust me."

Sam scanned the church parking lot as he pulled alongside the street, careful to keep his trailer out of the way. Apparently the church was having a full-on rummage sale, so there were quite a few browsers. He didn't see any family members, just a few people he knew from the church, working the sale. Word would definitely get back to his family that he'd been in town—it wasn't a very big church. Oh well.

He stepped from the truck and met Sadie around the other side. Despite her pestering, he had to admit he admired her determination. Some people would've sold the ring and pocketed the money. That idea never seemed to occur to Sadie.

Plus she hadn't seemed to mind riding in his work truck. Hadn't complained about the smell or poor suspension or rolled-down windows. Maybe she wasn't that bad.

There was Ms. Stapleton, a pale blue outfit hanging from her short, sturdy frame. Her white hair was cropped and winged, and there was that ever-present pair of readers perched where she could peer at you over top of them with those close-set eyes.

Sadie set her sunglasses in place. "Would it be better if she didn't know you were with me since she already turned me away?"

"Doesn't matter." He headed toward the librarian, who stood by the table with the cashbox, standing guard over it and her books like an eagle over a nest. "Let me do the talking."

"Sure thing. Whatever you say."

On the way across the lot, a couple of church members greeted him, giving him that pitying look he was so familiar with. He said hello but didn't stop to chat.

When Ms. Stapleton's gaze fell on him, she pressed her lips together and, yep, peered at him over her readers. "Well, if it isn't Sammy Ford. What brings you by the rummage sale? I haven't seen you in church in months."

"Hello, Ms. Stapleton. Good to see you." That was pushing it. "This is Sadie. I guess you met her yesterday."

"Hi!" Sadie's hand wiggled a little wave. "How are you? Beautiful day, isn't it?"

A frown creased the librarian's brow. "Hello." Her gaze swung back to Sam. "I suppose you're here about that book? That ring? I told her I didn't remember who donated it."

"All due respect, Ms. Stapleton, but we both know no one flutters a page in your library without your knowledge."

"Don't you be smart with me, young man, or I'll tell your mother. Now, do you want to buy some books and support this church, or are you just here to cause trouble?"

"I understand your reticence to disclose proprietary information to a stranger. But you've known me since I was toddling around the church halls. I figured you'd be more willing to help me find out who this ring belongs to." He withdrew a twenty and tucked it in the donation jar.

She sniffed. Crossed her thick arms.

Should've gone with the fifty. "I'm not trying to cause trouble. I just want to know who donated that book. Listen, this is kind of a big deal, so if you could just give me a name, we'll make sure the man gets his ring back."

Ms. Stapleton tilted her head and skewered him with the look that sent lollygagging kids scuttling right back to Sunday school class.

Beside him Sadie fidgeted like a sugared-up kid. But to her credit, she kept her mouth shut.

The librarian was being just as stubborn as Sam had expected. Good thing he'd accounted for that. He reached into his back pocket, pulled out the paperback, and slapped it on the table.

The woman stared down at the book. Her mouth slackened. Then her attention snapped back to him.

"I found it while cleaning out some stuff."

She picked up the old copy of *The Lion, the Witch and the Wardrobe* and smoothed the cover, caressing it the way she probably petted her three-legged cat.

"Shouldn't be any late fees since I paid you for the book years ago."

"That's not the point," she said, but she carefully tucked the book under the table. "I suppose you think you're entitled to that name now."

"I was hoping." He'd been holding on to that book for years, and it pained him to let her have it. Clearly she wasn't the only stubborn one around here.

Ms. Stapleton's spine straightened, making her a full two inches taller. "Fine. It was Mary McAllister who turned it in."

"Mary McAllister? What would she be doing with an engagement ring?"

"She's Joe Graves's daughter. He asked her to get rid of some of his late wife's old things, and high time—she's been gone a decade. That book came in the box she brought, and when I realized we already had three copies of it, I put it in the purge pile. A young woman, tourist by the look of her, bought the book on Wednesday. That's all I know."

Sam recalled some old gossip, bad blood between the widower and Ms. Stapleton. "Thanks for telling me. We'll be sure he gets the ring back."

"You're not doing this woman any favors, sticking her with that ugly last name. But that's not my problem. If you see your mama, tell her I said hello."

He was officially off her naughty list. "Thank you again, Ms. Stapleton. Good luck with your sale."

"Yes, good luck!" Sadie called as they stepped away. "It was nice seeing you again. Have a wonderful day. Thank you." She waved.

"All right, all right," he muttered.

"We got his name." Leaning close, she squeezed his arm. "We got his name!"

He resisted the urge to flex his muscle as her light fragrance teased his nose. “A sixtysomething widower. Not what I expected.”

“Me either, but I’m so excited we found the owner. We’re about to make that poor man’s day. Do you know where he lives?”

“I have to get back to work.”

“Oh, come on, it won’t take that long. He must live nearby. We should’ve asked for his address.”

Sam sighed. “I know where he lives. He’s a customer.” Tag usually serviced his lawn, but Sam had covered for him a couple times.

“Perfect. Let’s just stop by while we’re here and then we’ll be finished. We’ll have done a good deed and make those lovebirds very happy. What do you say?”

“You had me at ‘then we’ll be finished.’”

She gave his shoulder a shove. “Oh, you. I don’t think you’re half as curmudgeonly as you seem. So who’s this woman he’s seeing, and was it just me, or does Ms. Stapleton have some bee in her bonnet about Joe Graves?”

“The woman is Madeline Francis, and there’s definitely a bee.” They reached the truck, and since he was already on the passenger side, he opened her door for her.

“Why, thank you, kind sir.”

It took her a minute to climb up into the cab. She was short—but there sure was a lot of personality packed into that petite frame. And a pair of shapely legs didn’t go unnoticed.

He shut the door and came around to the driver’s side. After buckling in, he started the truck, checked for traffic, and pulled out onto the street.

"Well . . . ," she prompted. "You were about to tell me about the bee."

"Bee?"

"The bee in her bonnet. Come on, you can't just leave me hanging after I cooperated so nicely back there. I didn't say a single word and it was not easy. And what was up with that book you gave her? You'd think you'd presented her with a Holy Grail relic."

He signaled left. "Just an overdue library book."

"How overdue?"

"Ah, let's see . . . it'd be about nineteen years now."

"You kept a library book for nineteen years? For shame."

"It was lost."

"Well, thank God you had it. Clearly you know the way to that woman's heart. I think she would've given you her bank PIN to get that book back."

"She's strangely possessive about that library."

"Now, out with the rest. Tell me about Joe and Madeline and why Ms. Stapleton wrinkled up her nose when she said Joe's name. I want all the dirt."

He rolled his eyes. "I don't really follow the lives of the sexagenarians in the church. But I know Mr. Graves is a widower and Ms. Stapleton is said to have had a thing for him. When he finally got around to asking her out on a date, it went awry and shortly thereafter he started dating Ms. Francis."

"Went awry? I need details. That was one bitter woman back there."

"How am I supposed to know what happened?" Sam turned onto a residential street, found the house, and pulled up to the curb in front of a sprawling ranch. The man would get that ring back all because Sadie had taken it upon herself to hunt him down. He glanced at her wide smile, sparkling brown eyes, and choppy honey-blonde hair. He had to admit, she was kind of cute, all that enthusiasm and goodwill. And if he was honest, he was glad he'd had a small part in this. Glad he'd be here to see it work out.

"Is this where he lives? Nice large lot—and a very well-kept yard, by the way. Is that water behind the property?"

"It's the river."

They exited the vehicle and walked up the long shelled driveway.

She hugged her purse tight. "I'm so excited to return his ring. He's going to be so happy. So relieved."

"Don't pry about his history with Ms. Stapleton."

"I'd never do such a thing. But I might ask about Ms. Francis and his plans for the proposal. After all, we're kind of saving the day here—the least he can do is throw us a few juicy details."

When they reached the narrow walkway to the front porch, Sam set his hand on the small of Sadie's back, letting her take the lead. He wasn't sure why he did that, why he touched her, except that he wanted to. Strangely enough, she was growing on him. She was short and compact and always walked as if she couldn't wait to arrive wherever she was going.

Very different from Amanda's smooth, confident stroll.

He shook the thought from his head as Sadie knocked on the screen door. She toyed with the strap on her purse and shifted her feet around. This was going to make her day. Her week.

The front door opened and Mr. Graves peered out through the screen. "Can I—? Oh, hello, Sam." His high forehead furrowed. "Did I have a service scheduled for today? I didn't have it on my calendar."

"No, sir. This is Sadie, uh . . ."

"Goodwin," she said. "Hello, Mr. Graves. Would you have a few minutes to chat with us?"

"Well, sure, I guess so. I was just sitting out back enjoying the nice weather. Why don't you come on back, and I'll fix you up some of my iced tea?"

ELEVEN

In order for a romance plot to progress properly, you must generate setbacks for your heroine as she marches toward her external goal.

—*Romance Writing 101*

It was taking Mr. Graves forever to return with that tea, and Sadie could hardly contain her excitement. He seemed like such a nice man with his ready smile and friendly eyes. A real southern gentleman. She was about to make him a very happy man, and in return he would make his girlfriend very happy. Sadie did love a happy ending.

She set her hands on the armrests of the Adirondack chair and forced herself to settle down, to take in the peaceful surroundings. A grand live oak, draped with Spanish moss, dominated the backyard. It was the sort of tree that could shelter an entire wedding party on a sunny June day. She could just picture it. From somewhere in the yard a squirrel nattered and a robin tweeted. In the distance the river rippled by and a breeze stirred the air, carrying a hint of lilac.

"Calm down," Sam said. "Jeez."

She stilled her drumming fingers and cut him a sideways glance. "Didn't you know you should never tell a woman to calm down? First of all it doesn't work. Second of all it actually makes things worse. And how can I calm down when I'm holding that man's expensive ring, and my gosh, how long could it take to pour two iced teas? Is he *brewing* it?" Her gaze homed in on his face and she narrowed her eyes. "Did your lip just twitch?"

"You're kinda funny, you know that?"

"Oh, come on. Don't tell me you're not excited. I saw that look on your face when Ms. Stapleton came clean."

He was saved from answering by the appearance of Mr. Graves. *Finally.*

"Here we go," the man said. "Nothing better than a spot of iced tea on a hot, sunny day." He handed them their glasses and settled in one of the other chairs.

Sadie thought she'd burst when Mr. Graves began asking after Sam's family and the business. Sam was actually making small talk. What a terrible time to get chatty. She drained half the glass, then sat on her hands and waited for an opportunity to slide into the conversation.

But Sam beat her to it, segueing into the topic with the skill of a master communicator. "Speaking of your property, I believe we have something that belongs to you." He slid Sadie an expectant look.

"Oh! Yes, that's why we're here, in fact. I'm just visiting for the summer—staying on Tucker Island. And it so happens I'm renting the place next to Sam's—that's how we became acquainted. So this week I put up a Little Free Library—you know, one of those little boxes with books you see in neighborhoods sometimes. I put one up on the property, right on the beach. It's not officially registered yet, but I've already started the process and—"

Sam motioned for her to get on with it.

"Anyway, when I checked the library on Thursday there was a new book inside and, long story short, we tracked it back to you . . ." She whipped the book from her purse and handed it to him. "And here it is!"

He took the book and stared at it for a long moment. His brow furrowed. A breeze swept strands of thinning hair across his forehead.

The moment lengthened. Sadie's gaze flittered to Sam's face, which held the same confusion that now bloomed in her chest.

"I admit my mind's not as sharp as it used to be," Mr. Graves said. "But is this book supposed to mean something to me?"

Sadie's helium-filled hopes fluttered quietly to the ground. The disappointment was so profound she couldn't even rustle up the words to answer.

"This isn't your book then?" Sam asked.

"I don't recall ever seeing it before. Though I have heard of it. It's a beautiful book. You traced it to me, you said?" His gaze toggled between them.

"We traced it to the church first," Sam said. "To the rummage sale. Ms. Stapleton said she received it in a box of books that came from your house."

"Of course. Yes, I donated some of my late wife's things—among them a couple boxes of books." His gaze dropped to the novel. "But I've never seen this one. And Irene—my late wife—she only read nonfiction."

Had Ms. Stapleton been wrong about where the book had come from? If so, they were back to square one.

Sam leaned forward on his elbows. "Ms. Stapleton said your daughter brought in the books. Is it possible she might know something about it?"

"Well, she cleaned out Irene's bookshelves, so if it was in one of those boxes, I suppose she'd have to know something about it." He handed the novel back to Sadie. "Sorry I can't be of more help. Can I ask what's so special about it that you're tracking down its owner? Is it a first edition or something?"

"No, it's—"

Sam set his hand on Sadie's. "There's something in the book we felt the owner would want to have back. We'd like to reach out to Mary and ask about it if you wouldn't mind giving us her number."

"Of course. She likes to read just like her mama, and she does enjoy fiction—always had a book in her face all through high school. So maybe this was hers."

Mr. Graves rattled off her number while Sam put it in his phone.

"You might have a bit of trouble reaching her this week though. She left today on a Caribbean cruise with her boyfriend and his family."

"All right. Good to know." Sam stood and Sadie followed suit, then Joe escorted them around the side of the house.

"Thank you for your time and hospitality," Sam said.

Sadie swallowed back her disappointment. "Yes, thank you for letting us drop in unannounced."

"Of course." He addressed Sam. "You tell Tag that aeration was just what my lawn needed. It's never looked better."

"Will do, sir."

"You're welcome back anytime. The older I get the more I enjoy the company of youngsters. And I hope you find the owner of that book."

"We'll do our best," Sam said. "Have a good afternoon now."

"Thank you again. Bye." Sadie waved. "The tea really hit the spot. And you have a lovely property."

Mr. Graves lifted a hand.

When they reached the truck, Sam helped her into the passenger side. Her adrenaline rush had faded, making her hands shaky and her legs weak. She'd thought they'd found the owner. And what if Mary didn't know anything about the book? What if they couldn't even reach her?

Sam got into the driver's side and started the truck.

"I can't believe it wasn't his book. I thought for sure we'd found the owner."

"I know you're disappointed, but we'll call Mary and see what she knows."

"Well, it can't be her book, her ring! Even if she was planning to propose, she wouldn't have her own engagement ring be a part of it, would she? Or a coming-of-age novel about a young woman at the turn of the twentieth century?" A sudden thought occurred. "What if her boyfriend was planning to propose on that cruise? That must be it. And now it's going to be ruined."

"Don't jump to conclusions. We'll just call her and ask about the book."

"She's at sea! When I went on a cruise, I put my phone in the room safe and didn't take it out until we disembarked—do you know how expensive it is to use your phone at sea?"

"Then we'll just leave a message."

Sadie could hardly bear the thought of waiting a week. "But we can't mention the ring. We can't ruin the proposal—if that's what he's planning to do."

"We won't mention the ring."

"Why'd you stop me when I was going to tell Mr. Graves about it?"

"Because if his daughter's getting engaged, we shouldn't be the ones to tell him."

"You have a point, I guess. Give me your phone. I'm going to try to reach Mary."

But a few minutes—and one vague voice mail—later, they were no closer to finding that book's owner than they had been that morning.

TWELVE

> A *flashback* transports the reader back in time to a pivotal moment in a character's life to help the reader better understand his present-day situation.
>
> —*Romance Writing 101*

The heat was just one of the things distracting Sam from his work today. He shoveled out the last bit of pea gravel into the flower bed and spread it out. When he was finished he swiped his arm across his forehead. The temperature was in the midnineties today with not a cloud in the sky, and Mrs. Blevins's yard didn't have a single shade tree. He'd love to whip off his shirt and take advantage of the coastal breeze, but his dad drew the line at stripping in customers' yards. Go figure.

He pulled off his gloves and checked his watch. Almost quitting time. Just had to get one more bed done. He gulped the lemonade Mrs. Blevins had brought him. What was Sadie up to this afternoon? Had she managed to reach Mary?

Two days ago after their first unsuccessful phone call, Sadie had the idea of calling Mary's boyfriend instead. They just needed his number. But a phone call to Mr. Graves had proved unsuccessful, and Sadie had been unable to locate his information online.

Sam checked his phone—he and Sadie had exchanged numbers—but she hadn't reached out to him.

Tag, however, had sent him a text forty-five minutes ago. Hey, buddy. Just checking in with you. Mowed Mr. Graves's yard and he said you'd stopped by. Hope you're doing all right.

Sam frowned at the message, pocketed his phone, and got back to work with the wheelbarrow, shovel, and mound of pea gravel. He and his cousin were certainly back on speaking terms. After all, they lived in the same town, worked at the same business, and were related to the same people.

And it had been more than a year since that fateful day.

The memory surged into Sam's mind like a rogue wave. It was the kind of day a man didn't easily forget. He'd finished work early and decided to call it a day. He'd been dragging all afternoon—caught some virus, he suspected. But it was Friday and there was some beach party Amanda wanted to attend—a friend of hers on the island. He'd rather stay home, order in food, and watch a movie. But relationships required compromise. They'd both been busy lately and hadn't seen much of each other.

Since he knew it would be a late night and he had to work in the morning, he headed home for a quick nap. On the way he dropped his truck at Louie's Garage, just down the street from his apartment. Louie would change his brake pads, and Sam would pick it up in the morning. Amanda was picking him up at seven tonight. She preferred to drive her Mercedes rather than his work truck since it apparently smelled like sweat and grass.

Yeah, she was a little prissy, but she had a good heart. She'd worked hard to make something of herself. Had put herself through college and was now a paralegal at a prominent law firm in town. They'd met when she hired Ford Landscaping and Lawn Care to maintain the pristine lawn outside their new building.

He'd been thunderstruck at first sight of her—tall and thin with a sheath of black hair that sparkled like onyx and begged to be touched. She flirted with him and was quite adept at it. He was mesmerized by her sultry green eyes and the sensuous way she moved. Would she see a blue-collar worker as beneath her?

Apparently not. When he asked her out the next week, she said yes without hesitation.

Over the next several months he discovered that the woman beneath the sultry exterior was tough as nails. She'd had a rough upbringing, had been raised by her grandmother, and had clawed her way up through hard work and determination. She volunteered at the local nursing home where, he soon learned, she had all those old men wrapped around her little finger. The women liked her, too, especially when she gave them manicures and pedicures.

He walked home that day, smiling at thoughts of her. They'd been dating more than a year and things had gotten serious. On a whim last week he'd done a little searching online for engagement rings. They'd talked about the future and seemed to want the same things: meaningful careers, a marriage, a couple of kids. Maybe he'd give it a few more months and propose. Her upcoming birthday would be the perfect opportunity.

By the time he arrived at Tag's and his apartment, his nose was stuffed up and his head throbbed. Definitely coming down with something.

He turned up the air-conditioning, took a quick shower, and dropped on his bed.

When he woke up, the lighting in his room was different. The sun was low in the sky. He'd slept later than he intended and hadn't set his alarm since he never napped more than twenty minutes.

He sat up in bed, his head spinning, and checked his watch. He still had thirty minutes before Amanda arrived. Time to get some Advil into his system. Maybe a decongestant. He didn't want to cancel the date. He hadn't seen her in almost a week, and she'd been looking forward to this party.

He hauled himself out of bed, and the rush of air-conditioning felt so good. Maybe he had a fever. Oh well, the Advil would take care of that too.

He left his room and padded down the hall. The TV was on—sports, from the sound of it, so he expected to find Tag on the sofa.

What he hadn't expected to find was Amanda, wrapped up like a burrito in his cousin's arms. Engaged in a lip-lock.

He was hallucinating. He tried to blink away the image. Wavered on his feet. His pulse pounded in his temples. *Throb, throb, throb.* But the image remained. It was real. Tag and Amanda.

A red cloud rose inside him. "*What the . . .*"

The couple sprang apart.

Amanda covered her mouth—the same mouth that had just been plastered to his cousin's.

Tag jumped to his feet, his dark hair disheveled. "Sam. What are you doing home?"

Sam stepped closer, jaw clenched so tight his teeth ached.

Tears sparkled in Amanda's eyes. "This isn't—I'm so sorry." She put herself in front of Tag.

Because, yes, Sam wanted to pummel him right now. His hands clenched into fists. His breaths felt stuffed into his lungs. His brain worked to assimilate the facts.

Amanda and his *cousin.*

Making out.

Right under his own roof.

The past few weeks flashed in his mind, times when Amanda was unavailable and Tag was MIA.

"How long?" he grated out.

"Not long," Amanda said. "We tried not to—but we just couldn't help it. I'm so sorry. I was going to tell you."

"Oh yeah? When? When were you going to tell me?"

Tag put his hands up, palms out. "Hey, come on, buddy. We didn't mean for this to happen."

And that's when Sam's fist flew. Right into Tag's perfectly sculpted nose.

Now Sam stabbed the shovel into the pea gravel with more force than necessary. The memory wafted away like an ill wind. So, yeah, his cousin and his girlfriend had cheated on him right under his nose. And sure, maybe Sam could've handled the whole thing better. But the way he saw it, his cousin had gotten off easy with only a busted nose.

Tag and Amanda had since offered many apologies. Tag immediately offered to find another apartment, but Sam moved out instead. He had no desire to live with the ghost of that memory. In retrospect he could see Amanda had put some distance between them those last few weeks. He'd just been too busy, too naive, to realize it was anything more than busy schedules.

Tag had done everything he could to salvage his relationship with Sam. He admitted to grossly mishandling the situation. Tried to stay out of Sam's way for a while, even at work. He'd even, in a staggering moment of remorse and selflessness, offered to give Amanda up. Sam had been tempted to accept.

But in the long run she would choose who she wanted to be with, and it clearly wasn't Sam. And he wasn't so pathetic as to want her back.

Tag and Amanda had dated very quietly early on. It was months before Sam saw them together again. But over the past few months, Sam had seen the couple enough to realize they were madly in love. And though he'd probably never admit it aloud, they were better together than he and Amanda had ever been. Amanda seemed softer somehow. She'd lost that brittle edge and it suited her.

She was genuinely sorry she'd hurt Sam. Regretful that she'd handled her growing attraction to Tag so poorly.

And pretty soon, she would basically be his cousin-in-law.

THIRTEEN

New ideas often come along at the most unexpected times.

—*Romance Writing 101*

Baby Marcel pointed at the picture of the boat. "Bo!"

Sadie had found the board book in her Little Library this morning and grabbed it, thinking Marcel would like it. "Yes, that's a boat. He sure loves books."

"I read to him all the time," Keisha said.

Sadie continued reading. "So Jonah ran far, far away, all the way to the sea. And then he got on a boat and floated far, far away. But no matter how far, far away Jonah went . . . God was still with him."

"Fa, fa," Marcel said.

Sadie smiled. "Yes, far, far away. You're so smart."

Sadie's phone buzzed with an incoming call. She snatched it off the deck table, her spirits sinking when her agent's name flashed on the screen instead of Mary's. She'd been waiting three days for that call.

"You need to get that?"

"That's okay. I'll call her back."

Sadie finished the story and let Marcel have the book. He flipped through the pages, gazing at the pictures while Keisha told Sadie about her extended family.

"Well, it's getting late," Keisha said after a while. "We should get going." She stood and held her arms out for her baby. "Come here, little guy."

Sadie gave the toddler a squeeze. "Oh, don't take him away. I haven't gotten enough of his baby smell."

Keisha chuckled. "Stick around—the smells won't be so great. But I promised Derick chicken parm tonight, and I haven't even gone to the grocery yet. I'll stop by later this week if you're around. And I *will* take that walk on the beach. These thighs need some exercise."

"Stop it. You look great." Keisha had stopped by the Little Library to return the Higgins novel she'd borrowed, and the two had gotten into a lengthy book discussion that had preempted her attempt at exercise.

"You're lucky to be so tall. When you're short you can see every single donut."

"You don't look like you eat many donuts."

Sadie snorted. "Why do you think I jog?"

"Which book should I take next?" Keisha asked. "I'm in the mood for romantic suspense."

"Try the Coble novel—someone dropped it off last week. *Edge of Dusk*. But I'll warn you, it's the first of a series and you'll end up ordering book two."

"Ooh, sounds perfect. Thanks. It was fun chatting with you. Good luck with that plot."

Sadie had opened up to Keisha about her current writing dilemma—just not the part about her canceled contract. So humiliating.

After waving goodbye to Keisha and her sweet baby boy, Sadie awakened the screen on her computer. The sun was low in the sky, and though she now had a few pages of notes on her characters, the document for her actual synopsis was still blank.

She'd been sidetracked by that engagement ring. She opened up Google and searched again for *Rick Clemmons*—Mary's boyfriend still on that cruise. If she could just find his number, maybe she could get ahold of him without clueing Mary in about the proposal.

"Hi, Sadie." A woman waved from the pathway, wearing a huge pair of sunglasses on her delicate face. "I see you're hard at work again."

Sadie greeted the young couple. "You're back already." Nick and Anna had stopped by a few times since she'd put up the library. They lived on the island and had been dating two years.

"You have to enjoy the summer sunshine while it lasts." Nick's Braves cap cast a shadow over his smiling face.

Anna opened the Little Library's door. "We were out getting a bite to eat and decided to get a beach stroll in. Got anything new for me?"

"A friend of mine just returned a Jenny Hale novel. Have you read her?"

The woman found the novel and glanced over the back cover. "Don't believe I have. It looks good though."

"I think you'll like this one. It's romantic and heartwarming."

"Oh, come on now," Nick said. "I won't see her face for a week."

Anna swatted him with the book. "Don't be silly. I'll have it finished in a day or two." She addressed Sadie again. "I'll stop and grab it on our way back by."

"I'll guard it with my life." Sadie grinned at the pair as they waved and headed for the beach.

They seemed like such a happy couple, walking closely, hand in hand. Did they always get along so well? Did they ever get into loud arguments? Had Nick ever left for weeks on end as her dad was prone to doing?

Did Sadie have what it took to sustain such a long relationship? Her longest so far had only been five months, and that was an anomaly. She wanted true love—who didn't?

Caroline said she only looked for flaws in the guys she went out with. Maybe her friend had a point. But wasn't it also wise to go into relationships with your eyes wide open? Too many women projected positive traits on men they didn't really know. That only set them both up for disappointment.

Perhaps Sadie was too picky. But she wanted a man who was kind and forgiving. She wanted a man with a generous heart and a flexible spirit. She wanted the kind of devotion that promised they would work things out instead of just giving up.

He didn't have to be perfect. Heaven knew she had her own flaws. She could be a bit much—she'd been told that a time or two. She talked a lot, especially when she was nervous. She could be a little scattered. She wasn't good with numbers and she procrastinated on anything having to do with them—including paying the bills and doing her taxes.

But she loved people, she loved socializing, and she was a fun date. At least she thought so. Oftentimes she was the one turning down that second date. But there was no point in pursuing a relationship she didn't see as promising, and it was kinder to be honest about it up front.

Maybe that was the recipe for becoming a twenty-six-year-old who'd never been in love. But she just hadn't met the right man yet. She would surely recognize him when he came into her life.

She glanced at her laptop and woke it up again, brightened the screen. And yet somehow she'd agreed to write a romance novel. *What were you thinking?*

The phone buzzed with another incoming call. She checked the screen, hoping it was Mary returning her call. But no, it was her agent, and Sadie had already ignored two phone calls.

She accepted the call and forced some positive energy into her greeting. "Well, hello there. How are you, Gillian?"

"I'm doing well, thank you. How's the beach?"

"Oh, sunny and just perfect. The weather's been divine. And this house is to die for. Big huge windows overlooking the seashore. Rio and I are having a blast."

Hearing her name, the dog perked her ears and tilted her head.

"Lucky you. We've had nothing but rain in the city. Our lower level flooded a little and ruined some old mementos I had in boxes."

"I'm so sorry to hear that. How's your family doing otherwise? Are your kids stir-crazy now that school's over?"

"The kids are busy with summer activities, and Kyle and I are taking turns shuttling them around. I can't wait till Megan gets her driver's license—did I really just say that?"

Sadie chuckled. "It'll take the pressure off for sure. I know my mom was glad when I got mine. Not only did I drive myself to all those practices, I became her errand girl."

"That does sound tempting. But listen, I wanted to let you know that I spoke with Erin this morning, and she's eager to see that proposal from you. Thought I'd check in and see how it was coming along."

"Oh, it's going great. The juices are really flowing. These characters, they're just—" The cursor blinked on the blank page, mocking her. Sadie closed out the document with a jab. "They have me by the heart, what can I say? I should have something for her soon."

"Soon like later this week . . . ? She was hoping to have it in time to read over and present it at pub board, which is next Tuesday. So it would be great if she could have it no later than end of day Friday."

Friday? Sadie clutched her chest. That was only three days away! And she still had no idea what this story would be about. "Um, sure! Of course. It just needs a little tweaking is all. I'll flesh it out a bit and get it to her sometime Friday." She palmed her face.

"Perfect. She'll be so glad to hear that. I can't wait to see what you've come up with."

Me too. "You're going to love it so much. Just as much as I do."

After they said their goodbyes, Sadie's smile wilted as she face-planted into her keyboard. What was she going to do? She had nothing.

Nothing!

She'd been so focused on finding the owner of that ring, which was ever so much more fun and exciting than drafting a dry synopsis for a genre she'd never written before.

Fun and exciting.

The words gave her pause. The whole ring thing *was* exciting and interesting and unique. Certainly nothing like this had happened to her before. Could she weave a plot around that?

She bolted upright. *Write what you know.* Why not? Real life inspired fiction all the time, didn't it? There was even an engagement ring involved in this story—very romantic. She'd already decided on a hero and heroine who were staying on the beach next door to each other. They would go on a quest and end up falling in love!

It was perfect. The plot she'd been beating her head against a brick wall over had been right at her fingertips all along.

FOURTEEN

Just like in real life, characters reveal themselves through thought, action, and dialogue.

—*Romance Writing 101*

Sadie had a bucketful of nervous energy. So after dinner she took Rio for a walk on the beach. The poor thing had such short legs she couldn't accompany Sadie on her morning jogs.

The surf crashed against the shoreline, making the two of them periodically hurry up the beach. Rio had no interest in getting wet. She barked at the breaking waves. She barked at the seagulls and chased them as far as her leash would allow. She tried to get friendly with other walkers and dogs heading the opposite direction. Most of the time, they stopped to give her some attention. Who could blame them? She was just so darn cute.

Now that Sadie knew what her story would be about, she was eager to get the plot down on paper. But first she needed to organize her thoughts, and she did that best while she was busy doing something else.

When she reached the pier, she stopped and let Sadie sniff around the pilings and scare off the seagulls before she turned and headed back toward the house.

"Come on, Rio, let's head home! That's my good girl. Come with Mommy. Oh, you don't like those waves, do you? They just keep chasing you."

Sam would surely be home from work by now. She was eager to find out if Mary had called him. Even though Sadie had left her own number on the voice mail, she had called from his phone. It was possible Mary might call him instead.

The thought quickened her pace. Wouldn't it be wonderful if they could get their answer tonight? The man wouldn't get the ring back until they returned from the cruise, but at least the mystery would be solved and the ring would be returned to its rightful owner.

Perhaps the guy would propose on the cruise without the ring—would tell his future bride the tragic story of the lost ring and book. And wouldn't they both be so delighted when they discovered it had been found?

In her story she wouldn't have to follow the real-life version of things—that was the glory of fiction. She'd do whatever worked best as she wrote it. But, oh, it was practically going to write itself now. What a load off her mind. She hadn't realized the full weight of that pressure until it lifted.

The hero and heroine would make a bargain—the wedding date for his help—just as she and Sam had done. When they attended the wedding, sparks would fly. Could anything be more perfect? She'd felt sparks before, of course—that she could write about with confidence. The more touchy-feely emotions of love were going to require some imagination. But she'd read enough romance novels now that she was pretty sure she could fake her way through it.

When she reached the shoreline in front of the cottage, she spotted a man with a black Lab. The thirtysomething guy wore a fitted tee with a pair of board shorts. His golden-blond hair was just long enough to flutter in the wind.

Upon seeing the other dog, Rio barked and strained against her leash like mad.

Sadie chuckled. "Settle down. You want to be friends, don't you? Where are your manners?"

The man's face broke out into a perfect smile as his Lab tugged him closer to Rio. The dogs checked each other out.

"Beautiful Lab you've got there," Sadie said. "His coat's so shiny."

"He likes your little friend. Roscoe, take it easy, boy. She's littler than you."

"He's being very much a gentleman. Good boy, Roscoe." Sadie petted the dog.

"I haven't seen you around here," he said.

"I've only been here a week and a half. I'm here for the summer. Mostly I jog the beach in the mornings, but Rio wanted a walk tonight. It's so beautiful out. Do you live here?"

"About a mile that way." He gestured south.

"Lucky you. The island is beautiful."

"First time here?"

"Yes. What do you have to do to get a house on the beach?"

"I have no idea. I'm not *that* lucky. My girlfriend and I live inland a couple blocks. But we have access to the beach and enjoy mild winters, so we're not complaining. Where are you from?"

"Queens currently. I do not get to enjoy mild winters. But the snow is lovely to look at in the city. From the windows. In front of a fireplace. With a blanket, hot chocolate, and a book."

His chuckle rode the wind like a kite. "I'm Jared."

It had been a long day. Sam grabbed takeout from PJ's Clam Shack and ate it sitting on his sofa. He missed having meals with someone. Sharing about his day and listening to her talk about hers.

Today hadn't been so good. The work had been fine, but the memory of that day—of finding his girlfriend and cousin making out on the couch—had plagued him. He needed to completely let it go. Plenty of time had passed. No doubt they'd handled the situation badly, but people couldn't help who they loved, could they? Especially when life kept throwing them together.

He didn't love Amanda anymore. His heart didn't hurt when he saw them together. Instead there was just sort of a vacant feeling inside when he thought of her. And he wasn't sure he ever wanted to fill that empty spot with someone else. At least not for a long time.

When he finished his meal he stepped out onto the deck. Sadie was home and would no doubt come outside when she realized he was here. He was curious to know if she'd heard from Mary—though Sadie probably would've texted him twenty times by now if she had. Or called him and left a rambling four-minute voice mail.

He leaned against the deck railing and caught sight of her at the shoreline with Rio. She was talking to some guy while his black Lab got to know her lapdog. It appeared their owners were also becoming acquainted. Sadie didn't know a stranger. She was already on a first-name basis with at least a dozen people.

She drew people in. It had annoyed him at first. He'd come here to be alone, and suddenly strangers were sitting on his deck, stopping by to chat with her.

But really, that was a pretty handy skill she had. He admired it.

She threw her head back and let out a laugh he couldn't hear over the sounds of surf and wind. What had the man said to make her laugh like that?

She squatted and gave the Lab some attention. No doubt jealous, Rio jumped up on her knees and Sadie spread the love around.

A moment later she stood back up and resumed her conversation. Sam had seen the guy around but didn't know him personally. The island was too big to know everyone, especially with the influx of tourists from spring through fall. But he was probably single, judging by how engaged he was with Sadie. And he'd probably have her number before it was all said and done.

The thought pinched.

He pushed the feeling away. Maybe Sadie had grown on him a bit over the past week. He liked her optimism and ready smile. And she was certainly appealing to the eye. But he wasn't prepared for anything more than friendship. They were barely acquaintances. Anyway, she probably had a boyfriend back home. She was too good a catch to be single.

Movement on the beach signaled that Sadie was parting ways with the guy. Sam couldn't miss the way he glanced back at Sadie as she cut up the beach toward the cottage.

When she spotted Sam on the deck, her face broke out into a wide grin, and she gave an enthusiastic wave. He lifted a hand

and tried to view her as the man on the beach might've. Her feathery blonde hair, currently wind tousled, and a turquoise scoop-neck T-shirt that revealed shapely arms. It was tucked into a pair of shorts that sat high on her torso, accentuating her small waistline and hourglass figure.

How could the guy not be interested?

When she reached the yard she set Rio free, and the dog came running to him.

He gave her a little affection while Sadie made her way across the deck. "Did you hear from Mary?"

Her lips twisted. "Well, hello, Sam. My day was terrific—how was yours?"

"It was fine. So did you hear from her?"

"I was about to ask you the same thing if that answers your question. Shoot. They don't disembark for three whole days."

"Maybe she'll check her phone at one of the ports."

"That's the hope. Did you get a lot of yards done today? It was a hot one."

"Just two. I did some landscaping."

Her gaze flittered over him.

He glanced down to make sure he hadn't missed any dirt in his shower. Nope.

"Well, I really did have a terrific day. My agent called and said my editor wanted a synopsis by Friday. *This* Friday. And I panicked—only on the inside, mind you. I totally played it off like, of course! No problem! I'll get that right over to you. But then a few minutes after we got off the phone, guess what? An idea came to me—the perfect idea." She slid him an expectant look.

When he didn't say anything she added, "That's wonderful

to hear, Sadie. You must be so relieved. Why, yes, Sam, that's it exactly. I'm absolutely giddy with relief."

He arched a brow. "Do all writers do that?"

"Do what?"

"Carry on conversations by themselves?"

"What do you think dialogue is? Of course, most of my characters have been cowboys up to this point. That will be a real challenge for me—having modern-day people in my head."

Okay, then.

"Not real people. Characters and voices—and before you give me that look again, not *those* kinds of voices. It's all perfectly normal writer stuff. Sometimes a piece of dialogue will come to me, and I have to write it down *right now.* Otherwise I forget and it's gone forever." She snapped her fingers, then narrowed her eyes at him. "Now why does this always happen? I talk and talk and you say nothing, and now you know way too much about me, and I know practically nothing about you." She plopped down in one of his chairs. "It's your turn. Talk."

He turned at the railing and chuckled.

"You have a dimple. I said that out loud, didn't I? But I've never seen you smile and you have a dimple. Sit down. Tell me about your work. How'd your dad end up starting a landscaping business?"

She made him dizzy and he wasn't entirely sure he liked it. But he did as she asked and admitted, if only to himself, that it wasn't so bad having a little company in the evening. Especially after a day like today. Besides, he wasn't usually this taciturn. But when Sadie had initially arrived, he'd been busy sulking about sharing his sanctuary.

"Hi, Sadie!" A middle-aged lady waved from the beach pathway. "Oh, what's this? Is this new?"

"It's a Little Library. I just put it up a week ago. Help yourself to a book. There are some good novels in there."

"Oh, I wish! I'm working on my master's, and all my reading time is devoted to deadly dull material."

"Oh, poor you. This is my neighbor, Sam. Sam, this is Rhonda."

They exchanged greetings and Rhonda knelt to give Rio some attention through the fence.

After she was gone Sam just stared at Sadie. Seriously, he half expected the woman to be elected mayor in the fall.

"What?" she asked.

"What what?"

"Why are you staring at me like that?"

"I think you already know more people on the island than I do."

"Oh, I do not. I just enjoy conversations—real ones with real human beings. I find people interesting, don't you? And Little Libraries are great because you put one up and voilà! You have a common interest with a stranger. Nothing brings people together like books. I'd love to know your favorite book, but first you were going to tell me about your business."

"Oh, was I?"

"Only if you want. Otherwise, that favorite book." Sadie settled into the chair, lacing her fingers on her stomach as Rio flopped down on her bare feet. Two turquoise toenails peeked out from under the dog's head.

"The business story is pretty basic. My dad worked for another landscaping company in his younger days. He didn't like how it was run, how they ripped people off, so he decided to start his own."

"Were you and your sister born yet?"

"I was only eight, so she wasn't even a thought. Money was a little tight for a while. My mom got a part-time job at my school so she could help out financially but still be home for me. When I was thirteen I started helping Dad in the summer. My cousin came along a couple summers later. And now we have eight crews, lots of equipment." He closed his mouth. He'd practically given a speech.

"That's awesome. I love how your dad's dissatisfaction with something old became his motivation for starting something new. Sometimes being uncomfortable can be a good motivator for positive change."

"Hadn't thought of it that way."

"It gives me hope. Because I'm very uncomfortable writing in a new genre, and maybe that'll turn out to be a positive change too."

"You're an optimist."

"My best friend calls me delusional, but I like your word better. Is he your best friend—your cousin?"

That old knot tightened in his chest. "I guess you could say that." Their relationship had grown more distant in the past months, obviously. But they were working their way back. Sam wasn't sure it would ever be what it had been before.

"But you're not his best man?"

"He's got two brothers and a lot of friends. I'll bet you have a lot of friends."

"Yeah, I do. But just one bestie, Caroline. She's a dog walker in the city."

"What's she like?"

"Well, she's built a successful business around something

she loves, so clearly she's self-motivated and industrious. She's been happily married for all of a year—I was her maid of honor. We met in college. She got a business degree but she didn't love managing a coffee shop, and her side hustle ended up becoming her main gig. She's jealous of my summers off though, and I frequently rub her nose in it."

"You don't really have the summer off though, do you?"

"Well, not since I got my first publishing contract. But I'd rather write than have my summers off. Anyway, a teacher's salary is hardly enough to make ends meet in New York. Plus I have to do something productive or I get stir-crazy. Before the books, I wrote obituaries."

"What?" he said with a laugh. She was such a happy little thing he couldn't imagine . . .

"Yeah, it was a little depressing. But I did take joy in helping people express the essence of their loved ones. It was rewarding in that way. But I'd much rather be writing a story—of any genre."

"So is the goal a career as a novelist?"

"I definitely want to keep writing books, but I don't know if I'll ever give up teaching kiddos. I love it. If I could work during the school year and write a book each summer, that would be my ideal life."

"What about after you get married and have kids? Or is that not in the forecast?"

"Oh yes, I want all the above eventually. I guess I'll have to reassess at that point. That seems like a long way off though. I'm nowhere near that kind of relationship, and marriage and family are such important decisions—not ones I'd make lightly. What about you?"

"What about me?"

She rolled her eyes. "You're thirty-one—that's not exactly young. Don't you want a wife? Kids? Is there anyone currently auditioning for the part?"

The image of Amanda soured his thoughts. "Yes, yes, and no."

"You'll find her eventually. Caroline thinks I'm too picky. She's tried to set me up about a million times. What was your longest relationship?"

"Just over a year."

"What happened? Or is that too nosy? If it's too nosy, just tell me to mind my own business. Also, now that I'm writing romance, I should inform you that anything you say may be used as fodder for my story."

"You won't want to use this story. It ended badly."

She winced. "Ooh. I'm sorry. That must've been hard. How long ago was the breakup?"

"More than a year ago. I'm over it, over her. Life goes on."

"Have you dated anyone since?"

"Not really. Decided to skip the whole rebound relationship."

"Probably wise. Those usually don't turn out well, or so I hear."

The sun must've set on the other side of the house, as it was growing dark. The sky over the ocean had darkened, and fireflies were beginning to flash in the yard.

She slapped at her arm. "Well, the mosquitoes have come to visit—they love me, so that's my signal to retreat indoors." She stood.

Rio stood and shook, making her tags jingle.

"It was nice talking to you, Sam. And if Mary gets back with you, let me know, no matter the time of day or night. I'm dying to see how this turns out."

"Will do. Good night."

"Night." She navigated the barrier and headed toward the door, Rio on her heels, then turned suddenly. "Oh! You never said—what's your favorite book?"

He hesitated. "It's not some high-brow classic novel . . ."

She rolled her eyes. "I write genre fiction, Sam."

"*The Firm* by John Grisham."

"Aah." Her lips split into that wide smile. "And just like that we have something to talk about tomorrow."

FIFTEEN

A synopsis is your chance to sell the editor on your story, so put your best foot forward.

—*Romance Writing 101*

Thank You, sweet Jesus!" It was almost seven o'clock in the evening, but Sadie finally had a nice one-page, single-spaced synopsis. She leaned back in her deck chair. She'd have to go to the library to print out the document. She always did her editing on hard copy with a red pen—seeing the words on an actual page gave her distance and perspective.

But it wasn't due for two whole days yet. She had plenty of time to edit and tweak.

She glanced at her watch. It was almost time for Sam to return from work. She'd enjoyed their conversation the evening before. That part about his former girlfriend tugged at her heart. What exactly had he meant by "ended badly"? She'd seen the flash of hurt in his eyes when he spoke of it and wanted to give him a hug.

And what about those family and business tensions he'd mentioned before—the ones that had him hiding away on the island? She hoped he'd eventually open up to her about that. She was a good listener and not half bad at advice.

She thought back to their conversation. She'd almost told him she was using their ring search for the plot of her book. But what if he objected? He was now involved in that mystery—she'd invited him herself. What if he didn't want to be included in this story of hers? Of course, it wouldn't be *him,* not really. She'd certainly change the names to protect the victims—ahem, the innocent.

Obviously she could still write about it despite his objections. But she'd hate to strain their friendship just as they were getting to know each other.

No, it would be better to ask forgiveness than permission. She just *had* to write this story—mainly because it was the only idea she had. But also because it was a good idea. At least, she thought it was. She'd soon find out if her editor and agent felt the same.

She glanced down at her dog, who eyed a gecko across the deck. "Time to get some dinner, Rio. Come on, girl. Are you thirsty? Let's get you some water."

Sadie scrounged around the kitchen and warmed up leftovers. She ate inside with her playlist in the background. The berry salad was refreshing, and the meatloaf was even better than when she'd made it yesterday. She was almost finished eating when Caroline called.

"Hi there," Sadie said by way of greeting. "How goes it in New York? I hear there's been lots of rain."

"It's been an adventure. Lots of muddy paws and shaking dogs and wiping up foyers. But overall pretty good. I'm dog sitting for the Pearsons this week."

"Aren't they the ones with the eerie Doberman Pinscher?"

"He just stares at me. It's bone chilling. Believe me, I lock the bedroom door at night. And yes, I have to actually lock it because he can open these French levers. Tell me that's not creepy."

"You said he's never been aggressive with you."

"I know, but that stare! It freaks me out. He's looking at me now. He knows I'm talking about him. If you don't hear from me for a couple days . . ."

Sadie laughed, knowing her friend was mostly joking. "At least the job pays well."

"It had better since it's keeping me from my hubby. But also this place is gorgeous—lavishly furnished, all windows, sixty-fourth floor. The view! And the towels. I didn't know they made bath towels that big and soft. I'm not exactly roughing it—don't tell Carlos."

"What do these people do for a living?"

"She's a partner in a big law practice, and he's an executive with some brokerage firm. Maybe Duke will warm up to me this week. At any rate, I've decided to pretend this is Carlos's and my house."

"Boy, are you going to be depressed come Monday."

"I won't think about that. So what about you, Miss Smarty Pants—using real life to inspire your plot? How's that synopsis coming?"

"I actually drafted it today. Now I just have to edit and send it to Erin."

Caroline whooped, then lowered her voice. "Oh, he didn't like that. I didn't mean it, Duke. I'll be quieter. You can go back to sharpening your teeth on that . . . is that a femur bone? That can't be good."

"I'm so relieved to have that stupid synopsis done, I can't even tell you. The writing should be much easier now that I have a plot in place."

"And since you're kind of living out the story. See? I told you you could do it. And speaking of your plot, have you heard from that lady on the cruise? Also, side note, I need an update on the grumpy neighbor."

"No to the first question. As to the neighbor thing, I feel kinda bad about calling him grumpy. He's actually okay once you get to know him. And he is helping me to find the ring's rightful owner, after all."

"Don't give him too much credit—it was a trade. And you might regret it when you're stuck for hours at a wedding with a curmudgeon."

Sadie winced. She'd kind of exaggerated Sam's grumpiness and downplayed his looks. Otherwise Caroline would've been trying to set them up from afar the entire summer. "Well, it'll be worth it once we get that ring back where it belongs."

"Speaking of weddings," Caroline said. "I met someone last week I want to set you up with when you're back in the city. His name is Drew and he's in seminary at—"

"*No.* Absolutely not. I'm so tired of setups. I always wind up with duds and then I wonder what the so-called friend who set me up really thinks of me."

"But he's so nice. You'd like him, I promise."

"Not happening."

"Party pooper. Whatever happened with you and Carlos's friend Evan? He's so attractive and he's frugal like you."

"How quickly we forget. He took me to that Italian restaurant on Metropolitan and flossed his teeth after dinner. At the table."

"Oh yeah."

"Why can't it be easy? Why can't I just meet Mr. Right when we're hailing the same cab or something?"

"You wouldn't know Mr. Right if he sat on your lap, and you don't even believe in love at first sight."

"Yeah, there's that."

"Well, when he does come along you'll appreciate him all the more for having endured numerous letdowns."

"I hope you're right."

"I'm sure of it. Have you heard from your parents since you've been down there?"

"A couple times. They're in a good place right now. Next month, who knows?"

"That's good, I guess."

Her parents had been legally separated three times and divorced once. They regularly went through periods when they slept in different rooms. Then there were their good phases. Sadie found it easier when she had a little distance from the yo-yo relationship—part of New York's appeal.

Across the line a fancy doorbell chimed. "Hey, I gotta run. DoorDash is here and Duke looks ready to eat the poor delivery guy. Easy, Duke. He's bearing food. If you're nice, I might even share. See ya, Sadie. Congrats on the synopsis!"

"Thanks! Enjoy your digs."

After Sam finished his take-out meal, he went out on the deck. If Sadie was out there, that would just be a coincidence and have nothing to do with his decision to enjoy the beautiful evening.

Even though he'd been outside all day and the air-conditioning did feel pretty good.

When he stepped outside, Rio darted past the tree barrier and danced around his feet until he stopped to pet her.

"How was your day, dear?" Sadie asked from a lounge chair.

He straightened and blinked at her.

Sadie set aside the newspaper. "You know, 'Hi, honey, I'm home! How was your day, dear?' Never mind. I guess you didn't hear from Mary?"

"Ah, that's a negative."

"Me either. Oh, but I did finish my synopsis. There was much singing and dancing and shouting. I scared the seagulls away."

He stood at the railing, watching the evening beach strollers. "I guess congratulations are in order then."

"Don't congratulate me just yet. That's only my first draft—though admittedly the hardest one. Plus I still have to get my publisher's approval. But first I need to print that baby off and make some corrections. Is there a library nearby?"

"I brought a printer along. You're welcome to use it."

"Oh, isn't that handy. That's so nice of you. I'll definitely take you up on that, and if it wouldn't be too much trouble, I'll need to do some manuscript printing later."

"No problem."

"So how *was* your day? More landscaping or just mowing?"

"Mostly just mowing today."

"Your work must keep you in great shape, huh? I guess you don't have to jog on the beach so you can eat cheesecake."

Cheesecake? "Is that why you jog?"

"Not the only reason. There's my health, blah, blah, blah. And also there's donuts and ice cream and apple pie."

He lifted a brow as he made his way to a chair. "Sweet tooth?"

"Oh, that reminds me. I never did bake you those cookies. But I promise it'll be my first task right after I finish this synopsis."

"You don't have to do that."

She leaned forward to better see him around the barrier. "Of course I do. I haven't had cookie dough in weeks. Do you mind if I . . . ?"

She got up, joined him on his side of the deck, and plopped into the chair beside him. "Much better. The placement of those planters is so annoying."

He cleared his throat. "Meet any new strangers today?"

"Of course. Three of them borrowed books. Did you know the island has a horse farm? Well, sure you did—you live around here. I met someone who works there, training them. Also I met a bicycle courier from LA if you can imagine."

"Those still exist?"

"Apparently. He was in very good shape. I'll bet he gets to eat all the donuts he wants."

Sam stifled a grin. "Anyone ever tell you you're obsessed with food?"

"Please. You have an active job and you're, what, six one?"

Six feet two but who was counting?

"Naturally, I'm very active during the school year, on my feet most of the day. But the summers spent writing on my tush? I have to make an effort." She shifted toward him and propped her chin on her palm. "Anyway, you mentioned *The Firm* last night as we were parting ways. What did you like about it?"

He thought back. It had been a few years since he read it. "I like the legal aspects—the law firm, the courtroom. The plot was intriguing and unfolded rapidly. I was spellbound."

"I love a good page-turner. Who was your favorite character?"

"Mitch, of course. He's an upstart—a go-getter, and the firm was making an offer he could hardly refuse. But you could just see it all playing out, see the red flags and know he'll have major regrets. What did you think of it?"

"Oh, I haven't read it yet."

He did a double take. "What? You said we'd talk about the book."

"And we are. You're telling me all about it and I'm chiming in. I'm never short on things to say, especially about books."

He shook his head. "Well, surely you've seen the movie."

"I don't think so."

"Nineteen ninety-three? Tom Cruise?"

"Sorry. Missed that one *as it aired before my birth*."

Man, he was getting old. "Still, it's a cult classic. The book's better than the movie, of course. You should read the story. I think you'd like it."

"I'll be happy to do that, right after I finish writing my novel. Until that time, I'm on a strict diet of romantic fiction."

"And donuts? But what about the movie? Surely you can watch a movie."

Her head tilted to the side, a thoughtful look coming over her face. "Hmm. I suppose it wouldn't hurt anything as long as it's not a western. I'm having enough trouble keeping my thoughts in color."

He wasn't sure what that meant. "It's nowhere near a western."

She slapped the armrest. "That settles it then. We'll watch it tomorrow night. I'll stream the movie and you can provide the popcorn."

Wait. "What?"

"You didn't think I was going to watch it alone, did you? What fun is that? Besides, it was your idea."

He supposed it was. Oh well, what harm could come from it? And what else did he have to do? Besides, he hadn't watched it in years, and now that he knew her a little better, he found Sadie to be pleasant and kind of amusing.

"Fine," he said. "But let's watch it right after supper. Some of us have to work early."

SIXTEEN

A good writer gives her hero and heroine a time and place to become emotionally and physically closer.

—*Romance Writing 101*

The next day after work Sam found himself in a hurry. He ran by the IGA and picked up microwave popcorn, using the self-checkout lane, which he never did. He downed his take-out meal (hamburger, fries, strawberry shake) in the car on the way home—again, an anomaly. Then once home he rushed through his shower.

He wasn't hurrying because he was running late. He'd gotten off about his usual time. And he certainly wasn't rushing because he was eager to see Sadie. He was just impatient to watch the movie again, see if it still held the same appeal it had in his early twenties. Also, he wanted to get Sadie's impression of the movie.

He dressed in a black tee and his most comfortable jeans, slid on his flip-flops, and headed next door via the back deck. He was almost to her door when he realized he'd forgotten the popcorn and went back for it.

A minute later he tapped on her door. Maybe he should've bought drinks. Too late. He was overdue a trip to the grocery and could only offer orange juice or water.

The door slid open and Sadie beamed up at him. "Come in, come in. Got the popcorn?"

He held up the box as she ushered him inside. Rio danced around his feet, making movement difficult. He leaned down and scratched her behind the ears. "Settle down now. Jeez."

"She's excited to have company. Did you hear from Mary?"

He hated to extinguish the hope lighting her features. "'Fraid not."

"Bummer. Surely we'll hear from her tomorrow when the ship disembarks. Well, how was your day? I was awake early this morning—too early—and heard you leave. It was hardly even daylight."

"I'm an early riser. What woke you?"

"Oh, it was a text from my mom." Something crossed her features before her smile was back in place. "I had a great day though. I polished up my synopsis and I probably could've sent it to my editor, but I'm going to give it one last read-through in the morning."

"That's great." His phone buzzed with an incoming call and he checked the screen. "Speaking of moms."

"Go ahead and take it if you want. I'll get the popcorn going. Butter and salt?"

"Sure."

She headed toward the kitchen, just a few steps away. She looked comfortable in a loose pink shirt, a pair of leggings, and bare feet.

He accepted the call. "Hi, Mom. What's up?"

"Hi, honey. I was just having supper with your dad and talking about work. Thought I'd give you a call and see what you've been up to."

"Mostly just work. I'm putting in pretty long days—we have a lot of yards on the island."

"If it's too much, maybe we can hand some of those off to another crew."

"Nah, I prefer to stay busy. How's your week going? Any progress with the master bath?" His parents were finally doing some remodeling after twenty years.

"Oh, it's just a mess. The floor is torn up and there are tarps everywhere. I don't know what I was thinking doing this with a wedding coming up."

The microwave door clicked shut and began its loud hum. Sadie opened the fridge and bent down to peer inside.

He looked away. "Well, the renovation was in the plans long before the wedding was scheduled."

"I know, but . . . Well, anyway, did Hayley tell you she's thinking of becoming a teacher?"

She'd mentioned it several months ago. "She'd make a great teacher."

"I think the idea of being a coach also appeals to her. If she keeps her grades up, she could get a decent scholarship. Encourage her if you would. I just think she needs a little boost."

Sadie scurried around the kitchen like a woman who'd lived here for years. Sam still had to open multiple drawers to find basic things. Of course it didn't help that he got takeout most nights. Rio moved behind her, close as a shadow.

"If it comes up, I promise to be a positive influence."

"She's more likely to listen to you than your dad or me. How are you enjoying your time on the island? Are you getting enough rest?"

He rolled his eyes. "I'm doing fine, Mom. We're having good weather."

"I just worry about you, out there all alone."

He glanced at Sadie again. No way was he bringing her into the conversation. "I'm hardly alone, Mom—I talk to customers all day."

"But you've never been detached from the family for so long."

"Most families don't work together every day, you know. It's perfectly normal for most relatives to go a few weeks without seeing each other." Not to mention between all the texts and phone calls, they hardly left him alone for a solid hour.

"I know, but it's not what I've become accustomed to. We miss you around here."

"Well, you know I'm coming for lunch Sunday." He'd never miss Father's Day. "I'm looking forward to it."

Sadie returned to the living room with two drinks and flashed her pearly whites at him. She set the glasses on the coffee table, sat on the sofa, and went to work with the remote.

In the kitchen the popcorn started popping.

"I don't want to be a bother," Mom said, "but we're getting down to the wire on the RSVP count for the wedding. Have you given it any more thought?"

He turned toward the beach, wishing Sadie were back in the kitchen. He should've told his mom days ago, but he'd dragged his feet. "I'll be going, Mom. And you can go ahead and put me down for a plus one."

"Oh, that's wonderful, Sam." The relief in her tone was

obvious. "I know it won't be easy, but you won't regret going. It really is the right thing to do. And I'm so proud of you, honey, for putting family first. For being the bigger person."

If only his cousin had put the family first. Had been the bigger person. But no one seemed to hold him accountable for that. Well, that wasn't quite true. Tag had taken a lot of heat in the beginning—from Sam's parents. From his own parents and siblings. But in the end they'd all adjusted. What choice did they have?

What choice did Sam have? He needed to adjust too—and attending the wedding was the next step in that journey. Maybe that would put an end to this emptiness he felt inside once and for all.

"Sorry if I spoke out of turn, sweetheart."

He'd been quiet too long. This whole debacle wasn't his mom's fault. "You're fine, Mom. We'll get through this."

"I know, I just . . . Well, anyway"—she injected some cheer into her voice—"who's the girl you're bringing to the wedding? Anyone I know?"

Sadie's brows furrowed as she frowned at the TV screen. She muttered to herself as she juggled the laminated instructions and two remotes.

"No, no one you know."

"Well, what's she like? Are you dating her?"

He scratched his neck. "Ah, no, Mom. Just . . . a friend."

"Well, that's wonderful. I'm so glad you're coming and bringing a nice friend along. I've heard such wonderful things about the town. It'll be a fun weekend, you'll see."

Weekend. He glanced at Sadie, still battling it out with the remotes. He needed to come clean about that. He'd been putting it off and now he'd waited too long. At the root of his dread were the arguments he'd had with Amanda. Most of the time she was pretty calm, but when she got upset, man, could she lose her temper.

"Sam?"

"Yeah, Mom. Listen, I gotta run. Let me know what time on Sunday."

"Just come whenever you can. We'll eat at one. I'm making barbecue ribs, homemade mac 'n' cheese, and coleslaw—all your dad's favorites."

"Sounds great, Mom." They said their goodbyes and he disconnected the call.

The microwave kicked off, and the sudden silence gave way to Sadie's mutterings. "I already pushed that button. Which remote? Oh, for heaven's sake, could they have made this any more confusing?"

"Need some help?"

"There's something wrong with the TV."

The pout on her lips was kind of adorable. And called attention to the fullness of the lower one. "Let me take a peek."

He grabbed the remotes and pulled up the app screen.

"I haven't used the TV since I got here except for the regular channels. Also, I'm not very good with technology. Oh, that's the right screen, I think. It's on Netflix. Mrs. Miller has an account. How did you do that so fast?"

"The one next door works the same way." He painstakingly typed in the movie's title, then hit Enter.

"You'll have to show me what you did. I'll get the popcorn. Be right back."

Sam set down the remotes and surveyed the seating

arrangement. Just like at his place, a sofa sat opposite the TV. Sadie's phone sat on one armrest. She'd set his glass in the middle of the coffee table. He didn't want to imply this was a date by sitting too close. But the sofa was pretty big. If he sat in the middle there'd still be ample room between them.

This isn't rocket science, dummy—just pick a stupid seat.

He dropped onto the middle cushion, and Sadie appeared with a bowl of popcorn. Of course. They were sharing a bowl; they'd need to be somewhat close.

He felt pretty good about his choice, but guilt had pricked since the conversation with his mother. He should've been more forthcoming with Sadie about this wedding.

Sadie dropped beside him and set the popcorn bowl between them. "Okay, we're ready. Let's see what you got. Go sit down, Rio. No, honey, the kernels aren't good for you. Remember what happened last time? Mommy can't share. Go lay down. There's a good girl." She glanced at Sam. "Ready?"

"Yeah, um . . . before we start the movie, I, ah, have to tell you something."

"Ooh, that sounds ominous. You're not breaking up with me, are you?"

He blinked at her serious expression, his mind going blank.

Sadie took in Sam's obvious dismay and laughed. "You're way too easy, Sam. Come on, spit it out. How bad can it be? Is your printer on the fritz? Because I can always go to the library, you know."

"No, it's . . ."

He looked away, closed his mouth. Opened it again. Did it

have something to do with his mom or those family tensions? She'd heard bits of his phone conversation. But watching him now, she found his uncharacteristic uncertainty kind of cute. He scratched his neck when he was uncomfortable and avoided eye contact. She made a note to add those to her hero's traits.

"You know the, uh, the bargain we made?"

"Your help in exchange for my being your wedding date. Yes, Sam, I vaguely remember the bargain we made just last week."

"Right. Well . . ." His eyes locked on hers. "I didn't tell you quite everything."

She waited for him to expound. Got a little lost in those eyes. Flecks of caramel and dark brown swam in that golden sea. And those eyelashes. Good grief, why were the great lashes always wasted on men?

She gave herself a mental shake. "Okay . . . so it's something about the wedding?"

His eyes tightened in a wince. "Right, well, it's kind of not just a simple, ordinary wedding—it's kind of a weekend thing. A destination wedding, in fact."

A *destination* wedding? A million questions raced through her mind.

He held up a hand, palm out. "I'm sorry. I know I should've disclosed that before you agreed to the trade, and if you want out . . . I'll still keep my end of the bargain. But I'd really appreciate it if you'd—"

She nudged his shoulder. "Look at you, so serious. A destination wedding, are you kidding me? I'd love to go."

His brows shot up. Then he cut her a sideways glance. "Really? You're not upset?"

"Where is it? Hawaii? Jamaica? Bora-Bora?"

"Try Florida."

"I *love* Florida. Which part? How many days?"

"Anna Maria Island. It's a Friday-through-Sunday deal. You'll have your own room at the resort, of course."

"A resort? Two nights? Do they have umbrella drinks and swimming pools? Ooh, what about a hot tub?"

He rolled his eyes. "I would imagine so."

She loved going out, getting dressed up. She rubbed her hands together. "I need to go shopping. Where's Anna Maria Island exactly? And just so you know, I would've signed up for this without the trade. I probably shouldn't have told you that." She poked a finger into his chest. "You still have to help me with the ring."

"I won't quit on you now. The island's on the Gulf Coast near Bradenton and St. Petersburg. My cousin's grandmother lives there. I hope you like long car trips."

"We love long car trips." Her smile dimmed a couple watts. "Oh, what about Rio? Will I be able to take her?"

"I don't know. Didn't think of that. I'll have to check."

"Surely they wouldn't object to one tiny little dog. A resort! For two whole nights. I've never stayed at a resort before—or attended a destination wedding. How romantic." She swooned a bit, then caught his expression. "For the happy couple, I mean."

"Oh, right. So . . . we're okay then?"

She patted his thigh. So solid. "We're fine. No worries. Let's start the movie before it gets any later. I'll probably think of more questions."

"At least save them for after the movie." He grabbed the remote. "Anyway, I don't have a lot of specific information, but I'll find out more tomorrow."

"Guess I'll have to wait then." She turned off the lamp, ushering in darkness, and settled into her seat.

The movie started and they dug into the popcorn, but Sadie hardly even tasted it. She was too busy thinking about the wedding. She tried to follow the film (Tom Cruise was so young!), but her mind kept flittering back to the wedding.

Not only would this be a fun experience, but it would work perfectly into the plot of her story. A whole weekend together would allow time for her hero and heroine to grow closer. Add in a romantic wedding and a beautiful island setting, and the sparks were sure to fly.

She glanced at Sam, who was homed in on the screen. His face glowed dimly in the light. He was so handsome. How was it that he didn't have a dozen women he could invite to this wedding? Why had he chosen her? Maybe he wasn't interested in anything serious. And she supposed some women could get carried away at weddings—the whole affair conjuring up dreams of white picket fences and baby bundles. Maybe he wanted to avoid those expectations.

Before long her fingers scraped the salty bottom of the popcorn bowl. She set the bowl aside and forced herself to focus on the movie, which really was fast paced and interesting. She hung in there for the next hour, but before long her thoughts returned to the upcoming wedding.

What kind of clothes would she need to buy? Surely the bride and groom had a schedule that would clue her in to her wardrobe needs. Of course, there would be a rehearsal dinner, but Sam wasn't in the party, so they wouldn't be invited to that, would they? She'd definitely need a new bathing suit. Well, not *need*, but hello, it was a resort. A new bathing suit was practically a requirement. She'd only brought the one she'd purchased for that cruise a few years ago.

She smothered a yawn. She probably shouldn't have turned off the lights.

Would the wedding be held at night or during the day? Would it be formal or semiformal? Or would it be on the beach? Would the guests go barefoot? She'd need a pedicure! And a manicure, of course—that went without saying.

Somewhere between thoughts of swaying palm trees and spa treatments, she drifted away.

"Sadie," a voice whispered.

She groaned, pushed the outside away, and snuggled deeper.

"Sadie, the movie's over."

She fluttered her eyelids open. Blinked against the light of the screen, where names in a tiny font zipped past. Music filled the room. Sam.

She was leaning against his shoulder, cuddled up to his side. She'd probably drooled on his sleeve! She sat up and brushed the spot, relieved to find it dry. Still, her face warmed even while she relished the solid feel of his bicep beneath her fingertips.

"Whoops. I guess I fell asleep."

Apparently Rio had also found Sam to be the ideal pillow. She was curled up on his lap, snoring lightly.

Sadie ran a hand over her hair. "We both conked out on you. I'm so sorry. And here you wanted to share your favorite story with me. Why didn't you wake me up?"

Her gaze met his. They were still sitting close, and his face was in the shadows now that the screen had gone dark. The woodsy scent of his soap or shampoo beckoned. Tension crackled between them.

He looked away. "Uh, it's okay. You said you were up early this morning. Figured you needed the sleep."

Sadie pushed back to her side of the sofa. Good grief, how long had she been like that?

Rio stirred, stretched, and hopped off the sofa.

"I can't believe I did that," she mused. "I rarely take naps and now I don't know how the movie ended."

"Mitch ended up—"

"Shh! No spoilers. I'll finish it tomorrow, I promise."

"You don't have to. I enjoyed it as much as I did the first time." He shut off the TV. "Still not as good as the book though."

Sadie turned on the lamp, feeling vulnerable when light flooded the room. "Let me make it up to you. I'll cook you dinner tomorrow night if you don't have other plans, and we can have a full-on movie discussion."

Sam stood. "Nah, you don't have to do that."

"No, please. I feel bad for being such a rude host. Besides, don't think I haven't noticed all those take-out bags in your garbage can." He must spend a fortune at restaurants. "Don't you ever cook?"

"Doesn't seem worth it just for one."

"Tomorrow night then?"

He turned at the sliding door, the corners of his lips turning up. "If you insist."

She stooped and gathered Rio in her arms. "We absolutely insist, don't we, girl?"

"What can I bring?"

"Nothing but yourself. We'll whip up something tasty. Any allergies or dislikes?"

"I like just about everything except kale."

"Ew, no. We won't be using kale. It'll be fun. See you around seven?"

"Sounds like a plan. Good night."

"Night."

He slipped through the door and Sadie watched him go, the memory of that thick arm beneath her cheek filling her thoughts. How nice it had been to snuggle up with someone. Even if she'd been the one doing all the snuggling.

Rio let out a little whine.

Sadie kissed her head. "Know what, Rio? I think we like him."

SEVENTEEN

Minor characters enhance a story by revealing information or adding insight about your hero or heroine.

—*Romance Writing 101*

"I watched the ending of the movie," Sadie announced the second she let Sam inside the house the following evening.

Delicious smells distracted him from her proclamation, as did Rio, who danced around his feet, clamoring for attention. Sadie was also a little distracting, her hair tousled around her face. She wore a pair of white shorts and a roomy watermelon top that kept dipping off her shoulder.

He picked up the dog and forced himself to focus. "And what did you think?"

"I loved the ending. It was so exciting. Now I need to read the book—but not until I'm finished with my story." She headed toward the kitchen.

He followed, standing by the island while he scratched behind the dog's ears. Rio's eyes fell halfway closed in bliss. "Speaking of your story, did you get your synopsis finished?"

"Yes, sir, I turned it in at noon, but I haven't heard anything back from my agent or editor yet. I'm about to go mad with the waiting. Plus I haven't heard from Mary either." She gave him a hopeful look. "Did you, by any chance?"

"'Fraid not."

She huffed as she stirred whatever was steaming on the stove top. "Argh! I mean, she disembarked this morning. Surely she's checked her phone by now."

"She's probably been traveling all day. And you know how it is when you return from vacation—you're swamped trying to dig out."

"I know, but . . . what's my agent's excuse? How long could it take to read one measly page?"

She was kind of cute when she was impatient. "Maybe you should check in with her."

"I already did. She probably wants to get my editor's thoughts before she responds to me." Sadie covered her eyes. "Or she thinks it's the worst idea she's ever heard."

"Don't borrow trouble. Hopefully you won't have to wait till Monday to hear something."

"Gillian will contact me on the weekend, no problem. But Erin is a business-hours-only kind of person, so if she hasn't communicated yet with Gillian, I will end up waiting till Monday."

"Sounds like somebody upstairs is trying to teach you patience."

"Right?" She opened the oven and closed it again. "Now there's a fun lesson."

He glanced around the kitchen. "Could I do anything to help?"

"Could you set the table? It's almost ready."

"Sure."

They chatted about the movie while he gathered the supplies. He knew where some of the basic dishes were since their placement mirrored his own apartment. Music played lightly in the background.

Ten minutes later they were digging into delicious servings of shrimp scampi. The dish burst with flavors: lemon, parmesan cheese, and a hint of garlic. "Wow, this is really good."

"Thanks. I thought I'd take the opportunity to make some fresh seafood. This is a new recipe, but I might have to file it away for later. There's a great seafood market in my neighborhood."

"You definitely should."

They kept up a nice running dialogue as they ate: family, business, New York, their faith. He felt Sadie studying him while they talked. She was easy to talk to and a good listener. Conversation flowed easily, putting him at ease.

He was glad she was coming with him to the wedding. She would be a good distraction, and he even had a prayer of actually enjoying the event. He might even enjoy getting his arms around her on the dance floor.

Whoa there. While a summer flirtation held plenty of appeal, he wasn't ready to dip his toes back into the dating pool. Amanda—to say nothing of Tag—had wrecked his heart. He wasn't ready to trust another woman just yet.

However, he'd spent a good deal of today remembering what it had felt like to have Sadie cuddled up to him. He hadn't lied when he said he wanted her to get some rest. But also . . . he'd liked the slight weight of her against his shoulder. The softness of her pressed against his side. He had trouble concentrating on the end of the movie.

Even now, that shirt slipping from her shoulder again, his fingers itched to touch her skin. Was it as soft as it looked? What would she say? How would she react?

Sadie's phone vibrated with an incoming call, and he shook his thoughts away.

"It's my mom."

"Feel free to take it."

"I'll call her later."

As she pocketed her phone, a faint knock sounded. Sadie tilted her head, listening. "Is someone at the door?" Before he could answer she got up to check just as the knock sounded again.

Sadie peered through the sidelight. "Um, there's someone at your door. Do you know a tall teenage girl with dark brown hair? I think she's wearing a soccer shirt."

Hayley. He tossed his napkin on his plate and headed for the door. Once there he peeked through the sidelight and sighed. "It's my sister. Give me a minute."

After Sadie retreated he opened the door. Hayley, still in her soccer uniform, was returning to her old Saturn.

He scowled. "How'd you find me?"

Her gaping mouth was quickly replaced with a frown. "Wow, thanks for that hardy welcome. And I guess I didn't exactly find you since I had the wrong address, and what's with all the facial hair?" She hopped up the stoop steps. "Well, are you going to invite me in or what?"

He continued to block the doorway.

"Jeez, when did you become so rude?"

"Hi," Sadie said over his shoulder. "Hi there. You must be Sam's sister."

He expelled a long breath as his sister's eyes toggled between them, taking on an *aha!* expression he didn't like. Especially when she pinned him with a very arrogant *gotcha* look.

"I'm Sadie and this is Rio. Step aside, Sam, and let her in. Would you like to stay for dinner? We're having shrimp scampi and we just started."

"We're almost finished," he added.

"Why, I'd love to." Hayley seemed downright triumphant as she edged past him and introduced herself to Sadie.

They followed Sadie into the dining room, where Hayley caught sight of the setup and whispered, "Well, how cozy."

His withering glare didn't seem to faze her.

Sadie grabbed another place setting while he took a seat at the table, a sense of dread creeping over him.

Fifteen minutes later Sam's peaceful vibes were long gone. He sat back against his chair while Hayley and Sadie chatted like they'd known each other for years. Hayley was the picture of a gracious guest, complimenting Sadie on the food and asking for seconds. She bloomed under Sadie's attention. Especially when she discovered Sadie was a schoolteacher. That topic went on for another ten minutes while Sam waited for the other shoe to drop.

Why was he so tense? Was he worried Hayley would bring up

his former relationship with Amanda? Or that she'd say something else to embarrass him? And why did Sadie's opinion matter so much?

"—and he totally saved the man's life."

Sam tuned back in to find the other two staring at him. One with a smug grin, the other with a look of wonder.

"What?" he asked.

"You saved a man's life when you were there mowing his lawn? That is so amazing."

He scowled at Hayley. "It was no big deal."

Hayley pushed back her plate. "There was an article in the paper about it. He got a medal of commendation from the mayor and everything."

He rolled his eyes even as heat flushed his neck. "He had a heart attack. I called 911."

"Actually, he performed CPR for eighteen minutes and kept the man alive until the medics got there. He's kind of a hero."

He was gonna kill her. "Don't you have homework or something?"

"It's summer. Duh."

Sadie squeezed his wrist. "Stop it. She's right. You are a hero. What a wonderful thing to do."

His pulse fluttered at her touch before she removed her hand. "Thank you, but it was really nothing."

"Yep, he's a regular hero. Did you know he saved me from drowning in the ocean once when I was seven?"

Sam rolled his head back.

"Oh, tell me. I can't wait to hear this one."

"I'll do the dishes." Sam stood.

"You don't have to do that," Sadie called as he headed into the kitchen.

"Yes, I do," he muttered.

Sam began clearing the table and loading the dishes into the dishwasher. He was close enough to hear every word, but fortunately, once his sister finished the ocean story, the topic shifted to something unrelated to him.

"I love your nail polish," Hayley said to Sadie as he collected the last of the dishes.

"Thanks. It's Purple Rain. You should come over sometime and I can paint yours for you."

"She doesn't like that kind of—"

"I'd love that." Hayley shot him a smug look, then turned back to Sadie. "So you must be the one he's taking to our cousin's wedding."

At the sink Sam whipped his head around.

"That would be me, and I can't wait. I've never been to a destination wedding, so I'm really excited."

He directed a hot laser stare at his sister. Attempted mental telepathy: *Do not bring up Amanda and me.*

"I'm glad you'll be there. I helped make the table centerpieces for the reception. They're kinda cheesy, but whatever."

Sadie laughed. "Did you get a new dress? I'm definitely going shopping for this."

"Mom took me to the mall. I got an outfit for the breakfast too."

"There's a breakfast?"

Hayley nailed Sam with a look. "Did you tell her nothing?"

Sam grunted. Hayley was going to tell Sadie all about Amanda and him, and he'd come off the poor rejected schmuck. So, yes, that was apparently why he'd been so tense since his sister's arrival. He obviously cared a great deal what Sadie thought. He didn't even want to dissect that thought.

His sister was busy laying out the weekend schedule. "And after the rehearsal dinner, there'll be s'mores on the beach. There's a buffet breakfast on Saturday morning, and lunch is on our own, then it'll be time to get ready for the wedding. It's on the beach at sunset. I got a light blue sundress and strappy sandals, but I'll probably take them off at the beach. The hotel looks really nice and it'll be a full weekend, but I'm glad there's some free time. I love my family, but there's a great pool, and you never know when you're going to meet a cute guy."

"Maybe there'll be someone at the wedding you like. We'll have a great time, you'll see. And now I'll know someone else besides Sam."

He put the last plate in the dishwasher, aiming that laser at the side of Hayley's head. *Do not tell her.*

"Oh, my family is nice enough. It's big though. Lots of cousins. My mom has seven siblings, so—"

"Goodness. I can't even imagine. I have no siblings and only two cousins. A big family sounds like a lot of fun though."

"It's a lot of something," Hayley said dryly.

Sam closed the dishwasher door at the same time Hayley scooted back from the table. "Well, I really should run. I'm going to spend the night with a friend."

Hayley thanked Sadie again as the two said their goodbyes, sharing hugs, even. *Women.*

While Sadie started the dishwasher, Sam walked Hayley to the door.

She turned on the stoop and patted his cheek. "Relax, bro. I got you covered."

Then she turned and hopped down the stoop before getting into her rusty Saturn.

Hard to believe the girl was old enough to drive, much less appreciate the nuances of his complicated feelings. But apparently she was old enough for both.

EIGHTEEN

Like dominoes, each scene in your story should cause a toppling effect that keeps the action flowing throughout the novel.

—*Romance Writing 101*

What was taking that woman so long to return her call? Sadie's bare toes dug into the deep sand with each step as she checked her phone. On a leash, Rio trotted alongside her. The late-afternoon sun beat down from a clear blue sky, and a warm breeze fluttered her shirt and tugged at her hair.

She'd tried to call Mary twice today and had gotten voice mail both times—her inbox was too full to take another message.

On a positive note Sadie had gotten a text from Gillian this morning, raving about the synopsis. Sadie had danced a jig on her deck in full public view.

Unfortunately, Erin hadn't gotten back to her agent by the end of yesterday, so Sadie would have to wait till Monday to hear her opinion. Hopefully she loved it, too, and it would be approved at pub board on Tuesday.

If it was, Sadie could start writing the novel itself on Wednesday. That would give her just over two months to finish it—a challenge, for sure. But since the plot was based in reality, the writing should go quickly. She hoped.

She reached the public-access path and checked the Little Library on her way back to the house. New books appeared here and there. Someone had put a lovely conch shell inside the box.

Sadie straightened the books and headed back inside. The copy of *Christy* was safely tucked away in her nightstand drawer. If Mary would just call, they could get all this figured out. Sadie couldn't wait to return that ring and see the look on that man's face.

In the kitchen she refilled Rio's water dish and ruffled her fur. "Drink up, sweetheart. Can't have you getting dehydrated now, can we?"

Next she started dinner, which consisted of reheating last night's shrimp scampi. The evening before floated through her mind, inducing a wistful smile. Sam had been so funny. It was obvious he hadn't wanted his sister there. Why, she couldn't imagine. Hayley was delightful with her youthful energy and wry sense of humor. She obviously enjoyed tormenting her brother. Having no siblings herself, Sadie was intrigued by the relationship and enjoyed watching the dynamics between the two.

When the scampi was reheated, Sadie carried it to the dining room and sat down, scanning the empty table. She missed eating with her roommate on occasion. She'd love to go out to dinner and sample some of the island's restaurants, but it wasn't really in the budget. Besides, she disliked the thought of dining alone.

She briefly considered inviting Sam over. He was home—she'd heard his truck pull into the drive.

But she'd already invited him over to watch a movie and have dinner. The ball was in his court now. She hoped their friendship would continue though. She enjoyed his company and wondered if anything more could develop between the two of them.

More to the point: Did she want it to?

She'd never been in a relationship that had developed outside of traditional dating. She was accustomed to cutting things off after a first or second date when she realized the man in question didn't suit for whatever reason. And sometimes her date didn't ask her out again. Fair enough.

But she knew Sam fairly well now. And sometimes he did regard her in a way that made her insides flutter. Made her skin flush with heat. The moment she'd awakened against his side on the sofa, for instance. She'd definitely gotten the feeling he hadn't minded her closeness.

Was he interested in something more than friendship?

Her pulse thudded in her chest at the thought. Excitement? Fear? Maybe a little of both. With regard to Sam, she hadn't seen any red flags yet, though his recent failed relationship might still be a factor. Was he still in love with the woman? Hmm.

He was a little broody, but that seemed to have waned as they'd gotten to know each other.

The biggest obstacle in a long-term relationship with Sam was that she lived thirteen hours away—and that was a major complication. She loved her life in New York, and Sam obviously had deep roots here. She didn't know how that kind of hurdle could be overcome.

Look at her—not even a single date and she was weighing the prospect of a serious relationship with him.

"Good grief, Sadie. Get it together." Just as well. Obviously they had no future, and it was better to know that now.

Rio tilted her head and perked her ears.

"Mommy needs to chill out. All this romance writing is going to her head."

She took a bite of scampi, then grabbed her phone off the table to check it for the hundredth time today.

A voice mail had come in—and it was from Mary's number! She gasped and tapped Play.

"Hi, Sadie, this is Mary McAllister. You called me, uh, I guess it was last week, something about a book? Sorry it's taken so long to reply, but I'm back in town now. Give me a call when you get a chance."

Sadie's heart thrashed as she poised a finger over the Redial button.

But no. She should include Sam. He'd want to hear what Mary had to say.

She rushed out the back door, crossed to his side of the deck, and knocked on the sliding glass door. They were finally about to get their answer. They would have to be careful what they revealed to Mary—they couldn't ruin her boyfriend's proposal.

She knocked again, then cupped her hands on the glass and peeked inside. He was nowhere to be seen. "Oh, come on, Sam, you're killing me." She shifted back and forth on her feet. He must be upstairs. She knocked so hard it hurt her knuckles.

When that didn't help she tried the door. It slid smoothly open. She stepped inside. "Sam? Are you home?"

She slid the door shut and tiptoed toward the stairs. "Sam, I—"

He emerged from the bedroom and stared down from the second floor, wearing only a white towel and a frown. A pair of broad shoulders tapered down to a narrow waist where one hand rested on the towel knot.

"Whoops, I'm so sorry to intrude." But was she really? (Those pecs. Those *biceps.*) "I, uh, didn't mean to barge in like this, but Mary called and you didn't answer your door and it was unlocked—"

"Sadie."

"—so I thought you'd want to know that Mary left a voice mail, but she didn't really give me any information, so I have to call her back and I thought you might want to—"

"Sadie."

"Um, what?"

"Maybe I could get some clothes on before we have an actual conversation?"

"Not on my account." She put her fingers over her mouth. "I mean, of course. Yes, go ahead, I'll wait here. Is it okay if I wait here?"

He rolled his eyes before disappearing into his bedroom.

"But hurry, okay?" she called up the stairs. "Because I'm about to die from the waiting and I don't want to miss her. She could leave or have company and then who knows how long we'll have to wait for her to call back."

Sadie paced around the living room, trying to siphon off her excess energy. The image of his bare torso lingered. Tanned skin stretched over taut muscles. The broad expanse of his shoulders.

Stop that!

She turned her attention to his furnishings. She'd only been in his side of the house once, to print off her synopsis. It was decorated much the same as hers, and was—as it had been last time—neat as a pin.

His mail was stacked on the coffee table on top of a magazine: *Landscape Management.* His flip-flops sat by the back door. Other than that it was free of clutter. And so quiet. He could use a little music or something around here.

She checked the voice mail on her phone again as if she could manufacture more information about Mary and that ring. Nope, the woman's message hadn't left a single clue, and Sadie was so darn ready to return that ring to its owner.

She glanced up the stairs. "Sam? You almost ready?"

"Jeez, woman, hold your horses."

"Sorry," she muttered and returned to her pacing.

Five decades later Sam moseyed down the steps in a pair of shorts. Covering up in that navy blue T-shirt now seemed like a crime. He must've trimmed his beard this morning, but his wet hair hung around his face. Somehow the whole effect made the color of his eyes seem wilder.

She gave her head a shake and poised her finger above the Call button. "Ready?"

"Go for it."

She tapped the button and put the phone on speaker while he meandered into the kitchen and pulled a bottled water from the fridge. He offered it to her.

She shook her head. How could he think about water at a time like—?

"Hello?" a voice said from across the line.

"Mary? This is Sadie Goodwin returning your call. I hope

you had a lovely cruise." Maybe the woman would simply admit she'd gotten engaged.

"It was wonderful. That was my first and we'll definitely be going back."

"I took one a few years ago. It's a great way to travel. Well, listen, I have my neighbor Sam with me also, on speaker. We've kind of been working together to find the owner of that book I mentioned."

Mary and Sam greeted one another.

"Okay," Mary said, "so you were wanting to know where a book came from that was in with my dad's things? It would've belonged to my mother. I cleaned off her bookshelves last week and took them to his church for their library—he thought that's what Mom would've wanted."

"That was very kind of you. Well, there was a particular book in the bunch that your dad didn't think belonged to your mother. It eventually found its way into our hands, and we'd like to return it to its original owner. Your dad said you might know something about it. It's a copy of *Christy*, a burgundy hardcover with only the title and author's name on the cover. Do you remember it?"

"Oh yeah, of course. I actually put that copy and a few others in with my mom's things. Figured I'd clear off my own shelves while I was at it."

Sadie frowned at Sam. Mary obviously wasn't aware of the book's hidden compartment.

"Sure," Sam said. "Can we ask how you came to be in possession of the book?"

"Would you mind telling me why you're so eager to return it? Did you find a hundred-dollar bill in there or something?" Mary chuckled.

Sadie gave Sam a look. "No, but there were some . . . personal effects inside we felt the owner would want back."

"Well, that's nice of you to go to so much trouble. All I can tell you is that my son gave it to me. He found it in his apartment—I think it belonged to the last renter or something. I was visiting over there and he thought I might like to read it. It's not really my kind of story, but I took it anyway. Didn't want to be rude, you know. It was sweet of him to think of me."

Sadie closed her eyes. "Of course. When did he give you the book, do you remember?"

"I guess that'd be a couple weeks ago. I can give you his number." Mary chuckled. "I will say he's not real good about returning calls though. Or even answering his phone for that matter. Oh, what the hay, I can give you Aaron's address. My dad vouched for you guys."

"That would be great," Sadie said. "Thank you."

Mary rattled off the address and phone number. "He works from noon to midnight, so late morning might be the best time to catch him at home."

"Thank you," Sadie said. "We can't tell you how much we appreciate the information."

"No problem. I hope you find the book's owner."

They thanked her again, then Sadie tapped the Disconnect button and threw her hands up. "For heaven's sake. Who in the world does that ring belong to? It can't be her son's. He wouldn't have given away the book if he knew the ring was in there. And if it belonged to the former renter, why would he have left it behind?"

"I don't know."

Sadie huffed, all her frustration and impatience escaping

in a single puff of air. "Where in the world did that book come from?"

"We'll figure it out eventually."

"Well, we won't figure it out today. Aaron works till midnight. How could one little book have passed through so many hands so quickly?"

He homed in on her for a hot minute, then chuckled, his eyes softening, his dimple dimpling.

"What?"

"You are a very impatient woman."

She pressed her lips together. But it was impossible to work up much indignation when he was gazing at her with such affection. (And also when he was spot-on.) "I'm trying to do a good deed here, and I've been waiting nine days to do it. Think of how impatient that poor guy must be, searching high and low for that ring." That's exactly what she should be thinking of—and not those gold flecks in his eyes. Or the way the corners of his eyes crinkled when he smiled.

He blinked. "I guess you have a good point. But we can't do anything until tomorrow, so you may as well get on with your evening and try to put it out of your mind."

"Let's run by his place in the morning."

"Not too early. The man works till midnight. And I have lunch with my folks at one."

"That's right, it's Father's Day." She'd sent a new fishing pole to her dad and would call him in the morning. "I can be ready to leave at nine."

Water dripped down his neck and her fingers twitched to wipe it away. She clenched her hand in a fist.

"How 'bout ten? Let's let the guy sleep in a little."

"Nine thirty?"

The twist of his mouth and tilt of his head labeled her impatient once again. He wasn't wrong.

"Fine," he said. "Nine thirty. Can I go comb my hair now?"

"By all means." She headed toward the sliding door. "And, uh, sorry about the, you know, barging in part. That's probably a boundary issue—I'm working on it. See you." And with that, she slipped through the door.

NINETEEN

The scenes of your novel should ebb and flow. Some will be full of conflict and others will be full of rapport as your hero and heroine bond.

—*Romance Writing 101*

Sadie awakened at seven o'clock—and she used the term *awakened* loosely as she'd tossed and turned half the night, thinking about that ring.

She took Rio outside to do her business, filled her dishes with fresh kibble and water, and had a bowl of granola. She didn't always jog on the weekends, but she needed to run the clock down and expend some nervous energy. So she geared up in Spandex and hit the beach.

Everything about jogging was different here. The running surface challenged her every step. The waves rippled onto the shore, keeping her company, and the gulls scampered around her, seeking food. There were no honking taxis, no steaming concrete, no roaring jets overhead.

She could get used to this.

By the time she finished her run, she had just enough time to shower, get ready, and call her dad. "Hi, Daddy, happy Father's Day," she said when he answered the phone.

"Hi, punkin. Thank you. And thanks for the fishing pole. We'll have to plan a trip next time you come out to see us."

"I'd love that. How was your week? Did you get that old El Camino running again?" Her dad was a mechanic at a local garage. He was quite good and loved what he did, but her mother felt he could do better.

"I did. The owner picked it up yesterday. He was very happy with it. How are things in South Carolina? How's your story going?"

"It's going great. I got my synopsis turned in and I'm just waiting to hear back from my editor."

"Your mom mentioned that. I'm glad the switch in genres isn't throwing you off too much."

"Oh, it definitely threw me off. But thanks for your encouragement along the way. It means a lot."

"You're a gifted writer. I know westerns are your preferred genre, but I have no doubt you can pull this off."

"Thanks, Daddy."

"Speaking of literature, your mom told me about that ring you found in a book. What's up with that?"

She chuckled. "Your guess is as good as mine. I still haven't found the owner. But I'm not giving up yet. Are you and Mom going anywhere this summer? You're welcome to join me down here. There's a spare room and I'd love the company."

"Oh, thank you, honey. But I know you have a book to write. Besides, I think we're going to skip vacation this year. Get our savings built back up."

They'd purchased a new home in the fall. Sadie sensed there had been some discord over the two-story home situated in a prominent development. Sometimes navigating a relationship with her parents was like walking through a minefield. "I wish I could come out there, but this book has me pretty swamped the rest of the summer."

"Maybe Thanksgiving break."

"I'd love that. I miss Mom's cooking."

"She hasn't been doing much of that lately. Between the animal shelter and the nail salon she's been pretty busy."

"Her business seems to have grown a lot the past few years."

"Oh, it has. She's doing very well. I keep telling her she needs to hire more help, but you know your mom . . ."

Fearing she'd just stumbled upon another touchy subject, she changed the topic. "Did you get the picture I sent yesterday of the Little Library I made?"

"I did. I'm impressed."

"You taught me everything I know about tools."

"A woman should know how to take care of herself. Did your mom tell you that your aunt Doris read your books recently? She was raving about them at church Sunday."

"I'm glad she liked them."

"Well, they're really good, honey. Grandpa would've been so proud."

Her heart gave a tight squeeze. "Thanks, Daddy. He was a good man. I know a day like today must be hard for you."

"I miss him a lot. He was a good father to me."

"I miss him too. And Grandma. I have so many good memories at their ranch."

"It was a great place to grow up." Her mother said something in the background. "Mom says to tell you hi, and I hate to cut this short but we're gonna be late for church."

"Tell Mom I said hello, and have a happy Father's Day, Daddy. I'll call you later this week. Love you."

"Love you too, punkin."

By the time she hung up, it was almost time to meet Sam. She rubbed Rio's head. "Mommy will be back soon. Do not chew on anything that is not yours."

Rio lowered her head and gave Sadie a mournful look.

"I know. Mommy's so mean to leave. You be a good girl and I'll give you a treat when I get home."

She went out the front of the duplex, hopped up Sam's stoop, and knocked.

A few seconds later the door swung open. Sam's hair was still damp but he'd combed it off his face. "You're early."

"Are you ready?"

"Let me grab my keys. I'm driving."

A minute later he locked up the house and they headed toward his truck.

"Do you always have to be the one driving?"

He opened the passenger door for her. "Yep."

"Well, since you have such nice manners, I'll let it slide." She climbed inside the cab and waited while he rounded the front. She breathed in the scents of grass and gasoline, with a hint of leather—a unique bouquet she'd already come to associate with Sam. She wasn't overly fond of any of these aromas, but somehow, taken as a whole, the effect was quite addictive.

He got into the cab, donned his sunglasses, and started the truck. "Aaron's place is only ten minutes away. It's right downtown. Got the book?"

She patted her purse. "Right here. Though I don't see any scenario that would end with us handing it over to him."

"Not him, maybe. But he could lead us to the right person—apparently that former renter."

"I sure hope so."

As the miles passed, they chatted about their families. Sam obviously enjoyed a close relationship with his parents—even his sister, though they clearly liked to give each other a hard time. Sadie wondered about that family tension he'd mentioned before, but how bad could it be? He didn't seem to be dreading a meal with them today.

Hearing him talk about his family with obvious affection made guilt prick at her heart. She was in no big hurry to return to Pennsylvania. She loved her parents and they loved her, but the push and pull of their marriage had worn her down over the years. It was easier to maintain a relationship from afar where she wasn't so easily drawn into the drama.

Before she knew it they were heading into downtown. The heart of Tucker Island consisted of a string of old brightly painted cottages set close to both sides of the two-lane road. Shops and boutiques abounded: a surf store, a fudge shop, and a quaint flower shop called Bayside Blossoms, housed in a darling cottage painted cotton-candy pink. Farther down toward the marina, there was PJ's Clam Shack, a small gallery, a boat charter, and a shanty called Billy's Bar, sided with rough-hewn planks that seemed weathered by years of sand and wind.

Sam pulled along the curb in front of the art gallery, which was painted a pretty aqua shade and trimmed in white. Low-growing palms squatted under the plate-glass window alongside bright-blooming hibiscus bushes.

Sadie frowned at the building. "Is this it?"

"It's the right address. The gallery's new. This used to be a hair salon." He leaned toward her, peering out her window. "Looks like there might be an apartment above the shop."

"You're right. There are steps leading up to it. Let's go."

She grabbed her purse and exited the truck. The rickety staircase moved with her weight, and the paint on the handrails was peeling. The steps ended at a landing, and since there was no doorbell, she knocked on the white steel door.

Sam remained two steps below, putting them eye-to-eye. His sunglasses hid his eyes, but there was still plenty to recommend his face. A straight nose that flared gently above his short-cropped mustache. High, chiseled cheekbones and a groomed beard that called attention to a pair of lips that seemed impossibly soft.

"What?" he asked.

The door opened, obliterating her thoughts.

"Can I help you?" The tenant appeared to be in his early twenties. Dirty-blond hair hung attractively around a baby face, and a wrinkled T-shirt and khaki shorts hung from his slim frame.

"Are you Aaron?" she asked.

"Yeah, that's me."

"Hi, I'm Sadie and this is Sam. Your mother gave us your address."

"Right, right. She texted me, said you'd be coming by. Y'all want to come in? Place is kind of a mess, but it's my day off and likely to stay that way."

"Sure, thanks." Sadie followed the guy into his apartment. The living room was dark and gloomy even with the lights on.

Aaron pushed open the heavy curtains, and sunlight flooded in to reveal old wooden floors and white plaster walls. A hodgepodge of furniture sat around an area rug that had seen better days.

"Have a seat. Can I get you something to drink?"

"No thanks," Sam said.

Sadie perched on the sofa beside Sam. "Did your mom tell you we were asking about the book?"

Aaron scraped his hair off his forehead. "Sure, yeah. The one I gave her. I can't tell you much about it though. It was left behind when I moved in. The place was partially furnished and I found it inside that desk over there." He pointed to an old dark-stained desk with a sloped top.

"Mind if I take a look?" Sam asked.

"Help yourself."

Sam walked over to the desk and lifted the lid.

"What's in there now is my stuff. Far as I know the desk was here when the other tenant lived here. I guess he forgot to clean it out or didn't want the book. I'm not much of a reader, so I gave it to my mom."

"Do you happen to have his or her name or contact information?" Sadie asked.

"Sure don't. Haven't gotten any stray mail either. But I'm assuming it was a guy because of some stuff left behind—stray socks and whatnot. I reckon my landlord might know something about him though. I can give you her information."

Sam closed the lid. "That would be great. Thanks."

"What's so special about that book?" He gave a dry grin. "My luck, it's a first edition worth a million bucks."

"Nothing that exciting," Sadie said. "It just had some personal effects inside and we'd like to return it. About when did you find the book?"

He hitched a shoulder. "I guess it was a few weeks ago. I'd just moved in. Beginning of the month—first or second, I'd say."

Aaron pulled out his wallet and looked through his things. "The owner of the building has the gallery downstairs, but it's closed today. Here's her card. You can have it; her information is saved in my phone."

Sadie took the card. "Thank you."

Sam pulled out a business card and handed it to Aaron. "If you happen to hear from the former tenant, could you let him know we're trying to reach him?"

"Of course."

They made small talk about the island for a few minutes. He grew up in Brighton Beach but preferred Tucker Island. He was working at a nearby factory.

When the conversation petered out, Sadie hitched her purse on her shoulder and stood. "Well, we should probably let you get on with your day. Thank you so much for your help, Aaron. We sure do appreciate it."

"No problem. Hope you find him."

They said their goodbyes and left. Once inside the truck Sadie turned to Sam. "Let's call the landlord." She glanced at the card. "Merilee Owens."

"Be my guest." He started the truck and got the air going.

Sadie tapped the number into her phone and put it on speaker. It rang once. Twice. Three times. Then it clicked over to voice mail. "*You've reached the voice mail of Merilee Owens. I'm not available to take your call at the moment. Leave a message or call me back during business hours, nine to five Monday through Friday and nine to one on Saturday. Have a wonderful day."*

Sadie wavered briefly, then tapped the Disconnect button.

"Don't want to leave a message?"

Sadie slouched in her seat. "I'm tired of waiting for people to return my calls. I'll try her first thing in the morning."

"Another setback. Are you disappointed?"

"It's not a setback, really, just a delay. But yes, I'd hoped to resolve this today, despite the unlikelihood. It has to belong to this guy though, right? The former tenant? He's the man who's going to propose to his girl—if he hasn't already."

"That's the assumption I'm working under."

"Then we'll just have to wait until tomorrow. We'll get a forwarding address and pay him a visit."

TWENTY

Nothing clarifies a person's romantic interest
quite like the threat of competition.

—*Romance Writing 101*

Happy Father's Day." Sam stepped inside his parents' home and gave his dad a hug.

In his midfifties, his dad was the same height as Sam, a big bear of a guy. His skin was bronzed, his body in good shape from his work outdoors. The physical labor, however, hadn't prevented time from wreaking havoc on his hairline.

"Thanks, Son." Dad pushed up his wire-framed glasses, calling attention to his brown eyes and the laugh lines fanning out from them.

"Get over here and give your mama a hug." Mom appeared and swept him up in an embrace. She was petite with a delicate bone structure and blue eyes that sparkled when she was happy and flashed when she wasn't. The only thing Sam had inherited from her was his thick black hair.

"Hi, Mom. Good to see you."

She pulled away and swatted his arm. "'Bout time you showed your face around here. I had to hear about your visit to town from Eleanor Stapleton. You couldn't have dropped by to see your dear old mom?"

He showed her his best hangdog look. "Sorry, Mom."

She shelved her hands on her hips. "That's all I get? And who was the woman you brought to the rummage sale? Do I know her?"

Dad wrapped an arm around Mom's shoulders. "Let's not scare him away, honey." He kissed her temple. "Come on, Son. You should see the new flooring in the master bath. We shoulda had it done years ago."

"The food smells great, Mom," Sam called as he headed down the hallway with his dad.

The remodel was still in an ugly phase, with tarps and dust. But the new ceramic flooring looked great. His dad showed him the paint colors and fixtures they'd chosen. After they were finished, they headed back to the living room.

Hayley entered through the garage door. "I'm home. Happy Father's Day, Dad." She kissed him on the cheek. "Hello, Brother. So glad you deigned to visit your childhood home."

He gave her a hug. "Yes, Meatball, it's been so long since I've seen you."

She blinked up at him innocently. "Did you bring your girlfriend?"

"Girlfriend?" His mom entered the living room.

Sam cut Hayley a glare.

"Is that who you brought to the church? Are you seeing someone, Sam?"

He'd have to be visually impaired to miss the hope scrawled across Mom's face. He got it. His loved ones were eager to see him move on from his heartbreak. "She's just a friend, Mom."

"You'll have to tell us all about her over lunch, which is ready by the way. Come and get it, everyone."

As the siblings followed their parents to the dining room, Hayley sent him an innocent grin and he mouthed *Thanks a lot.*

At the table his mom said a heartfelt prayer, thanking God for the wonderful man who was her husband, then they all dug in.

"The food looks great, Mom." Sam wasn't kidding either. After all the take-out meals he'd had recently, he appreciated the home-cooked meal.

"Thank you. I hope the ribs are tender. It's a new recipe."

Dad loaded his plate with ribs and a heaping spoonful of mac 'n' cheese. "Smells wonderful, honey. The meat's practically falling off the bone."

"So who's this girl Hayley mentioned?" Mom asked. "Is she the one you're taking to the wedding?"

Sam grimaced. He'd hoped she might forget about Sadie.

"Her name's Sadie," Hayley said, "and she's his neighbor on the island. She's really sweet and fun." She gave Sam a meaningful look. "*And* drop-dead gorgeous."

His mom beamed. "Well, how nice!"

"We're just friends."

"And how did you meet her, honey?" Mom asked Hayley.

"I stopped by the other night, and they were having supper together at Sadie's place."

Sam scowled at her. If it wasn't summertime he'd bring up her grades. He snatched a rib and took a bite. "These are great, Mom."

"So what brought her to the island?" Dad asked. "Or is she a resident?"

Sam swallowed the bite. "She's just here for the summer."

"She's from New York and she's a schoolteacher. She teaches art to elementary kids. Doesn't that sound like a fun job? And she's a published author too."

"Well, how interesting." Mom tucked her hair behind her ear. "What does she write?"

"She's had a couple westerns published." Sam had actually ordered them last week and they'd arrived yesterday. He was curious to read her work.

"I can't wait to meet her."

"She's looking forward to the wedding," Hayley said.

"She sounds lovely, Sam. You should have her over here for supper. We'd love to meet her before the wedding, wouldn't we, honey?"

"Sure." Dad was too busy gnawing on rib bones to say anything more.

Sam needed to lower his mom's expectations about a million notches. "Thanks, Mom, but I barely know her. She's only going to the wedding as a favor."

"But she's living next door and you were having supper together."

He opened his mouth.

"They're *just friends*." Hayley's eyes twinkled as she shoveled a forkful of mac 'n' cheese into her big mouth, smiling around it.

"Well, I'm sure she's a lovely person. I can't wait to meet her."

Sam didn't disagree. But he wasn't about to offer his mother any encouragement. He liked Sadie. Maybe he could even like her a lot. But his heart wasn't yet ready to take that risk.

The afternoon passed in a blur. After lunch Sam and his family watched the Braves defeat the Pirates. His mom only brought up Sadie one other time—when he was leaving.

"I meant what I said about inviting your friend over. She's welcome here anytime."

"Thank you, Mother." He resisted the urge to remind her they were only friends.

By the time Sam got home, it was suppertime, but after the big lunch, complete with homemade apple pie and interrogations, he wasn't hungry. Instead he found himself eager to see what Sadie had been up to. He tried to ignore the way his pulse raced upon seeing her car in the drive.

He went straight through the house and out the back. Sadie was nowhere to be found, but her pink flip-flops sat on the bottom step. She must've gone for a walk on the beach. He wished he'd gotten home a little earlier. He could've gone with her.

He wanted to tell her about his afternoon with his family. The way Hayley lit up when she talked about teaching someday. The way his dad, so reflective and stoic, had sprung from the couch when the Braves scored a grand slam in the last inning.

He'd obviously been hiding out on the island too long without company. Or maybe he'd just been too long without female companionship.

Brimming with energy, Sam stood at the railing. The sun warmed his skin even as the ocean breeze cooled it off. His gaze drifted over the beach crowd, soaking in the last rays of the day. A father and son tossed a Frisbee at the shoreline. A couple with young kids worked on a sandcastle. A man jogged by at the waterline.

Farther down, a couple walked with their—no, that wasn't

a couple. It was Sadie and the man he'd seen her with last week, the one with the Labrador.

He frowned at the two of them, who seemed engrossed in conversation. Had they planned this little walk on the beach, or was it just a chance meeting? Had Sadie spent the entire afternoon with the guy?

And why did Sam care so much?

And he did care. Especially when Sadie threw her head back and laughed. He wanted to be the one making her laugh. There was no mistaking the dull twist in his stomach or the fervent wish that the guy would take a hike.

The feelings were familiar—and not in a good way.

Of course this little twinge of jealousy didn't have the teeth the situation with his cousin and Amanda had. He wasn't in love with Sadie, and she wasn't betraying him with a man he loved and trusted.

But it was a good reminder that he never wanted to feel that way again. He never wanted to have a woman and then realize in a terrible moment of clarity that he didn't have her at all.

He scratched his neck. Where had these feelings come from? He'd barely known Sadie two weeks.

She and the man stopped directly in front of the house, still engaged in conversation. Sadie squatted to play with the black Lab while Rio danced around the man's legs until he picked her up.

Sam frowned.

She'd really managed to get under his skin quickly. And it seemed like he wasn't the only one. The guy on the beach didn't seem to be in a big hurry to part ways with her. He wore a pair of board shorts with a white T-shirt. He was fit, if a little on the short side. Then again, even barefoot he still stood a head above Sadie.

Was the guy asking her on a date? Would Sadie entertain the idea of a new relationship when she was only here for the summer?

Now there was a pertinent question. Equally relevant, was Sam open to the idea of dating Sadie?

No, he decided on the spot. His heart wasn't ready for a serious relationship, much less one that would be over come summer's end.

TWENTY-ONE

A *slow-burn* romance is a story in which the love relationship develops organically, at a gradual pace.

—*Romance Writing 101*

As Sadie returned from the shoreline, she spotted Sam at the deck railing and gave a big wave.

He nodded.

So understated, all those minimal movements and short sentences. She needed to remember that when she started writing her story this week—provided Erin and the team liked her proposal. *Please, God.*

Eager to chat with Sam, she bypassed her Little Library and headed straight for the deck. "How was lunch with your family?"

"Well, I'd say it was a mixed bag."

She set Rio loose and the dog went straight to Sam. "Do tell."

He picked up the dog and leaned against the railing. "The food was great, but Mom acted as if she hadn't seen me in a decade. My dad was his typical reflective self, and my sister was up to her usual tricks."

Sadie joined him at the railing. "Oh, come on. Hayley couldn't be nicer. What trouble could she possibly cause?"

He snorted. "You're clearly not her brother."

"That's no answer. Come on, I'd tell you."

"Of course you would." He said nothing else, just arched a brow.

"How very enigmatic of you. Fine, don't tell me then. It's not like I don't have enough unknowns in my life at the moment. The ring mystery hangs in the balance, as does my writing career, but don't you worry about little old me."

"I have a feeling you'll be just fine on all fronts."

She tilted her head. "That sounded vaguely complimentary."

"Well, you don't exactly exude a helpless vibe."

His words warmed her, probably more than they should've. Did he admire her independence? He seemed to, though some men seemed threatened by it.

"Hello there." Anna and Nick waved from the public-access path.

"Well, hi, Anna! Hi, Nick. What are you doing out and about today?"

"We had lunch with Nick's family over at PJ's Clam Shack."

Nick slipped his arm around Anna's shoulders. "And now we're going to enjoy a quiet walk on our favorite beach."

Anna opened the Little Library. "After I peruse your bookshelves. You were so right about that Jenny Hale novel. Do you have anything else by her?"

"I don't think so, but there's a Debbie Macomber novel you might enjoy."

"Oh, there it is." She flipped the novel over, then slipped it back inside the box. "This looks great. I'll pick it up on my way back. Is this your husband? I didn't realize you were married. What a charming couple you make."

Sadie's hands fluttered about. "Oh no, he's not . . . I didn't . . . we're not . . ."

"I'm Sam—Sadie's co-tenant for the summer."

"Oh, I'm so sorry. I'm Anna and this is my boyfriend, Nick. When I'm not taking romantic strolls on the beach, I enjoy putting my foot in my mouth."

Nick gave her a squeeze. "I can vouch for that."

"No worries," Sadie said. "Enjoy your walk. It's such a beautiful evening."

"It was nice meeting you, Sam," Anna said. The two waved and were off on their stroll.

"They seem like a nice couple," Sam said.

"They're regulars at the beach."

"And at your library?"

"Well, she is a voracious reader and I'm happy to introduce readers to new authors. So did your dad have a nice Father's Day, despite your sister's mysterious antics?"

He arched a brow at her but otherwise ignored her efforts to pry. "I think so. As long as his family's there and he's being well fed, he's a pretty happy guy. How about your dad? Was he having a good day?"

"I think so. I sent him a new fishing pole—that's his favorite hobby. Something we used to do together."

"It's too bad you can't be with him today."

"Yeah, I guess. I don't think my family is like yours though."

He pinned her with a look that made her squirm. "In what way?" His voice was low and sincere, his gaze fixed and warm.

"I don't know. We're not especially close. I live so far away—but that's my fault. When I graduated from college, I took a job that put me in New York where Caroline lived."

"Do you miss living near your folks?"

She wavered. "Yes and no. They have kind of a complicated relationship, so let's just say I don't mind the distance."

"Sorry to hear that."

"They're terrific people, don't get me wrong. They love me and made sure I knew it. But their own relationship is inconsistent. I thought that was normal until I started staying over at friends' houses in junior high and got to know other families. I was surprised to find my friends' parents had never been separated or divorced."

His brows winged upward. "Yours have?"

"They were divorced once when I was really young. And separated three times that I can remember. Each time when they got back together, I thought, *Okay, everything will change now.* But no, the cycle would just start all over again. They never seem to learn from their mistakes. It's as if they can't be together but they can't be apart either." She gave her head a sharp shake. "Anyway . . . sorry. I didn't mean to unload on you. They're having a good spell right now, so hopefully that'll last awhile."

"But that must leave you waiting for the other shoe to drop."

Her gaze shifted to him, zeroing in on his tender expression. He seemed to get it somehow, and that made her feel inordinately understood. The thought put a pinch in her chest. "That's it exactly. It's hard to enjoy the good times because I know what's coming."

"That must've been unsettling for you as a child."

She forced a smile. "Well, at least their feelings for me never wavered. They always made sure I knew their problems weren't my fault. That they loved me. But going away to college taught me that it's better to love them from a distance. I hope that doesn't make me sound like a selfish brat."

"Not at all. You're entitled to live your own life. And believe me, even with a healthy family, sometimes a little distance doesn't hurt." He released a wry grin.

She was glad for the slight shift of topic. "Hence your extended stay on the island."

"Well, I can't really move to New York because of the family business."

"I guess you can't." It must be expensive to maintain a home and also rent out a beach cottage. "Do you ever regret that—working with your family? Is there something else you'd rather do?"

"Not at all. I love working outdoors. And most of the time, working with my family."

"What do you like about it?" *Other than it obviously keeps you in great shape.*

When Rio squirmed he set the dog down. "I guess there's something satisfying about taking someone's property and making it beautiful. Or even taking a brown, untended lawn and making it flourish."

She nodded. "I get that. Sometimes when one of my students understands and implements a simple art concept, I feel so proud of my work. It makes it all worthwhile."

"Exactly. Customer satisfaction is a big deal to me. Seeing someone's pleasure with what I've done. Probably the way you feel when a student feels good about their own work."

"That's right." Her eyes sharpened on him, taking in his steady gaze and engaged expression. "You know, you're not at all who I thought you were."

"Oh yeah?"

Remembering when she'd stumbled off the stoop, she chuckled. "When we first met I thought you were at best a hermit and at worst a world-class jerk."

"Wow, no need to spare my feelings."

She nudged his shoulder. "You made me feel like an imposition, and I was trying so hard to be friendly since we were going to be flat mates for the whole summer."

"You're friendly with everyone." He looked away and nodded out toward the sea. "Case in point, you've already found a walking buddy."

She frowned as she followed his gaze. "Oh, Jared—and his lovely sidekick, Roscoe. We met last week and ran into each other again tonight. He's an islander who works at the marina and, ironically, doesn't own a boat."

"Interesting."

"Roscoe and Rio are so cute together. Roscoe lets her run right underneath him, plus they're aligned in their mutual distrust of all seagulls."

"Is that so?"

"I've always loved Labradors. But the city—not to mention my tiny apartment—isn't a place for a big dog. Jared's street has no sidewalks. Anyway, the beach is such a nice place to walk."

"And to meet new people."

At his strange tone she sent him a sideways glance. Was he jealous of Jared? Mentioning that he had a girlfriend seemed presumptuous. "People are so friendly here. I love that you can start conversations with random strangers. My mom said I was like that even as a baby, before I could talk. I'd smile at strangers and get them to engage with me."

"That I can believe." He cut her a glance. "I'll bet you were an adorable baby."

She laughed. "I was very chubby and had a terrible cowlick, which I fortunately outgrew. But that wasn't my worst phase—that would've been my third and fourth grade years, and okay, probably half of fifth grade too. I had acne and these awful thick-framed glasses. Also my hair was always greasy. Why didn't I just wash it?"

He chuckled, the low, throaty timbre making something squeeze tight inside her. "Because nobody cares about personal hygiene at that age. Well, obviously you grew out of that stage. No acne or thick glasses in sight."

Her gaze locked on his, holding for a long moment that made her want to take a dip in those beautiful eyes. Possibly drown. The way Sam gazed at her . . . Did he want to kiss her? Did she want to kiss him?

Whoa, Sadie. Rein it in. Not happening, remember?

She cleared her throat and pulled her gaze away. "Um, so . . . what about you? I'll bet you never had an ugly phase. I'll bet you had all the girls chasing after you."

"Nothing as dramatic as that. Actually, I was short through most of school. I had a late growth spurt my senior year."

"Are you kidding me? You're over six feet tall."

"Well, I was about your height through most of school. It was a good thing I worked out and played baseball—although playing shortstop, I got my share of ribbing."

Sadie chuckled. "Oh no."

"It was mostly in fun. Plus my cousin had already hit six foot and was on the football team, so he always watched out for me."

"Your cousin—the groom-to-be?"

"Tag. Yeah, that would be him." Sam stared out toward the ocean.

"It's nice that he had your back like that."

"Yeah, it sure was." But the tone of his voice hinted at something else.

TWENTY-TWO

Begin each chapter with a sentence that draws the reader in, and end each chapter with a sentence that entices her to turn the page.

—*Romance Writing 101*

Sadie paced the living room as her watch ticked away the last minute. At precisely nine o'clock she dialed the number for the art gallery. All she had to do was convince Merilee Owens to give her the former tenant's information, and she'd be able to return that beautiful ring to its rightful owner.

Merilee answered on the fourth ring. "Island Art, Merilee speaking."

"Um, hello. My name is Sadie Goodwin and I got your number from Aaron—your tenant above the gallery?"

"Yes, of course. How can I help you?"

"This is kind of a long story, so you'll have to bear with me. I'm visiting the island for the summer and put up a Little

Library on the beach—you know, those little book boxes that have popped up in neighborhoods . . . ?"

"Right. Yes, I've seen them around."

"Well, about a week and a half ago, someone left a hardbound book that has some personal contents inside. Long story short, I'm certain the owner would want the book back, and I traced it all the way to Aaron, who said he'd found the book in an old desk that was left behind by the former tenant. I was hoping you might be able to give me that renter's information so I can return the book to him."

"An old desk . . . how intriguing. I'd love to help you but I only recently purchased the building. The apartment was furnished but the last tenant was already gone, so I'm afraid I didn't have any contact with him."

Sadie's stomach flopped to her feet. "Oh, I see. Well, maybe you could give me the previous owner's information. He or she would surely have his former tenant's phone number if not his address."

"I actually purchased the property from a bank. But now that I think of it, I remember someone mentioning that the previous owner passed away before the bank seized his assets."

"Oh no. I'm sorry to hear that. But what about his family? Surely they'd have records regarding his previous tenants . . ."

"I really couldn't say. I don't even know the owner's name."

"Well, I guess only the bank has the information I'm looking for then." That was better than nothing.

"I'm sure they do. But whether or not they'll release that information might be another matter." Merilee gave her the name and address of the bank, which fortunately was right on the island.

"Thank you so much, Merilee. I appreciate your time. And

I'll definitely come take a peek at your gallery soon. I'd love to have a souvenir of my time on the island, and trust me when I say my apartment in New York could use some help."

"I'd love that. We have some unique artwork, and all of our pieces are made by local artists and artisans."

"I can't wait to check it out."

After Sadie disconnected the call, she swept Rio off her feet. "Well, girl . . . I guess we'll just have to visit the bank and hope for the best, won't we?"

Rio yapped and licked her chin.

"That's right. But maybe we should wait for Sam. He might know someone who works there, and I have a feeling we'll need a connection to break through the red tape."

She sent him a text using voice-to-text. The gallery owner doesn't know who the former tenant is. However, SunTrust does. I don't suppose you have a local connection there?

About an hour later she received a reply. No connections that I know of. But I can go with you tomorrow morning. Maybe I'll recognize someone.

Sadie took Rio for a walk on the shore, then after lunch she took a dip in the ocean and lay out on the beach with a romance novel for an hour—that was about as long as she could sit still. She constantly checked her email for a letter from her editor. Tomorrow was pub board. Why hadn't Erin responded to her proposal yet?

Midafternoon she texted Gillian to see if she had news. Nothing yet, kiddo. Have faith. We'll know soon enough.

"Argh!"

Rio's eyes opened from where she napped on a sunny spot of the living room floor.

"Why hasn't she written me, Rio? Doesn't she know I'm dying down here? My whole career hangs in the balance."

Clearly used to Sadie's monologues, the dog's eyes fluttered closed again.

She might as well clean the house. It would pass the time—and there was perhaps more sand on her floor than on the beach. She changed into comfortable leggings and a loose-fitting T-shirt.

Two hours—and a million email checks—later, Sadie's apartment was sparkling clean and it was almost dinnertime. The New York office would be closing in a matter of minutes and still no word from Erin.

She'd heard Sam pull into the driveway a while ago—a short day for him, though he usually started just after sunrise.

Sadie sighed. "We may as well start dinner, huh, girl?"

Rio had followed her around the apartment as she cleaned. Her little sweetie was the best company. Sadie had taken breaks only to text with Caroline and her island friend Keisha, who'd decided to start a mommy book club and wondered if Sadie had any advice. Oh boy, did she.

On her way to the kitchen, she checked her phone to see if Keisha had responded to her last text and saw a new email. She opened the email app.

"It's from Erin!" She plopped down on the barstool as she opened the message. Her stomach wobbled at its short length, and she held her breath as she read.

Hi Sadie,

Sorry to take so long to respond to your proposal. I love

your story idea. I'll be taking it to pub board tomorrow and will let you know Wednesday how it went.

Have a wonderful evening!

Erin

Sadie leaped up from the barstool, screaming. She twirled around in a circle. "She liked it! She! Liked! It! Wooooo! Wooooo! Aaaaah!" Her head spun with pleasure—and also with dizziness.

She stopped whirling but the room kept spinning. "She's taking my story to pub board, Rio! She liked my idea! She really liked it!"

The dog barely glanced her way before resuming her nap.

Sadie whooped again. She was smiling so hard her jaw ached. Erin was a senior editor and the team usually backed her recommendations based on her stellar track record (Sadie's western novels notwithstanding). She was so blessed to be getting a second chance.

"Thank You, Jesus! I'm going to write a romance novel, Rio! Just wait and see. Woo-hoo!"

A knock sounded just before the patio door slid open. Sam stuck his head inside. "Sadie, you okay?"

"Sam! She liked my proposal!" She flung herself into his arms and squeezed him tightly. "I just got an email from my editor, and she's taking my story to pub board tomorrow."

"Wow, that's great news. Congratulations." His breath fanned the tip of her ear even as his arms tightened around her.

"I waited all day to hear from her, and the email just came in." Her heart pressed against his chest, thudding quickly. She really should pull away, but the embrace felt so nice. So solid and comforting. "I was afraid I'd be back to square one and I don't have another idea. I'm so relieved and so happy."

"I can tell."

At his droll tone she drew back.

His eyes lit with humor and that dimple came out to play. "I heard you screaming from my apartment. I thought the ceiling must be caving in."

She laughed. "Whoops. Guess I got a little carried away."

He smelled faintly of leather and some pleasant earthy scent. His hands still warmed the small of her back and the spot between her shoulder blades. She slid her hands down, pressing his lapel—then realized he didn't have a lapel.

She gave his chest an awkward pat, then drew away. "My heart's beating so fast. Because of the email, I mean! The good news," she added, just to be clear. She turned away and winced. Although, yes, it had felt very nice to be wrapped in his arms.

"No, you should be. That's, uh, some great news, Sadie."

"You want to stay for dinner? I was getting ready to make something, and I'm in the mood to celebrate. I splurged on a couple of steaks. They're in the freezer but I could thaw them out really quick and grill out—if you don't mind showing me how, that is."

"That sounds great but"—he rubbed his neck—"I actually have plans tonight."

"Oh." Her stomach sank a little, but she forced a smile. "That's okay. No worries."

He checked the time. "We're still going to the bank in the morning though, right?"

"Right, yeah, of course. It opens at nine. That won't interfere with your schedule?"

"I'll make it work." He backed toward the door.

Come back. Stay with me. Celebrate with me. She took a step toward him, then blinked. What was wrong with her? Since when was she so needy for companionship? She'd always relied on her female friends, especially Caroline, to fill that role.

He opened the door and turned, flashing that dimple again. "Congratulations again on your proposal. I hope the rest of the team likes it."

"Thanks. I'll see you in the morning."

Sadie laid her hand over her heart as she watched him go, feeling it throb against her palm. When had she gotten so attached to Sam? And why was it that when she had her happiest news in weeks, she most wanted to share that moment with her neighbor?

TWENTY-THREE

Give your protagonist setbacks so the reader will keep flipping pages to find out if she prevails.

—*Romance Writing 101*

All that for nothing.

Sam opened the bank door for Sadie, and she stepped out into the bright morning sunshine. She'd even worn the most professional outfit she'd brought with her—an ice-blue fit-and-flare dress. She'd twisted her hair into a chignon and donned a pair of heeled sandals so she'd look as respectable as possible.

And still a *no*.

"Sorry I couldn't be of more help." Sam opened the passenger door of his truck.

"Not for lack of name-dropping. How can you not have any connections with the staff on an island this small?"

"It's not as small as you think." He closed her door and rounded the vehicle.

She was getting a headache. She took the pins from her hair and shook it loose.

Sam settled in the driver's seat, staring at her strangely.

She blinked at him. "What?"

"Nothing." His fingers fumbled as he started the truck.

"Now what are we going to do? The bank's our only connection with the previous owner of that building."

"Not necessarily. I was thinking while that guy pontificated about their privacy policy . . . Property sales are public record. We could find the man's name online and possibly locate his family that way."

"That's a great idea. Why didn't I think of that?"

"That'll give you something else to do while you're waiting to hear back on your proposal. You must be on pins and needles."

"Today's going to drag by so slowly. I keep praying it goes well, but I'm pretty sure God's getting tired of me."

"I don't think that's possible." His smile, the look in his eyes, seemed full of affection.

A round of butterflies cut loose in her stomach as he pulled from the parking lot. Sadie's heart gave a thump. She recalled the way she'd felt in his arms last night. The hug had turned into something more. Something longer. Of course, that was only because she hadn't let go of him, but still. His effect on her was . . .

Well. Let's just say it had been difficult to distinguish between the excitement of her news and the feelings he provoked.

In the quiet of the cab, she couldn't deny the special spark between them. She recognized the common feelings of attraction, of course. But there seemed to be something more. Their friendship was shifting in a new direction.

Did she want it to?

A summer fling might be good for her in so many ways. She'd never experienced the rush of love—not that she was feeling that now. But there was the possibility of it.

She did want to find love someday. Settle down with a man and start a family—she adored children. She longed for something very different than what her parents had. She wanted a consistent, drama-free relationship that withstood life's inevitable troubles. She wanted to have enough in common with a man that they didn't argue over every little thing. Enough money—and unity on the way it was spent—that financial troubles didn't put them in separate beds for weeks on end.

Or land them in divorce court.

But Sam's life was here and hers was in New York. Was there any point in pursuing a relationship with him when it would predictably end come summer's end?

Definitely not. She was going to have to put a lasso on this and wrestle it to the ground if need be.

Before she knew it Sam pulled along the curb in front of their house. "Don't be disappointed. I'll bet you can find the owner online."

He'd apparently mistaken her silence for discouragement. She dredged up a smile as she opened her door. "I'm sure you're right. I'll keep you up-to-date via text."

It was midafternoon when Sadie admitted she'd hit a dead end. She pushed her laptop away and flung herself back against the Adirondack chair. The sun beat down on her bare shoulders, making beads of sweat pop out on the back of her neck. A slight breeze ruffled the hair that had escaped her bun.

"Well, Rio, I guess we've hit a roadblock."

The dog opened her eyes but didn't lift her head from her paws.

Sadie had found the previous building owner's name almost immediately and quickly located a short obituary. (Not very well written, she had to say.) It had been published several weeks ago in the *Tucker Island Gazette* and contained a long list of relatives by whom he'd been predeceased.

The man had no one who'd survived him? No wife or kids or grandkids? How was that possible? She'd even looked him up in online directories and made some calls, but his name, William Brown, was a common one, and she'd found no one who knew the man she was searching for.

Finally she'd texted the results of her research to Sam but hadn't heard back from him yet.

She glanced at her watch. Four o'clock. At least the research had kept her mind occupied most of the afternoon, and the business day was almost over. The pub board had already decided her fate—she just didn't know what it was yet. This was her only chance at another writing contract. She didn't have time to come up with a new plot, and after the dismal sales of her Lonesome Ridge series, no other publisher would touch her.

Even if the team approved her proposal, she'd only have about ten weeks to turn in a manuscript. But she had to return to school the third week of August, and she'd need three weeks for the rewrites. So that meant she'd have roughly five weeks in which to write the first draft.

Her nerves jangled at the thought. She'd never cranked out a book that quickly, much less in a genre she'd never written in.

But since the plot so closely reflected real-life events, maybe she could pull it off.

If only the team liked her idea.

Her phone vibrated in her pocket with a call. She checked the screen. Sam. Despite her discouragement about their search for the ring's owner, she smiled because he'd never called her before. "Well, hello there."

"Hey, I'm sorry you haven't had much luck with your search."

She imagined him cooling off in the shade of his truck, the air on full blast. "Yeah, I've looked high and low, and I can't find any information on the guy."

"I had an idea after I got your text. I could check around with other business owners in town. Surely someone knew something about him."

"Oh, that's a great idea. His name's William Brown. Do you have any idea of how many William Browns live in the area? Seven. And I know because I called every last number listed online, and none of them knew the William Brown who recently passed. And I don't know if he went by William, Will, or Bill for that matter."

"It sounds like you were pretty thorough. Listen, I'm just about done for the day. I'll head downtown in a bit and ask around. I know a few people who work in the area. Maybe we'll hit pay dirt. Want to tag along?"

Her heart thumped at the invitation. After all, they'd worked together so far, and it was nice that he wanted to keep it that way. "I'd love to . . . but I have a date tonight." She wasn't sure why she'd used that word, but she couldn't seem to keep herself from testing the waters. And maybe it had its desired effect, because there was a long pause before he responded.

"On a Tuesday night?" His voice gave nothing away.

She chuckled. "It's your sister's only free night this week. We're going shopping for wedding clothes."

"Oh . . ."

"What's wrong? Afraid she's going to divulge your deepest, darkest secrets?"

"Actually I'm shocked she has any interest in shopping at all. She's always been kind of a tomboy."

"Well, it was her idea and I wasn't about to turn her down. It's no fun to shop alone."

"I'll take your word for it. Listen, I'm at my next job. I'll keep you apprised on my investigation."

"I'll keep you apprised on my shopping venture."

"Not necessary," he said drolly.

TWENTY-FOUR

At the heart of every romance novel is the concept of thwarted desire.

—*Romance Writing 101*

Sam walked with purpose toward his truck. It was getting later in the day and businesses were starting to close. He'd already stopped by PJ's Clam Shack and spoken with PJ herself. She'd known William Brown only vaguely and had no idea if he had family in the area. But she did confirm he went by "Will." The manager on staff at Billy's Bar had never met Will Brown.

Finally, Sam realized that the building's previous retail tenant, the owner of the hair salon, definitely would have known her own landlord. But the salon had apparently moved across the island.

When he reached his truck he got in and headed that way. He thought of Sadie and Hayley, even now hitting the stores in search of wedding clothes. He wasn't worried anymore that Hayley would divulge his previous relationship with Amanda.

She seemed to understand the hurt and humiliation the whole situation had caused him. And while embarrassing him was one of her favorite pastimes, she'd never humiliate him.

Sadie was probably wondering about his progress, but he didn't want to update her until he had something positive to share. When they began this venture he hadn't dreamed it would be this hard to hunt down that book's owner. And he'd never dreamed that making Sadie happy would come to mean so much to him.

He didn't want to let her down.

He let that thought soak in for a long minute. When had pleasing Sadie become so important to him? She was such a positive person by nature. It had been hard to see her disappointed this morning. He'd felt like a failure when he'd been unable to make a connection at the bank that would loosen that red tape.

Sadie was obviously coming to mean something to him, and he'd already decided he shouldn't pursue that relationship—despite how nice that hug had felt last night.

He shook the memory from his mind. They'd solve this mystery, then he would leave her alone. With any luck she'd have a book to write, and surely that would consume the rest of the summer.

Of course, there was also the upcoming wedding. There was no way he was attending that alone. He'd just have to stay strong. Keep the relationship on friendly terms.

How hard could it be?

A few minutes later he turned into the parking lot of the Hair Gallery. A Cape Cod home had been transformed into a business. Conforming with the island's pastel palette, it was painted sea green and trimmed in white. The wide porch was welcoming and bore a hanging shingle with the names of the salon and business owner.

He entered the building and found a wide-open first floor decorated in neutral shades. A blow-dryer hummed in the distance, and the scents of eucalyptus and lemongrass teased his nose. A few hairdressers buzzed around their stations, but he stepped up to an old fireplace façade that had been repurposed as a front desk.

A twentysomething woman with an airbrushed face and at least three sets of earrings greeted him. Her blood-red lips parted in a professional smile. "Hello, welcome to the Hair Gallery. Need a trim? We're a little backed up right now, but we could get you in, say, in twenty minutes?"

"Thank you, but I'm not here for a cut. I was actually wondering if I might speak with Chantilly Thomas?"

The woman tucked her short bleached-blonde hair behind her ear. "That would be me. But it's just Tilly. What can I do for you?"

"My name's Sam Ford. I work here on the island, and I'm trying to find a phone number for your former landlord, Will Brown. I thought you might be able to help me."

Her face fell. "Oh, I'm sorry to tell you, but Will passed away a while back . . ."

"Right, I know that. I guess I should've said I'm wanting to reach his family. I have something that belongs to a former tenant of his and would like to return it, but I can't find the renter's current information. I was hoping his family might be able to help me."

"Yeah, I don't think he had any family. At least, that's what he told me. His wife passed away a long time ago and they never had any kids. Word has it everything he owned was sold and the proceeds donated to some charity. No beneficiaries." The phone on the desk rang. "Excuse me just a minute."

Frustration, from both the bad news and the interruption, pinched at Sam's nerves. If what she said was true, how would they ever reach that tenant? He had to find some connection, some trail that would lead him to that renter.

Tilly hung up a moment later. "Sorry about that. Where were we?"

"You mentioned a charity—do you happen to know which one benefited from Will's passing?" Maybe he could find the man's family through them.

"Sorry, but I have no idea. I wish I could help you out."

Just as disappointment began to settle in, an idea came to him. His spine lengthened. "Wait, the tenant I'm trying to reach lived upstairs when your salon was downtown. You must've met him at some point."

"Oh, that guy." A pair of dangly earrings jingled as she shook her head. "I never actually met him, only saw him in passing. I didn't know his name or anything. I was busy trying to get my business off the ground, and I didn't see him very often. I had the feeling he kept irregular hours, like maybe he worked second shift or something."

"Is there anything else you can tell me about him? Did you ever see him with someone else, someone you might've known or recognized?"

"I never saw him with anyone else. But like I said, I was pretty busy. Sorry I can't be of more help. You have something that belongs to him, you said?"

"Right. It's actually pretty valuable, so I'm sure he'd want it back. Could you tell me what he looked like?"

She hitched a slim shoulder. "Late twenties, maybe? Brown hair, medium build. Sorry, I guess that's not very helpful."

He pulled out a business card. "That's okay. I appreciate your time. Can I leave this with you? If you happen to see him around or come upon his contact information, could you call me?"

"Sure thing." She pocketed his card. "And if you find yourself in need of a trim . . ."

"I'll know where to go."

The phone rang again.

"Thanks again for your help. I'll let you get back to work."

As he left the shop, dismay hit him like a tropical-force wind. He'd exhausted all avenues and was no closer to getting the name of that tenant than he'd been when he started tonight.

Worse yet, their search seemed to have reached a complete dead end—and Sam would have to break the news to Sadie.

Shopping always lifted Sadie's spirits, and shopping with Hayley lifted them even higher. They'd gone off island to the shopping mall and hit all of Sadie's favorite stores. Hayley might be a tomboy, but she had great taste in fashion.

Sadie found the perfect dresses for the wedding and rehearsal dinner, and better yet, she'd found them both on sales racks. She'd also bought a new bathing suit. She would've loved to have splurged on new heels, but she could make do with what she had. She was already pushing the limits of her budget, considering she might have to pay back that advance.

She and Hayley had capped off the night at the mall's ice

cream shop, where she'd indulged in a hot fudge brownie sundae and lots of laughter.

It was almost nine by the time she turned into her driveway. Sam's truck was parked on his side of the house. He'd never updated her on his progress tonight with the neighboring businesses. Maybe he wanted to share the good news in person.

Instead of heading toward her apartment, she grabbed her bags, made a beeline for his door, and rang the bell. Not only did she want that update, but after spending an evening with Hayley, she had plenty of material to tease him about.

He answered a long minute later, wearing khaki shorts and a navy blue Braves T-shirt. His hair was a little damp, the back just starting to curl up. "Hey. Come on in."

She followed him into the foyer and set down her bags. "You never texted me. What happened? Did you learn anything helpful?"

His gaze dropped to the shopping bags just before he headed into the living room. "I didn't want to interrupt your shopping spree, which appears to have been a great success."

She followed him, her sandals clicking on the tile. "It was. I had a great time, but the suspense is killing me. What did you learn?"

He turned in the living room and stuffed his hands into his pockets. His expression telegraphed his answer long before his words. "Sorry to say I came up empty. I visited all the downtown shops, and all I gleaned is that William went by Will and he had no family."

Sadie frowned. "None at all? Are you sure?"

"I located the owner of the salon that used to rent the lower space in his building."

"Oh, that's a great idea—she would've been his tenant."

"Right. She's the one who told me Will had no family. His entire estate went to some charity."

Her hopes shriveled up like an old prune. "Oh no."

"She didn't know which charity, so that's not useful information. She had seen the tenant we're searching for, but only in passing, and her description of him didn't exactly set him apart from the crowd." His eyes turned down at the corners, mirroring his lips. "I'm sorry, Sadie. I'd hoped to find something helpful, but it seems like we've reached a dead end instead."

Sadie felt deflated herself but forced a smile and touched his arm. "Hey, you tried. That's all you can do, and I really appreciate your efforts."

"I left my card with everyone I talked to, so I guess we can still hope to hear something. Or maybe we'll think of something else, some other trail to follow."

Her hand still lingered on his arm. And though she didn't want to, she pulled it away. "That's right. There's always hope." But Sadie's usual optimism was nowhere to be found. She had a terrible feeling that the mystery man they'd been searching for would never recover his beautiful engagement ring.

TWENTY-FIVE

Along with setbacks your heroine should also enjoy wins that have your reader rooting alongside her.

—*Romance Writing 101*

What was taking so long? Almost the entire day had ticked away one slow second after another. It was almost close of business day, and Sadie still hadn't heard from her agent or editor.

She'd started her day with a jog on the beach. Then, inspired by total boredom, she went to a hobby store to buy an embellishment for her Little Library, feeling guilty the whole time about the money she was spending. When she got home she added the shingles, and by the time she finished, her Little Library was adorable and more weatherproof.

Later she had Keisha over for coffee and cookies, and Sadie got her fill of baby snuggles. When Keisha left, Sadie checked in with Caroline via text and her mom via phone. All was well back home.

Once the sun sank lower in the sky, she took a walk on the beach with Rio, making sure her phone was set to ring, the sound turned all the way up—not that she'd be able to hear it over the crashing waves. But she had to stay busy or she would go crazy.

She ran into several people she'd previously met, thanks to the Little Library: Ellen, a suspense fan; Doreen, a romance reader; and Hildy and Dave, who read aloud to each other in the evenings. Each of them greeted Rio, and before they parted ways, Sadie encouraged them to stop by the library and check out the new books—as well as the structure's new embellishments.

When it was almost five o'clock, she came upon Jared and Roscoe, and they walked with her for a while. They were almost back to the house when Sadie's phone vibrated with a call. She whipped it out and gasped at the name on the screen.

Erin!

"Um, I have to take this," she said to Jared. "I've gotta go. Come on, Rio. Sorry, I'll catch you later. Bye, Roscoe!"

She barely heard Jared's response as she turned toward the house and answered the call.

"Hi, Sadie. I'm sorry it's taken so long to get back with you. Oh my goodness, what a day. How are things in South Carolina? Still enjoying the sunshine?"

"Oh yes, it's been great. The weather has been divine. How are things around the office, other than busy?" She normally enjoyed the niceties of conversation, but right now she wanted to skip straight to the point.

"Mostly good. We found a replacement for Tina in the marketing department and she's fitting right in. And Josie, one of our associate editors, announced her engagement today. Is that the ocean I hear? I'm so jealous."

"That's what it is. I just took Rio for a walk on the beach. I'm getting spoiled but I have to admit, I couldn't ask for a more ideal setting in which to write a romance novel."

Erin chuckled. "Nicely done—I couldn't imagine a more perfect segue. And I'm happy to say that's exactly what you'll be doing. The team loved your proposal, Sadie."

Yes! Sadie spun around on the sand, pumping her arms. Rio's leash wove around her legs, nearly tripping her. Sadie stepped over Rio, untangling herself. "That's wonderful news." Despite her best efforts she sounded as breathless as she felt.

"I'm pretty stoked about it myself."

Sadie mamboed her way into her yard and all the way up the deck while Erin gave her a complete rundown of the team's commentary—all positive.

"I can hardly wait to get started." Once on the deck, Sadie stopped dancing, but excess energy had her bouncing on her toes. "I can't tell you how inspired I feel about this story. I hope I can bring it to life on the page."

"We never doubted your ability to do just that. But since the schedule is a little tight and the genre is new to you, I thought maybe you could send me the story in batches. That way, if there are any major issues we can catch them as you go."

"I'd love to have your input as I write. How many pages would you like to see at a time?"

"Oh, whatever you're comfortable with—seventy-five pages perhaps? Or one hundred?"

"One hundred sounds great. That should give me time to lay down the premise and get the story off the ground."

"When can I expect to see the first pages? I know you're on a tight deadline, and if I get it in my schedule, I'll be able to provide quick feedback."

Sadie did some quick mental math. She'd have to write sixty-five pages a week, so she should be able to easily produce a hundred pages in less than two weeks. But the destination wedding fell during that time, and she wouldn't get much writing done there. She should also work in a little wiggle room in case she struggled with the story. "How about July seventh? Will that work for you?"

"That would be perfect. I'll pencil you in. We're so delighted you're going this direction, Sadie, and I can't wait to read your story."

Sadie beamed. "Thank you for all your in-house support, Erin. It means so much to me and I can't wait to write this story."

After they said their goodbyes, Sadie let out a loud whoop, then looked up into the heavens. "Thank You, thank You, thank You!"

Her gaze fell on her dog. "I can't believe it!" Rio stopped sniffing the sea oats long enough to glance at Sadie. "They liked my proposal and now I'm going to write a romance novel and hopefully it'll sell a bajillion copies, and I won't have to pay back my advance. Woo-hoo!"

Rio went back to sniffing.

She had to tell Sam. She rushed toward his door and knocked, barely resisting the urge to barge inside. He must be home by now, but he was taking forever to answer. *Come on, Sam. You're killing me here.*

A moment later he slid open the door, seemingly fresh from his shower.

Sadie flung herself into his arms. "They liked my proposal! I'm going to be a romance writer."

His welcoming embrace was like a warm bubble bath at the end of a difficult day. "Hey . . . that's great, Sadie. I'm so happy for you."

"It's going to be a whirlwind—I only have eight weeks to produce a whole novel, but I couldn't be more excited even though I'm a little scared. What if I can't do it? What if I get writer's block? Oh my gosh, what have I done?"

His husky chuckle stirred the hair at her temple—and her heart. "You can do it. I have no doubt."

She smiled against his chest. She could've stayed on the beach with Jared when the call came in—then she would've been able to share her news with him. She'd told him she was on the island to write, after all. But she hadn't wanted to share this moment with Jared. She'd wanted to share it with Sam.

Because he'd become such a good friend.

Her friend's heart thumped in her ear. Once again her celebratory hug seemed to have shifted into embrace territory. How did that keep happening?

She had to be more careful. It wouldn't do to fall for a man she could have no future with.

Sadie slipped from his arms, meeting his gaze.

His eyes crinkled and his dimple was out in full force.

She fought against the magnetic pull. "Sorry. I seem to be beside myself with excitement and nerves right now. I guess I'm kind of a mess. I truly can't wait to get started. I can't believe I'm saying that about this novel—but I'm actually dying to get started."

"Go for it. Write when the inspiration strikes."

She stepped out his door. "You're right. I'm off to work. Wish me luck."

"Have fun. And congratulations."

If he said anything else, she didn't hear it. She was already beating a path for her apartment and the laptop she'd left sitting on the living room sofa.

TWENTY-SIX

A *crucible* is a plot device that causes tension by forcing your hero and heroine together. Increase the story's tension by throwing your couple into a marriage of convenience or sending them off on a road trip.

—*Romance Writing 101*

Sadie squirmed under Sam's pointed gaze. She'd just handed him a garment bag with her two wedding outfits, pushed an elephant-sized suitcase his way, then handed him a tote bag.

"Snacks," she said.

He arched a brow and lifted the fifty-pound suitcase as though it were a clutch. "And all the rest of this?"

"It's not as if I'll have to pay baggage fees."

"Did you pack everything you brought to the island?"

"And then some. I can't really know what I'll need, so I'm bringing a little bit of everything." Sadie situated Rio's car seat on the cab's small rear bench. She gave Sadie a wounded look. "I know, I know, Mommy's so mean. But we have to keep you safe, sweetie."

Sam had only a garment bag and a toiletry case that wouldn't even fit the shoes she'd brought. Men had it so easy.

After buckling Rio in, Sadie climbed into the passenger seat and got settled. She had her laptop handy, just in case inspiration struck during the seven-hour drive. She wasn't holding her breath.

They would arrive on Anna Maria Island just in time to freshen up for the rehearsal dinner, which Sam was apparently invited to even though he wasn't in the wedding party. She was looking forward to meeting the rest of Sam's family and enjoying a party-like atmosphere for an entire weekend.

When Sam was finished loading the truck, he got in and pulled from the drive. In the week and a half since her editor's call, she'd only seen him in passing.

Time had flown by. Sadie wrote every day, Monday through Saturday, and oftentimes ideas or bits of dialogue woke her in the middle of the night. The story had come pretty easily at first. She mostly kept the plot true to life, only changing details here and there. With a September first deadline, *write what you know* was her mantra. However, her hero was a genuine alpha, more like she'd assumed Sam to be in the beginning. But he maintained that rakish hair, sexy stubble, and delicious dimple. And if Sophie had been transformed into a leggy, blue-eyed blonde . . . well, who could blame her?

Initially the writing had gone so well, she'd hoped to have those hundred pages to Erin before the wedding. But the past few days Sadie had struggled to fill even a page. She was getting deeper into the story where the romance must develop. And everything she wrote about the protagonist's inner desire for the hero sounded so cliché. She hadn't stood for poor writing in her westerns, and she wouldn't stand for it in her romance novels. Her editor certainly wouldn't, much less her three devoted readers.

But what could she do when she didn't know what falling in love actually felt like? It was certainly more than mere attraction. And how could she distinguish between the two when she only knew what one of those felt like?

So the past few days her flowing fountain had slowed to a depressing dribble.

Reading a hundred romance novels hadn't prepared her for this. How could she describe in a fresh way a feeling she'd never before experienced? It was different than pulling off the emotions of a gunfight or a fall into a raging river. After all, she'd felt fear and exhilaration before. Who hadn't?

She'd felt love as well, of course, but romantic love was altogether different. Or at least she assumed it must be. Why else would there be a billion novels featuring the emotion?

Maybe she just needed a short break from her story world—and she would be getting just that. Maybe a romantic wedding would be just the inspiration she needed. She was counting on it, because time was a luxury she didn't have.

Following the GPS instructions, Sam turned onto the highway. They were well underway, but Sadie had been uncharacteristically quiet. She'd been so busy writing since she'd gotten the go-ahead from her publisher. Whenever he saw her working on the deck—and he did, often—he didn't disturb her.

Not even when he wanted to share something that had happened that day. Or when he just wanted to know how her story was going.

He'd missed her.

The revelation sent a shot of anxiety through his veins. He'd come to depend on her company. That was something he might feel for a friend, of course. But a friend wouldn't notice the sway of her hips as she walked or the way her lips looked lush when she bit them in concentration.

And now he was fixing to spend a long car trip—and a romantic wedding weekend—with her. Never mind that he'd have plenty of other distractions.

He rolled his eyes. How ironic that he'd originally counted on Sadie to *be* a distraction from those things. He shook his head. "So how's your story going? You're sure putting in the hours."

"Well, it was practically writing itself until a few days ago. Now I can't seem to write a decent page."

"I'm sure you're just being too hard on yourself."

"No, seriously. It's taken me three days to write one page. And the longer this goes on, the more anxious I feel, because I need to meet my daily goals if I'm going to finish this novel on time."

"Maybe the pressure's just getting to you."

"Oh, no doubt. But that deadline is very real, so I can't just block it out. Besides, it's the content that I'm struggling with. The new genre. This has never happened to me before, and it wouldn't be happening now if I were writing a western."

"Anything you want to run by me? I mean, I'm sure I won't be much help, but we do have many traveling hours to pass, and sometimes just verbalizing the problem can help you solve it."

"Thanks for the offer but, uh, I don't think that'll be helpful in this case. I'm sure to find inspiration this weekend though." Sadie peered out her window. "Have you heard anything about the ring from anyone you left a business card with? I've been too busy working to delve into it any further."

"Sadly, no. But I'm still hoping we hear from someone."

"Maybe after I turn in my first hundred pages I'll do a little more searching." She glanced at him. "In the meantime . . . after talking with your sister I have some juicy material that'll keep us busy for quite a few miles."

He happened to know Hayley had called Sadie once or twice, presumably to talk wedding stuff. "Somehow I'm teetering between needing to know what she said and never wanting to hear it, ever."

"As if I'm going to give you a choice. But before I get started . . ."

He groaned.

"I just have to know . . . do you still use a night-light? Because I have an extra in my apartment I could loan you."

He sighed. It was general knowledge in his extended family that he'd slept with a night-light until he was twelve. "I watched horror flicks as a child. I couldn't seem to stop myself even though they scared me silly."

"Your parents let you watch those?"

He cut her a chagrined look. "They didn't know."

"Okay, well, that clears that up. So on to the bed-wetting that continued till you were *ten*."

"Oh, jeez. How long have you been holding on to that one?"

"Since the shopping spree." She sipped from her water bottle. She'd brought along an entire case for the road. "Any explanations, or are you just going to let that one ride?"

"I had a small bladder. I was short for my age, remember?" He scratched his neck. "Are we almost done here?"

"Just getting started. You never told me, for instance, about that time on your very first date when you saved up your money for a month to take out the popular girl you were crushing on and ran smack into the glass door on your way out of the restaurant."

"It was very clean—and I was a little distracted."

She chuckled. "Hayley said you had a knot on your forehead for a week."

"She was only two at the time—my mom has a big mouth."

"Poor baby. Did you get another date with the girl?"

"You kidding me, after that boneheaded move? She was five inches taller than I was, but apparently that didn't stop her from using me as a tool to make her ex-boyfriend jealous. The good news is—it worked. They were back together the next week."

"Aw, that's not cool. Did she break your heart, Sam?"

The warmth in her tone stirred him. "Only a little." Truthfully Lindsey had been a little boring. He was too blinded by her beauty to realize how superficial she was. A lesson well learned. "I guess I don't have to worry about my family embarrassing me this weekend. My sister's already given you my entire backstory—at least the humiliating parts."

"What are little sisters for?"

"No fair—you don't have any little sisters."

Her melodious laughter filled the cab. "Kind of great the way that worked out."

"For you," he said, but he couldn't keep from smiling. "So much for being fourteen when Hayley came along. Apparently my parents have ratted me out. If I ever get your parents all to myself, you're in for it."

She gave a smug grin. "I guess I'll just have to make sure that never happens. Did you really forget you were supposed to be babysitting Hayley when you were fifteen and *leave the house*?"

He still winced at that one. "To my credit she'd fallen asleep under the end table while I was gaming, so I kind of forgot about her. My friend called and invited me to the movies. But I'm sure Hayley filled in every juicy detail."

"I'd rather hear your side of it. Your parents came home to find you gone?"

"Not only that, but they didn't see Hayley at first either. It was terrible. They were frantic when they called me during the middle of the movie. And then, while I was rushing from the theater, they found her under the table. They were furious. I was grounded for months."

"Well, I'd hope so. I'll bet they never asked you to babysit again."

"I'll admit they made sure I'd grown up a little before putting me in charge of her again. Does that conclude the humiliation portion of this trip?"

"As it happens I've run out of stories—for now. I hope to glean more from your other relatives though."

He groaned. "Come on, you have to give me something in return. Tell me at least one embarrassing story from your childhood. You owe it to me."

"I guess it's only fair. Let's see, which one shall it be? There were plenty, I assure you."

"It has to be legitimately embarrassing—something you wouldn't ordinarily tell anyone."

She thought a minute.

He glanced over and caught a grimace. "Tell me that one. The one you're thinking about right now."

"Aw, jeez. Not that one."

"Let's recap: bed-wetting, night-light, dating mortification, babysitting fiasco . . . It can't be worse than mine, at least not collectively."

She appeared to waffle. "You make a good point. All right, fine. But you can't tell anyone."

"I'd make you promise the same, but my family already knows all my dirty secrets. But yes, I promise. Lay it on me."

She heaved a sigh. "Well, let me start by saying I sleepwalked as a child. A lot when I was younger, but I started growing out of it as I got older. When I was thirteen I went to a friend's house for a sleepover. I was new to the school and Mackenzie was my first friend. That night I sleepwalked and was apparently trying to find the bathroom because I wandered into her baby sister's room instead and I"—she covered her face—"I peed in her stroller."

Laughter bubbled up inside. "I'm sorry, what was that? I thought you said—"

"Yes, yes, I peed in her stroller. Are you happy now? I can't believe you made me tell you that."

"Oh man," he said through a chuckle.

"Of course, I didn't remember it at all. But the next morning Mackenzie's mom discovered the stinking, wet stroller, and my mom had ever so helpfully notified the woman that I occasionally sleepwalked. The entire family was present at breakfast when they put it all together."

"You're right, that is pretty bad."

"Actually, it's even worse than you're thinking because

Mackenzie had this hot older brother on whom I had a huge crush, and of course he was present to witness my humiliation."

He winced through the laughter. "Okay, you win. That's awful."

"She never invited me over again."

"Go figure."

She smacked him in the arm. "I was sleepwalking. I couldn't help it and it was a very traumatic event."

"Okay, okay. I'll stop laughing now."

"And a change of subject would be just great, thank you."

"I'm not the one who brought up humiliating childhood moments."

"I'll accept full responsibility if you'll allow me to shift topics and promise to never bring it up again."

"Scout's honor. I'll even throw you a bone and change the subject with a confession of my own."

"I'm learning a lot about you recently."

"That's true, but this isn't about me so much . . . I read your books."

Her eyes widened. "You did?"

"Don't tell anyone, but I'd never read a western before. I was impressed, Sadie. You're a really good writer." A quick glance betrayed a sweet flush on her cheeks.

"Well, thank you. I can't believe you read them. I have all kinds of questions. Like which one did you like best, and who was your favorite character? Ooh, and how did you feel about the ending of *Sundown at Lonesome Ridge*? Was it too much?"

"Slow down there, pardner. One question at a time."

Over the next thirty minutes he answered all her questions, and they chatted at length about the books. He hadn't been exaggerating. She really was a good writer—he hadn't been able to put the books down.

When they finally exhausted the topic, she brought up the wedding weekend ahead. "So who will I be meeting this weekend? Is there a drunk uncle who hits on inappropriately young girls or a matronly aunt who'll ask us when we're getting married?"

At the thought of the weekend ahead, his smile wilted. But he still gave her the full rundown on his parents, cousins, uncles, and aunts, including those who tended to be matchmakers.

"What about the bride? Amanda, right? Is she nice? Do we like her?"

"How'd you know her name?"

"I asked Hayley for their registry information. I got the happy couple a very nice votive holder."

"You didn't have to do that. I was planning to put your name on my gift."

"They're including me in their big weekend—the least I can do is spring for a nice gift. So tell me about Amanda. Does your family love her? Did she and Tag date very long?"

He cleared his throat. "Yeah, sure, my family likes her just fine. She's a career-oriented woman, very smart. She and Tag dated for more than a year." He was pleased that talking about the couple didn't cause that hollow spot to open up in his chest. Progress. Maybe there was hope yet.

"Why did they decide to have a destination wedding, especially when they practically live on the South Carolina coast?"

"They both favored a smaller production, and a destination wedding has a way of paring down the guest list. Plus Tag spent a lot of time on Anna Maria Island as a child, so it's a special place for him."

"That's so nice."

As a teenager Sam had made the trip twice with his cousin. They fished right from the shore and played around on the Jet Skis until they ran out of gas, getting golden brown under the summer sun.

"And the wedding is at his grandma's cottage?"

"The wedding *and* reception. But I'll warn you the cottage is more like a mansion. It's on the beach and has some great sunset views."

"Oh, it sounds amazing. I can hardly wait."

Sam was less than enthusiastic about the weekend. But he was grateful to have Sadie at his side—even if she was proving to be a little more of a distraction than he'd initially planned.

TWENTY-SEVEN

Romance novels are famous for the "almost kiss" because it prolongs the suspense, ratcheting up sensual tension.

—*Romance Writing 101*

Sam tried not to give away his pounding heart or unsteady legs as he escorted Sadie across the hotel foyer toward the restaurant.

He hadn't seen Amanda since Tag had brought her to the family's annual Easter brunch. He still recalled that awful ache inside upon seeing her at his cousin's side. It had been the pivotal event that drove him to the island. Well, that and the wedding invitation.

He wasn't sure how seeing them together tonight, this weekend, would affect him. But he was determined to keep his pain to himself. The last thing he wanted was more pity. And despite all they'd put him through, he didn't want to spoil Tag's wedding weekend.

Truth was, he missed his cousin. They'd been so close all these years. Sam's mom had been right. It was time to put the ill feelings aside and get on with life. If only he could convince his heart to cooperate.

Sadie cut him a sideways glance as they entered the restaurant. "Are you all right?"

"Of course. I'm fine." He forced his muscles to relax, his lips into a smile, and told the hostess the party's name. She led them through the restaurant toward the back, where a rented space opened to the beach. The wedding party and family milled around a beautifully set table that stretched the length of the open-air room.

Hayley, only a few steps away, was the first to spot them. "Sam. Sadie. You're here."

As Sam hugged his sister his gaze swept the room, settling on Amanda and Tag. They were engaged in conversation with Tag's parents.

"You're so pretty," Sadie told Hayley. "I love the sundress, and that blue is great on you."

"Thanks. You look amazing too. I'm so glad you chose the pink one. Doesn't she look gorgeous, Sam?"

He tore his gaze from Amanda, but Sadie cut in before he could respond. "He already complimented me on my appearance like the wonderful date he is."

"I'll take your word for it," Hayley said. "You're sitting by me. I made sure of it."

Sam swallowed as his parents noticed them and headed their way. When they arrived he introduced them to Sadie. She was charming and congenial, saying all the right things and sparing him from having to make conversation.

As they talked he was painfully aware of Amanda and Tag's changing positions in the room, working their way closer to Sam's group. He half hoped the party would be called to the table before the awkward meeting could occur and half hoped he could get it over with already.

Amanda wore her black hair up in a simple twist, exposing her long neck. The green dress wrapped around her slender waist and stopped midthigh, exposing long legs that ended in a pair of very high heels. Even so, Tag topped her by a couple of inches.

But the thing he noticed most about Amanda was her radiant joy. Even though this was her big event and she must have a million details on her mind, she seemed . . . *relaxed.* And that was not a word he ever would've used to describe Amanda Borden.

"Sam?" Mom said. "What do you think so far?"

He jerked his attention back to the conversation. He had a feeling that wasn't his mother's first effort to get his attention.

Sadie hooked her arm through his. "We agree. The rooms are beautiful and they've been great about Rio—they even left her a doggie bone and a water dish. Isn't that nice?"

He gave Sadie's arm a grateful squeeze. "It's a beautiful hotel."

Tag stepped into the circle. "You made it, Cuz. How was the drive?"

They exchanged a man hug. "It went by fast." When they separated Sam spotted Amanda at Tag's side. He forced a smile and greeted her with a hug. When he pulled away, he set his hand on Sadie's back, urging her forward. "I'd like you both to meet Sadie. Sadie, this is my cousin Tag and his soon-to-be bride, Amanda."

Sadie exuded warmth as she exchanged brief hugs with the couple. "I'm so thrilled to be here. You've chosen the perfect location for your big day, and I'm so blessed to get to be a part of it."

"How kind of you." Amanda's smile was genuine. "I love your dress. Don't you just love empire waistlines?"

"Thank you. Yours is beautiful too—that color is amazing on you. And those stilettos. If I could walk in those, I'd wear them every day."

Amanda laughed. "The pain is so worth it."

"Okay, everyone," a young woman called from the doorway. "It's time to take your seats. Dinner is served."

As Sam and Sadie made their way toward their seats, she leaned in close and whispered, "You left out *gorgeous.*"

He supposed he had. He shrugged. Amanda's striking looks had diminished for him in the wake of their disastrous breakup.

But taking stock of his current emotional state . . . he felt nothing but relief. And ironically, that only generated more relief. The most awkward part of the evening was over and he'd handled it well. Now he could concentrate on other things, like possibly enjoying himself.

"I had a really good time tonight," Sadie said hours later as they exited the elevator and headed toward their adjoining rooms. Some of the others had gone out for a night on the town—in a golf cart. There were more carts on this island than cars.

But after a three-course meal and s'mores on the beach, Sadie needed to check on Rio. Plus it was getting late, and the socializing, while energizing, had eventually drained her. "Your parents are nice, and your whole family is so much fun.

I thought I'd lose it when your uncle showed us his long gray chest hair. Gross."

"He whips it out on the regular. Aunt Betty has tried to uproot it more than once."

Sadie chuckled.

"At least he waited until after supper this time."

"Your great-aunt Georgia is a trip too. She cornered me when I went to the restroom and interrogated me. I could practically feel the hot lamp shining in my eyes."

"Rest assured, she's already picked out our wedding invitations and named our firstborn son."

She waggled a finger at him. "See now, that's where I draw the line—my first son will be named Logan. I refuse to compromise on that."

"Interesting choice."

"He's my favorite cowboy from Louis L'Amour's Sackett series."

"Of course he is." He aimed a charming smile her way. "Do you have a cowgirl name for your future daughter as well?"

They reached her door and she slid her key card in the slot. At the noise Rio barked on the other side of the door. "I should probably let my husband name at least one of our children."

"Very fair-minded of you." He unlocked his own door and opened it. "Did you hear we're meeting for brunch at ten?"

"I'll be ready to go."

"After that we'll pretty much have the day to ourselves until time to dress for the wedding."

"I can't wait to try out that beautiful pool."

After they said good night, Sadie slipped inside, gave Rio some much-needed attention, then leashed the dog and took her outside. When she returned to the room, she changed into her yoga pants and cami and spread out on the king-size bed with her dog and the remote control. She needed to wind down before she was ready to sleep.

As she channel surfed she replayed some of her conversation with Sam, and that led to his complimentary review of her books on the trip down. Her work was so personal, and knowing that he'd derived pleasure from it warmed her from the inside out.

"I'm impressed. You're a good writer."

His words lifted her spirits as she flipped from channel to channel.

"What do you think, Rio? The local news, *Dateline*, *Hawaii Five-0* . . . Ooh, a serial killer show. No, wait, I need to sleep tonight. Baseball—that's a hard no." A western popped up on the screen. She gasped. "*Red River*. Oh, the cruelty. John Wayne, you're killing me." Whimpering, she forced herself to change the channel.

"*Family Feud*, *The Golden Girls*, *Ridiculousness* . . . Oh!" She stopped at the familiar scene from *The Firm* that preceded Sam's favorite part of the movie—a scene sequence repeating the line, "No associate has ever failed the bar exam."

She grabbed her phone and texted Sam. Quick, turn your TV to channel 32.

She tapped her fingers on her legs as the scene progressed. Checked her phone a minute later. Finally she hopped off the bed, opened her adjoining door, and knocked on Sam's door. "Sam! Open up."

She peeked at the TV. It was almost time for his favorite part. She grabbed the knob and pushed. "Sam, *The Firm* is on channel—"

The door suddenly fell open. Sadie stumbled forward.

She squeaked just before she face-planted into Sam's chest.

"Whoa." He stumbled backward. Caught her by the waist.

She grabbed Sam's arms, steadying herself as he gained his footing. "Oops. I didn't mean to . . ." As she looked up, their gazes met.

Tangled.

"*The Firm* is, uh . . . it's on TV." Her voice seemed to be breathless.

"Yes, you, ah, mentioned that."

"It's almost to that scene you like where . . ."

His hand shifted at the small of her back.

Heat flared from the epicenter of his touch. She sucked in a breath. Her words died in her throat. She grappled for them. But it seemed there were no words to replace them.

What were words again?

Awareness crackled between them. She kept finding herself in his arms, even if accidentally this time. But there was nothing accidental about the way his gaze raked over her face. Or the way his hand pressed her closer.

Her breath caught. Her gaze fell to his lips. It wasn't the first time she'd wondered what they'd taste like. Or pondered how he would kiss her—softly or firmly or reverently or masterfully. She'd place her money on the last one.

Her heart knocked against her rib cage. Noisily. Insistently.

Oh, never mind—someone was at the door.

Sam's gaze followed the sound. His hands fell to his sides.

She blinked and stepped away. "I, uh, should let you get that."

Rio had apparently slipped through the adjoining doors as she was currently at the entry door, barking her head off.

Sadie rushed over and picked her up. With the dog quivering in her arms, she headed back toward her room. "It's okay, sweetheart. There's nothing to get excited about."

Except that Sam had almost kissed her.

Hadn't he? She glanced over her shoulder.

He seemed perfectly collected as he told her good night and closed the door between them.

Once the connecting door was shut, Sam leaned against it and composed himself. *What the heck was that, Ford? You've hardly figured out how you feel about Amanda, and you're putting the moves on Sadie?*

He ran a hand over his flushed face. Because, yes, that's exactly what he'd been about to do. So much for being unprepared to trust another woman, for avoiding a relationship with someone who lived all the way in New York. She was just so darned tempting with her pretty eyes and sweet scent. Even her clumsiness was adorable. He banged his head against the door.

Another knock sounded. He pushed himself upright and answered the door. Troy was on the other side of the threshold, duffel bag in hand. "Hey, Cuz, can I stay with you?"

Sam opened the door wider. "Sure, come on in. Did you figure out Brendan snores like a freight train? Why do you think no one else wanted to be his roommate?"

Troy dropped his bag on the unclaimed bed. "He's sick. He barfed right after supper."

"What?" Tag's brother hadn't joined them for s'mores, but Sam figured he was just tired from the travel.

"He said he'd been feeling a little queasy all day, but he thought he was just car sick. Then he remembered his coworker came down with the stomach flu a couple days ago. And now Troy's got a fever—at least that's what Aunt Georgia said."

"That's not good. Does Tag know?"

"What do you think?"

Besides being a retired RN, their great-aunt was also queen of the family grapevine. "Good point."

"Aunt Georgia's staying with Brendan tonight—whether he wants her to or not. I, for one, couldn't get out of there fast enough. I hope Tag and Amanda don't get whatever he's got, because it's not pretty up in room 321."

Sam felt awful for Brendan—and for Tag and Amanda. Since Brendan was the best man, this illness would disrupt the wedding.

The thought lingered as Troy got ready for bed. If the couple's relationship had developed in any other way, Sam would've been in Tag's wedding party—if not his best man.

As it was, Tag had never put him in the position of having to say no. And Sam would've done just that.

But now, all these months later, he no longer felt so adamant about that. Seeing Amanda again hadn't been the torture he'd expected. Not even close. When Tag's father had toasted the couple tonight, Sam had caught the intimate glances between Tag and Amanda.

She'd never looked at Sam that way.

He would've expected that realization to send him spiraling into misery. But instead he felt a twinge of happiness for his cousin. Even for Amanda, because she seemed different—kinder, softer somehow—than she'd been when Sam had dated her. Tag seemed to have brought out the best in her. And who was Sam to begrudge them that?

He mulled over the situation while *The Firm* played out on the TV screen. Troy had been asleep for a long while by the time Sam grabbed his phone off the nightstand and texted Tag.

TWENTY-EIGHT

Your character's *internal goal* is a want or need that has been denied her because of an *internal obstacle*, resulting from a previous negative experience. The events of your story should force her to realize and confront this obstacle so she can finally attain her goal.

—*Romance Writing 101*

Sadie might as well have watched the serial killer show. She tossed and turned all night—but it wasn't because she feared someone would slip into her second-story hotel room and murder her in some heinous way.

No, it was something much more pleasant—yet somehow just as scary—that had her counting sheep well into the night. Had she and Sam not been interrupted by that knock on the door, he would've kissed her. A part of her thrilled to that knowledge. Longed to have his gaze sweep sensuously over her again. And soon. He was all too tempting.

But she'd already determined their relationship was a dead end—her specialty, apparently. In a city of more than eight million people, why couldn't she find one nice guy who shared common goals and to whom she was attracted?

She'd have to untangle that knotted rope another day. For now she just had to prevent the romance of this tropical wedding from going to her head so she could stay focused on her summer goal: writing her novel.

By the time she finished dressing in a sleeveless fuchsia top and white skirt, her pep talk had worked. First the brunch, then an entire day of hanging out by the pool—with Sam, his darling dimple, and his perfect physique.

Oh dear. She fanned her face.

A knock sounded on the entry door.

She took one last glance in the mirror before crossing the room, Rio underfoot and yapping. "Hush now. Be a good girl and no chewing on the drapes. Here's Mr. Mouse. I'll be back and we'll go for a nice walk around the town."

At her favorite word the dog's ears perked and her entire rear end wagged.

"Not right now but in a little while. Mommy will be back soon." She tossed the toy across the room and while the dog was distracted, she slipped into the hallway.

When she turned, there was Sam, looking very handsome. His white polo set off his tan, and his black shorts made the most of his muscular legs. The hair at his nape was still damp, and her fingers itched to comb through those curls.

"Morning," he said.

"Good morning." She cleared the frog from her throat. Heat flared in her cheeks.

His gaze swept over her casual outfit and chic ponytail. "You look nice."

"Thank you." She opened her mouth to return the favor, then figured her ten-second ogle had probably been sufficient.

"I didn't think it would be possible to be hungry this morning," she said as they headed toward the elevator. "But I was wrong."

"Should be a nice spread." When they reached the elevator he punched the Down button. "Listen, Sadie, about this afternoon . . ."

The elevator doors opened. They stepped inside, joining a middle-aged couple and two teenagers.

The button for the first floor was already lit, so Sadie settled into the front corner next to Sam. The doors swept shut, closing their occupants inside the hushed confines, and the elevator gave a small jolt as it descended.

She wasn't about to continue their conversation in the quiet. Was he about to ditch her for the afternoon? Was he avoiding her because he regretted their almost-kiss?

Possibly so. And that would probably be for the best.

Her weighted stomach belied the thought. But the last thing she needed was more time with an attractive man who wasn't right for her. This was why she always cut things off as soon as she realized a man wasn't right for her. There was no reason to tempt fate.

That's exactly what had happened to her parents. They'd met on a mission trip to Ecuador and lost their hearts to one another with no thought to how they'd reconcile their very different lifestyles. Her mom left her dream life in New York City and moved to Scranton to marry her father.

And see how that had turned out.

But like it or not, Sam was her date for the weekend—and her neighbor for the remainder of the summer. Not to mention her partner in the possibly doomed engagement ring mystery. How was she supposed to avoid temptation for another month?

His arm rested against hers in the confined space. The elevator seemed to have grown hot and stuffy, the walls pressing in on all sides. She focused on breathing and resisted the urge to fan herself.

She cut a glance Sam's way. What was he thinking over there?

And why the heck was it taking so long for this stupid elevator to travel *one floor*?

Not a moment too soon the doors whooshed open, and Sadie stepped from the confined space into the gloriously spacious and air-conditioned lobby.

"Hang on a minute." Sam guided her out of the flow of traffic, and they stopped beside a table with a beautiful pink peony arrangement.

"As I was saying before . . . Tag's brother, Brendan, came down sick last night—a stomach flu or something."

"Oh no. That's terrible."

"He's the best man . . . so I offered to step in, fill his shoes so to speak."

"That's very nice of you. Oh, wow, you have a lot to do. You'll need to get fitted for a tux—you'll have a speech to write."

"I know, there's a lot to get done this afternoon. I really hate to desert you like this . . ."

She waved him off, predictably disappointed and relieved at

the same time. "Not at all. I'll be perfectly fine. There's a beautiful pool right outside and a novel with my name on it."

He flashed his dimple. "Thank you for being so understanding."

She fought the urge to kiss his cheek right there in that hollow spot. "Not at all. I'm glad you'll be able to help out."

They headed toward the restaurant. This was definitely for the best. Less time together equaled less temptation. And if the news had deflated her, it only proved that she needed to avoid his company even more than she'd suspected.

Sam finished buttoning the shirt and slid into the black jacket. As far as he could tell, it was a good fit. Tag had been grateful he'd offered to step in. His cousin even offered to move someone else into the best man slot and allow Sam to serve as simply one of the groomsmen.

But Tag had always been closer to Sam than anyone else in the party, and if the bride were any other woman, Tag would've asked Sam to fill the role.

He pushed the curtain aside and joined his mom and cousin outside the fitting room. Unused to wearing a buttoned-up shirt, Sam tugged at the collar.

Upon sight of him, his mother clasped her hands at her chest, and laugh lines fanned from her eyes. "Oh, you look so handsome, honey. It's a perfect fit, don't you think, Tag?"

"I think so, but maybe we need an expert opinion. Could you go get the saleslady, Aunt Beth? I think I saw her over there by the ties."

His mom scooted off, eager to be of assistance and no doubt brimming with joy that Sam had stepped in to save the wedding—surely a sign he was ready to mend fences with Tag.

"I wanted a minute alone with you." Tag's brown eyes sharpened on Sam. "I haven't had a chance to thank you in person for what you're doing. I can't tell you what it means to me."

"We've been through a lot. It's time to move forward."

"I know I don't deserve your generosity." A shadow flickered in Tag's jaw as it tightened. "But I appreciate it—and so does Amanda. I wanted you to be my best man all along, but I couldn't ask you after what I did."

Something in Sam softened at his cousin's contrite expression. He gripped Tag's shoulder, staring him square in the eye. "She was never meant for me, Cuz. I can see that now."

"I wish I could do things over again. I handled it so badly. I'm ashamed of that. I hope you know I never meant to hurt you." He blinked back tears. "I know that doesn't change anything or excuse what I did, but . . ."

"I know you didn't. Let's just rebuild from here, all right? We all need a little grace sometimes. I've needed it from you a time or two."

Tag's mouth quirked to the side in a droll smile. "Not like this, you didn't. But if you can find it in your heart to forgive me, I'll strive to be more like you. You're a good man, Sam."

Sam swallowed hard as he clasped Tag's hand and pulled him in for a shoulder bump. "Already forgiven, Cuz."

"Thank you." His voice sounded choked. He drew back, making eye contact. "You don't know what that means to me. There's one other thing . . . We haven't talked about the best man speech yet. I can have Troy do the toast if you'd rather. He's already offered."

Sam regarded his cousin closely. Saw the boy he used to go fishing with and the man who owned up to his mistakes. "Thanks, but . . . I'd like to do the honors tonight, if that's all right with you."

TWENTY-NINE

> Will your hero and heroine fall in love instantly, over the course of years, or somewhere in between? The choice is yours.
>
> —*Romance Writing 101*

On the boardwalk Sadie kicked off her sandals alongside the other shoes and took the arm of a handsome teenager. He escorted her down the sandy aisle to a white wooden chair on the right-hand side.

In the distance the sun sank toward the horizon, cooling the air and streaking the sky with striking shades of pink and purple. It was a beautiful evening for a wedding.

The rows of chairs ended at a canopy, its corners draped with chiffon and dripping with wisteria. To the left of the structure, a woman in a beautiful blue gown tickled the strings of a violin. In the chairs ahead Sadie spotted people she'd met over the past twenty-four hours, though most of them were in the wedding party.

She scratched her bare shoulder and soon felt the sting of

sunburn. She'd relaxed by the pool most of the day, book in hand. Afterward she took Rio for a long walk on the shore and treated herself to an umbrella drink from a busy beachside bar. When she returned to the resort, she had a snack to tide her over till dinner, then began getting ready for the wedding.

She took her time with her makeup, curled her hair, swept the sides back and secured them with a tortoiseshell barrette. Her cerulean-blue halter-style dress clung to her waist and flared about her knees in cascading ruffles. The dress was meant for the dance floor, which was perfect because she couldn't wait to get her groove on.

The preacher appeared, taking his spot under the center of the canopy. The thirtysomething man wore sideswept bangs, black-rimmed glasses, and a congenial smile.

Sadie thought she might see Sam in passing today, but she hadn't. He checked on her via text a couple of times while he was busy with best-man obligations. She thought of the wedding party swap. Why hadn't Tag moved someone else forward in the lineup? After all, Sam hadn't even been in the party.

Before she could follow the thought, a rustle off to the side alerted her to the groomsmen's arrival. Sam led the way, gorgeous in that black tux, beard trimmed neatly, dark hair fluttering in the breeze. The well-fitted suit made the most of his broad shoulders and trim waist.

When he neared her seat he glanced her way, and his lips tipped up at the corners just before he was eclipsed by the setting sun.

Sadie's breath caught. She resisted—barely—the urge to cover her heart, which was ready to burst from her body. She couldn't take her eyes off Sam as he strode to the front and took his place on the canopy's right side.

Tunnel vision erased everyone and everything except his beautiful face. She couldn't seem to get control of herself.

A weird fluttering stirred in her stomach. She felt as though her body had just released, in one glorious dose, all the endorphins from every mile she'd ever jogged.

Perhaps the hormones permeated her mind as well, because it spun with a thousand thoughts, none of which made a wit of sense. Her heart swelled right along with the moving melody. The visceral sensations overtaking her body were . . .

Wonderful.

Overwhelming.

Exhilarating.

Hopeful.

Terrifying.

And brand new. She'd never felt this way before. Not even close. But if that was true . . .

Then how could she know with such certainty that this was exactly the way it felt to fall in love?

The wedding guests gathered later behind the beachside cottage under a starry canopy. Sam sat at the head table, which perched on the deck along with the open bar and soundboard.

On one side of the backyard, wedding guests clustered at tables, eating, drinking, and socializing, and on the other side stood a makeshift dance floor, waiting for its moment.

Sam carried on a conversation with Tag and Amanda beneath the twinkle lights that sparkled over the tables.

As a melody ended the DJ spoke into the microphone. "All

right, everybody, it's now time for the toasts. Please turn your attention right over here to the best man—Sam Ford, cousin of the groom." He gestured toward the head table. "Sam, take it away."

His moment had come. He wiped his mouth, pushed back his chair, and rose to his feet.

Silence fell over the group. Almost everyone present knew about his former relationship with the bride. They were probably worried about what he might say.

He spotted Amanda's parents and sisters but didn't let his gaze linger—he was nervous enough. Instead he located Sadie at the nearest guest table and found strength in her encouraging smile.

Gathering his notes he drew a breath and addressed the crowd. "Hi, everyone." He also gave a small wave and mentally rolled his eyes. Sadie must be rubbing off on him. "Obviously I've known Tag all my life, so rest assured I have enough humiliating material to entertain you all night."

The crowd released a nervous chuckle.

"Trust me, you wouldn't be bored. But for the sake of brevity I've narrowed it down to a couple of my favorites—mine, not necessarily Tag's. Sorry, Cuz."

Tag covered his face to the delight of the group.

"You might not know this, but Tag has the sense of direction of a blind bat. When we were eighteen we decided to take a spring break trip to Wilmington, North Carolina—I know, Party Town, USA, right? Unfortunately, I let Tag drive. He set the GPS and I promptly took a nap—and woke up in . . . Tennessee. Because yes, folks, there's a Wilmington, Indiana, and we were already halfway there."

The crowd chuckled.

Sam glanced at his cousin. "Seriously, Tag, we're glad you made it to the island in time for your wedding."

Tag shook his head.

"Another thing Tag is not known for—his culinary skills."

His cousin groaned.

"Yeah, that's the sound Amanda makes when you offer to cook."

Laughter swelled as Amanda gave an emphatic nod.

"Tag and I took a cooking class together in high school, and he talked me into being his partner for Italian Day. It was more of a bribe, really, as no one else wanted to partner with him. When we were shopping for the spaghetti dinner, I sent him off for ground beef. I knew I was in trouble when he returned empty-handed and asked me where to find the beef that's 'crumbled.'"

He paused as the crowd chuckled. "He made a chocolate pudding cake for my twenty-first birthday, and to this day it makes me sick—literally—to even talk about it. He once managed to ruin *Jell-O.* Who does that?" Sam gave Amanda a wry grin. "In short, I highly recommend you keep him out of the kitchen, Amanda."

Laughter floated across the yard. Someone whooped. Another hooted.

"Speaking of Amanda . . . Isn't she a beautiful bride?"

The crowd applauded enthusiastically.

"Yeah, sorry, Cuz, you're totally outclassed."

Tag nodded sheepishly, threw his hands up in surrender.

"Seriously . . ." He paused as the crowd grew hushed for the solemn part of the toast. "Amanda and Tag are a couple who were clearly meant to be." Sam drew a breath as he gazed at the pair.

"I've always thought your partner should make you the best version of yourself. And since Amanda and Tag have been together, I've seen my cousin grow in ways that defy time and expectation. That's because of you, Amanda.

"And who can miss the radiance on your face today? You've always been a smart, strong woman, the kind of person who can achieve anything—maybe even teach him how to cook . . . Okay, probably not. But there's something softer and calmer about you since he came into your life. Something good. You make each other happy. You make each other better. Just the way it should be.

"So let's raise our glasses to the newlyweds . . ." Sam lifted his goblet and gazed down at the happy couple. "To Tag and Amanda . . . and a lifetime of love and joy. May you always champion the best in each other. Cheers."

"Hear, hear!" The crowd saluted the couple and sipped their drinks.

Tag's eyes filled with tears as he stood and embraced Sam. "Thank you. I love you, buddy."

Sam pounded his back, swallowing against the lump in his throat. "Love you too, Cuz."

Sam approached Sadie's table and caught her just as she put the last bite of cake in her mouth. "Wanna dance?"

She covered her mouth as she chewed. "Um, sure."

When she stood he led her onto the dance floor as the soft strains of "Just the Way You Are" began. He placed his hands at her waist as she put hers on his shoulders, keeping a bit of space between them.

He'd only seen her from a distance today, and he'd missed her. Had been looking forward to getting his arms around her. "Sorry I haven't been much company tonight."

"It's okay. Your toast was beautiful. If I didn't know better, I would've thought you'd been working on it for weeks." She watched the couples dancing around them.

"It's not so hard when you have so much history together."

Silence settled between them, stretching out through the song's first verse.

Strange. She usually had plenty to say. "Did you have a good day?"

"Sure." She smiled at his bow tie, then stared off toward the beach where a bonfire flickered.

"Maybe we can make s'mores later. Satisfy that sweet tooth of yours."

"That would be fun."

"Are you finding much inspiration for your romance novel?"

"Definitely."

He waited for her to expound. When she didn't, he frowned at her. Not that she noticed as she hadn't so much as glanced at him once since he'd asked her to dance. "Sadie?"

"What?"

"You okay? You're awfully quiet tonight."

She let loose a shaky laugh. "I guess I'm just, uh, tired from the sun." Her gaze bounced off his face.

It hadn't been that long since he'd had a woman in his life—he'd done something wrong. The question was, what did he need to apologize for? "Are you upset with me for leaving you alone today?"

Her fingers tapped out a nervous cadence on his shoulder.

"Of course not. I'm glad you helped out your cousin. Besides, I had a good day even if I did get a little sunburned as you can probably tell, but not enough to really hurt or blister or anything. I read almost the entire book I brought and it's really good, and I took a short nap by the pool, and then Rio and I walked all the way down to the public beach, which was very cool. It was crowded and lively with beach volleyball and a beach bar, and I have to say the weather was absolutely perfect."

She continued to fill him in on all the details of her day. She'd gone from practically mute to talking nonstop. And she was still moving stiffly in his arms. Plus there was practically a canyon between them, and while they'd never danced together, that didn't seem like Sadie.

And she still wouldn't look at him.

Was she freaked out over their almost-kiss the night before? Should he address the subject? Get it out there on the table? Or would that only make things more awkward? Anyway, what would he say? His only regret was that they'd been interrupted.

This weekend had been a big breakthrough for him. He'd realized almost immediately that he was over Amanda—a huge weight from his shoulders. Add to that the closure he'd gotten with Tag today, and he was practically giddy.

All he could think about while getting ready for the wedding was spending time with Sadie tonight. He'd even hoped to turn that almost-kiss into a real one. A summer fling wouldn't hurt anything, right? Get back on that horse—as Sadie might say.

But she seemed uncomfortable with him now. Detached in a way she'd never been before. Her demeanor was definitely not inspiring romantic thoughts. Maybe she wasn't interested in him that way. Maybe last night had made her realize she didn't want anything beyond friendship with him. His chest tightened at the thought.

Just when he'd connected with an amazing woman. Just when he was ready to try again. Judging by the size of the knot in his stomach, he'd already grown very fond of her.

Sadie was still talking about her day as the song's final notes trickled out. The up-tempo lead-in to the "Cha-Cha Slide" began, and guests rushed the dance floor.

"Oh!" Sadie drew back. "I have to find Hayley for this one." And then she was gone, dodging dancers on her way to his sister. Sadie fell in line beside Hayley at the front of the pack and picked up the dance.

Clearly he was out of practice. Sam tugged at his collar. What the heck was going on with Sadie?

THIRTY

Romantic tension, mounting intimacy, and the warring of desires versus obstacles build anticipation for the couple's first meaningful touch. In other words, a good first kiss begins on page 1.

—*Romance Writing 101*

Sadie had managed to avoid Sam most of the evening. They'd danced twice more and mingled a bit. But he had plenty of family and friends to fraternize with—every time she caught sight of him, he was busy talking or dancing.

From her spot in line at the bar, she brushed a few tendrils from her face. A rousing country tune played and the dance floor was packed. Another group gathered around the bonfire on the beach. Smaller cloisters congregated here and there across the deck and yard. The sounds of chatter and laughter rang out in the space between songs.

All evening Sadie had felt dazed. Dancing with Sam had

been pure torture. How could this have happened? How had she fallen in love in only four weeks? More to the point, how had she fallen in love with a man who lived five states away? Instead of avoiding her parents' fate, she seemed to be repeating it.

A mild breeze blew, stirring the hair at the back of her neck. She couldn't keep avoiding Sam. But she was terrible at hiding her feelings. She needed to figure out a way to act naturally—neither spouting monologues nor staying mute as a block of wood. For crying out loud, how hard could it be to find a happy medium? She ran a hand over her heated face at the memory.

"Having a good time, Sadie?" Sam's mom and dad appeared at her side.

Sadie pushed away her embarrassment and greeted the couple with a smile. "Oh yes. It's been a beautiful event from start to finish. I adore a lively party. Mrs. Ford, you look stunning in that gown. I love the way the fabric falls around your legs."

The woman smoothed the beige skirt. "Thank you. I was telling Dave how much I like your dress. It was just made for dancing in."

"Right? Who can blame me for hogging the dance floor?"

"Not at all. I'm glad you're having so much fun." Mrs. Ford touched Sadie's arm. "Honey, I'm so glad you came with Sam. Weddings can be so difficult—"

Mr. Ford put his arm around his wife. "Remember our wedding day, honey? It was very simple compared to today's events."

"It was a cake-and-punch affair," the woman told Sadie. "I wore my mother's gown, we used flowers from his aunt's garden, and a friend offered to take the pictures—they actually turned out pretty good."

"Don't forget the canned music," Mr. Ford said.

"It cut out as I was walking down the aisle."

"Oh no. What did you do?"

"I hardly even noticed." Mrs. Ford beamed at her husband. "We had love and that was all we needed. Right, honey?"

"You said it, sweetheart." He kissed her temple.

Sadie smiled wistfully. Sam's parents were so different from hers. So affectionate. "How long have you two been married?"

"Thirty-two good years," Mr. Ford said.

His wife elbowed him. "Oh, stop that. We've been married thirty-five years next Saturday."

"Well, they can't all be good," he said. "And thirty-two out of thirty-five ain't bad."

Sadie laughed at their good-natured ribbing. She imagined a sense of humor came in very handy in marriage.

Mr. Ford's eyes caught on something down on the lawn. "Honey, Amanda's parents are waving us down. We should go mingle with them for a while."

"Duty calls," Mrs. Ford said to Sadie. "Have fun, dear."

"You too." Sadie stepped forward in line at the bar. She was still smiling when Amanda appeared at her side, still looking fresh and beautiful despite her energetic dancing.

"Is the bride allowed to cut in line?" she asked Sadie softly.

"My friend, the bride is allowed to do anything she wants. And you should definitely take advantage of that while you still can."

Amanda chuckled. "I like you already."

They'd spoken briefly in the receiving line after the ceremony.

She seemed like a nice woman. Sadie admired her confidence and the feline way she moved about, so lovely and sensual.

"Wasn't Sam's speech the best?" Amanda said. "It moved me to tears."

"It really was beautiful."

Amanda touched Sadie's arm. "I'm so glad he brought you, Sadie. We've all been worried about him. I felt just awful about the way things went down between us. Horribly guilty. Tag and I handled it so badly."

Sadie's mind spun at the bombshell Amanda had just dropped. The fragments snapped quickly into place.

"For the longest time we were afraid he wouldn't even come to the wedding."

The couple in front of them cleared away, and Sadie automatically stepped forward and ordered her drink.

Amanda did the same. "I'm sure you know Sam's an amazing man. He deserves a special woman." Her knowing smile assumed Sadie was that woman.

"Um, thank you. He is an amazing man."

Her mind worked as Amanda turned away to reply to another guest. It was all making sense now. The bad breakup Sam had once alluded to. His retreat to the island weeks before his cousin's wedding. The family tensions he'd mentioned when they first met. And Mrs. Ford's obvious relief that Sam had brought Sadie along this weekend.

Sam's beloved cousin had stolen the woman he loved.

The bartender handed Sadie her drink. She slipped a few bills into the tip jar and saluted the bride even though part of her wanted to smack the woman upside the head. "Enjoy the rest of your evening."

"You too, Sadie."

She walked unseeingly away from the bar, crossing the crowded deck. Hayley had given Sadie plenty of dirt on her brother, but she'd never breathed a word of this. That his sister hadn't revealed this particular secret was no doubt a testament to the depth of his hurt and humiliation.

And yet Sam had not only attended his cousin's wedding, he'd stepped in as best man and delivered what now seemed like the most gracious toast she'd ever heard.

His speech played back in her head—not a hint of hostility in his words or tone. She stopped at the top of the steps, palming her chest. He's said such wonderful things about the people who'd hurt him so badly. His generosity made her ache for him. If there had been a shred of doubt that Sadie was in love with him before, it evaporated now.

Her vision cleared suddenly . . . and there was Sam. He stood alone for the first time tonight, just past the yard and on the beach, staring toward the bonfire. The moonlight shimmered off his dark hair and puddled on his shoulders.

Sadie's heart expanded at the sight of him. All those grand emotions that had swelled inside her before the ceremony returned, along with others: respect, admiration, awe.

Her feet moved of their own volition, carrying her down the steps. She crossed the flagstones leading toward the beach, her gaze focused like a laser on him.

As if sensing her presence, he turned. At the sight of her striding his way, his lips lifted in welcome.

Every fiber of her being needed him right now. The feeling swelled like the ocean, engulfing her with the force of a tidal wave. She was helpless against the strength of it.

As she neared, Sam's ready smile faltered. His brow furrowed. A question lit his eyes.

She had a ready answer for him. She set her drink on a bench and took his face in her hands, barely feeling the scruff of his beard before her mouth covered his.

He hesitated only a moment. And then he returned her kiss, his lips warm and pliable. She rose onto her toes. Wound her arms around his shoulders and kissed him like a woman in love.

Something about the thought distracted her from the delicious moment. She fought the urge to follow it and lost. She was in love with Sam, but for all she knew he was still in love with Amanda. Beautiful Amanda with the intelligent eyes, impossibly long legs, and graceful bearing. Sadie couldn't see *her* stumbling awkwardly down a porch stoop or sprawling through a door and into a man's arms.

Was Sam returning Sadie's kiss only to salvage her pride? Or maybe she was simply a stand-in for his true love—a woman he couldn't have.

Heat flushed her skin and she pushed back, breaking the kiss. "I'm sorry. I shouldn't have—"

He gathered her close and took her mouth with his.

Sam had no idea what had sent Sadie striding his way. At the moment he couldn't care less. Her lips were soft and delicious. The slight weight of her was a welcome embrace.

The blast of a firework interrupted their interlude. More explosions followed.

He drew away, found himself breathless. Sadie's heavy-lidded gaze made him downright heady. Another firework exploded. "You have impeccable timing."

She breathed a laugh. Her hand slid down to his chest where she could surely feel his heart pounding for want of her.

"You've been avoiding me all night."

She looked down, but before she could pull away, he tightened his grasp at her waist, not ready to release her just yet. "Have I kissed you speechless?"

"I believe so," she said in a thready whisper.

Wedding guests flooded the beach, intruding upon their space.

Reluctantly, he pulled away and took her hand. "Let's find a quiet spot."

He grabbed a blanket from the nearby stack and spread it out a distance from the others. They kicked off their shoes and he welcomed Sadie when she settled between his knees and leaned back against him.

The fireworks shot from a barge out on the water into the sky, blooming above them. But his mind spun with questions. What had compelled her to kiss him like that after avoiding him all evening?

She turned and gazed up at him. A *boom* resounded and the blooming firework cast a golden glow over her features. "Why didn't you tell me Amanda was the woman who hurt you?"

Vulnerability rose inside him. His walls went up. Of course he'd known it was possible she might learn about Amanda tonight. But he'd hoped the elephant in the room would remain invisible. However, it wasn't humiliation from the betrayal that made his heart shrink two sizes.

He forced himself to voice his fear, but he stared at the sky as he did it, not wanting to see the answer in her expression. "Please tell me that wasn't a pity kiss."

"*What?*" Sadie turned his face toward hers. Their gazes clung for long seconds. "*No.*"

Her affection for him was written all over her. In the way her eyes softened. In the release of a breathy sigh. In the gentle touch of her fingers.

His heart answered her silent declaration with a convincing tug. Relief flowed through his veins like wine.

"You're a wonderful man, Sam. I knew it before today. I admired and respected you, and . . . I cared about you. But what you did for your cousin after what he did to you?" She shook her head. "You're not just wonderful. You're remarkable. And I needed to show you how much I believe that."

He was glad it was dark so she couldn't see the heat that no doubt flushed his neck. He looked away.

She turned his face toward her again, leaned close, and swept her lips across his in the most tender caress. "Don't be embarrassed. It's true." She settled back in his arms, still gazing up at him. "Now, why didn't you tell me about you and Amanda?"

He tried to put words to his feelings. "I just . . . I guess I wasn't ready to talk about it yet. The whole thing was . . . painful and humiliating. I didn't talk much about it at all. My trust in people took a dive for a while."

"No wonder. I can't even imagine the betrayal you must've felt. I'm so sorry you went through that."

He understood why she might want answers, but he didn't want Amanda and Tag inside their private bubble tonight. "Can we table this conversation for a while? A lot has happened this weekend—all of it good—but . . . I just want you all to myself right now."

When she stroked his face, every cell came to life. "Of course. Let's just enjoy the evening."

THIRTY-ONE

Write your couple into a corner—then find a way to get them out.

—*Romance Writing 101*

It wasn't until the next day that fear struck Sadie. But the bustle of packing and saying goodbyes at the hotel usurped her time and focus. Now she and Sam were alone for the first time this morning.

He reached across the truck's cab and took her hand.

She laced her fingers with his. The merest touch from him made her heart fight its confinement. She cut a glance his way as he turned onto the interstate, heading home.

In the back seat Rio settled into her new reality with a heavy sigh.

Sadie's thoughts turned to the previous evening. They'd sat on the beach, talking and kissing, until long after the smell of fireworks faded from the air. Despite his intentions, he told her about the day he'd found Amanda with his cousin. She ached for him as he shared and marveled at his ability to put the betrayal in the past.

Later he walked her to her door and sent her to bed with a kiss that kept her tossing and turning all night. She reveled in his kisses. In the intensity of these new feelings.

But now, reality was setting in. She and Sam could never work out. Their lives were simply too far apart. She could never give up New York, and she could never ask him to leave his family's business.

The memory of her parents' bitter arguments, stony silences, and long separations plagued her. As a child she'd never known what was going to happen next. During the times they got along, she waited anxiously for the other shoe to drop. There was no stability in that. No assurance that all was well or ever would be. Just a constant uneasiness about what would happen next. And what would happen to her if their family eventually splintered apart for good.

Sam squeezed her hand. "You're quiet this morning."

"Sorry. I didn't get much sleep last night."

"I didn't either. A certain someone was on my mind."

She pushed her troubled thoughts aside and returned his flirty glance. "Anyone I know?"

"Are you trying to cause an accident with that sultry look of yours?"

"Maybe you'd better keep both those hands on that steering wheel, mister."

He shot her a sly grin. "At least you got plenty of romantic inspiration for your book this weekend."

"Was that the intention of all those stolen kisses? To inspire me?"

"Let's call it a happy by-product. But maybe your writing will come more easily when we get home."

"It had better. I don't have time for writer's block." She *had* gotten inspiration—and in ways she'd never planned or expected. The deadline loomed, the pressure returning with each mile of their trip.

"You'll find the words—I know it." They shared a smile. "But now that we're alone, maybe we should talk about us. About how we're feeling. I've been sensing some reservation from you this morning."

She gazed out the passenger window. She wasn't sure if she was ready to put words to her thoughts and feelings.

"Am I wrong?"

The fluttery feelings and new sensations were overwhelming. The thought of being with Sam was exhilarating and . . .

Terrifying.

"I—I guess I'm just concerned about what's next. I'm uncertain about your expectations."

"Fair enough. Let me be clear then—I'd like to be with you, Sadie. I enjoy spending time with you. I'd like to see where this could go."

Her heart gave a tight squeeze. She met his gaze. "I'd like that, too, but . . ." She wasn't sure how to complete the thought.

"Are you worried I still have feelings for Amanda? Because I don't. This weekend put that question to rest for me."

"I believe you. I'm worried about something else—we live so far from each other. I've never dated anyone outside the city."

"I understand your reservations. But feelings like this don't come around every day. At least, not for me they don't."

"Believe me, I know that."

"Maybe we shouldn't jump ahead of ourselves. All relationships have obstacles. But when it matters enough, people work through them."

She didn't see how this particular obstacle could be overcome. She wouldn't leave the city and he'd made it clear his future was in South Carolina.

She caught his glance and found his gaze warm and full of affection. She drank it in. With a mere look he gave her heart wings. How could she not allow these feelings to develop when they were so very enticing? The magnitude of their pull was impossible to resist.

And if you let these feelings play out, a seductive voice whispered, *wouldn't that be good for your story?*

She already knew what the first flush of love felt like. But what came next? It could be the most important research she would ever do for her novel.

She shook away the self-serving thoughts. Sam was a wonderful man and she really did enjoy spending time with him. She loved having his arms around her. Even if their relationship couldn't last, maybe she could just enjoy this romantic encounter for what it was—a lovely summer romance.

She smiled at him. "You're right."

He lifted her hand and pressed a kiss to the back of it. "My two favorite words."

She had only seven weeks until she had to return to prepare her classroom for the school year ahead. She'd enjoy these wonderful feelings while they lasted and push back any fear of repeating her parents' mistakes—because she would never allow things to go that far.

THIRTY-TWO

Give your heroine opportunities to understand and face her inner fears.

—Romance Writing 101

The first thing Sadie did after Sam left for work the next day was move those infernal trees separating the deck. With the barrier gone, she dragged the table to the center and arranged the Adirondack chairs together.

"There," she said to Rio, who was currently barking at the waving sea oats. "Isn't that much better?"

Sadie spent the day writing. The block had apparently disappeared in the wake of her revelations. Her feelings seemed to inspire all sorts of ideas—and reality played out on a page or three.

She had to write like the wind to get those first hundred pages done before the deadline—only three days away now. She was so glad she'd included a buffer.

She was in the middle of a scene, the dialogue flowing like an open faucet, when a call came in. She checked her screen. Mom. Sadie was tempted to ignore the call, but her mother rarely called during the middle of the day. Something could be wrong.

She pushed back from her laptop. "Hi, Mom. How are you?"

"Hi, honey." Her voice quivered. "I could be better, to tell you the truth. I hate to tell you this while you're at the beach, but your dad and I are taking a break. Things came to a head late last night and he left."

Sadie's heart sank, the unwelcome feeling all too familiar. "Oh, Mom. I'm sorry." She quelled the jaded side of her that wanted to ask her mother what she'd expected. This outcome was as predictable as the earth's orbit around the sun.

"I'm not going to drag you into our problems, but I knew you'd want to know. He's staying at Ernie's apartment." Her dad's divorced friend always seemed to have a spare bed for him.

"Is there anything I can do?"

"No, I'll be fine. As will your dad. I'm sure we'll work it out. We always do." She cleared her throat. "Well, I'm tired of feeling sad. Let's talk about you, sweetheart. How's your writing going? Are you finished with your book yet?"

Her mom always seemed to think books materialized from thin air. "It's going well. I'm closing in on the first hundred pages. I'll be sending them to Erin later this week."

"That's wonderful. I can't wait to read it, honey. How's Caroline? Have you heard from her recently?"

"Just quick texts. She's had a busy couple of weeks with her dog-walking business, plus her mom just had surgery on her shoulder so she's helping her out."

"That's very kind of her. And how are things with that handsome neighbor of yours?"

Sadie had texted with her mom yesterday as they were returning to the island. "They're going well, but we're not really serious."

"Oh, why not? You deserve to find someone special, and I can tell by the sound of your voice that you like him."

"I do like him . . ." More than liked him. Her pulse fluttered at the very thought of him.

"But . . ."

Sadie huffed. "But he lives five states away, Mom. What kind of future could we possibly have?"

"Take your time and try not to think so far ahead. Your address is just a matter of geography."

Just a matter of geography? Never mind that it had contributed to a lifetime of conflict between her parents. Never mind that it had left Sadie insecure and uncertain about her family the whole time she was growing up.

She shook her head. "How can you say that, Mom, when it's caused so much division between you and Dad?"

"What do you mean?"

"You left the city for him and you came to regret it. You've resented it all these years—resented him for taking you away."

"Honey . . . that's not at all what happened. I don't resent your father for—What on earth made you think that?"

"You talk all the time about when you lived in New York, and you speak about it in such a wistful tone. You've made no secret of your dislike for Scranton. You made New York sound so glamorous. So amazing. And you gave it all up to marry Daddy."

Her mom laughed. "Oh, honey, I was in my early twenties when I lived in New York. Of course it felt glamorous—all that energy and excitement. I was young and on my own for the first time. But you've lived in the city long enough to know it's not all rainbows and sprinkles. The traffic, the smog, the crowded subways, the cost of living. I hardly had two pennies to scrape together. I never regretted leaving the city, not really."

"Then why? Why are you and Dad always fighting? Why are you always splitting up and getting back together and doing it all over again?"

"Don't you think I've asked myself that a thousand times? Sweetheart, I think we just have one of those relationships with a lot of ups and downs. The ups are so, so good."

"I know, Mom, but who can stand that kind of roller coaster? Growing up I hated it." She winced at her harsh words, but it was how she felt.

"Sadie . . . I'm so sorry. I don't know what to say. We tried to keep our problems from you. But we see things so differently, your dad and me. We tried not to fight in front of you."

For the most part they had, but the vent in their bedroom carried their words straight into Sadie's room. She used to block them out by putting a pillow over her head. "I've heard you argue about money. Is that what pulls you apart?"

Her mom laughed. "The only time we argue about money is when your dad makes me mad, and I retaliate by blowing money on something we don't need. It's not really about the money for me. I get angry and lash out where it hurts him most—right in the wallet. Not my finest quality, I'll admit."

How sad. Sadie shook her head again. "Mom, have you guys thought about counseling? Maybe you and Dad could work out some of your issues and head off these major disputes."

"Of course we've thought about it. I guess I've been reluctant to tackle our problems. I think part of me gets a rush out of our ups and downs. And we've gone on this way for so long . . ."

"It's never too late to work out your problems."

"These arguments used to . . . energize me somehow. I'm embarrassed to say it. But I'll admit it's getting old. Maybe *I'm* getting old, but I don't think I have the strength to live this way anymore."

"Think about finding someone to talk to, Mom, okay? You and Dad deserve to be happy."

She and her mom talked a bit longer, then said their goodbyes.

Sadie leaned back against the chair, her heart heavy at the thought of her parents' relationship. She prayed they'd seek counseling this time and set a different course for the future.

THIRTY-THREE

Each barrier your heroine overcomes should bring her closer to her ultimate goal.

—Romance Writing 101

Sam had missed the call.

He'd been mulching a bed of primrose and pink verbena. The afternoon sun beat down relentlessly, making beads of sweat pop out on his arms. The clouds overhead promised rain, and he could only cheer them on. He could continue working in the drizzle. But the weather radar promised an afternoon storm, and he had another yard he hoped to finish before he returned home.

Home.

Funny how the island rental had claimed that honorary title. But it wasn't the house, really—it was Sadie. Things had been great since their return from Florida four days ago. They'd eaten together each night. He brought home takeout or she cooked. One night he'd taken her to PJ's for their wonderful crab cakes.

They'd spent hours on the deck talking and laughing. He was delighted that she'd removed the barrier dividing the deck and finally admitted he'd been the one to put it there. They'd shared a good laugh.

Aware of his dopey grin, he spread out the last heap of mulch, then gathered his tools and headed back to his truck. After loading up he turned the key and welcomed the cool blast of air. He checked his phone. He had a voice mail. He tapped Play.

"Hi, you don't know me, but my name is Michael Davis. I got your number from Aaron Carpenter. Could you call me back as soon as possible, please? It's about the book you found."

Sam leaned forward, his pulse kicking into gear as he hit Redial. This was the call he and Sadie had been waiting for. He tapped a tattoo on the steering wheel as the phone rang.

"Hello?"

"Hi, is this Michael?"

"Yes, it is."

"This is Sam Ford. I just got your message."

"Thank God. I'm so glad you called back. I rented Aaron's apartment before he did, and I accidentally left a book behind. He said you'd stopped by looking for me."

"Yes, my friend and I did. We have the book."

"And the ring?"

"Yes, of course. It's in a safe place."

"Oh, thank God." The man's breath rushed out. "You have no idea how relieved I am to hear it. I was so afraid I'd lost it for good. I had to move out in a hurry, and I totally forgot about putting the book in that desk."

How could a man forget an engagement ring he must've spent a fortune on? "Well, no worries. We'll be happy to return it to you. My friend and I have been on that book's trail for weeks. I hope it didn't spoil your proposal."

"Oh no, it's not *my* ring." He chuckled. "I'm not even dating anyone. A friend of my dad's hired me to make the secret compartment in the book—I guess you could say I'm a bit of an artisan-slash-woodworker. I have the tools and skills required for the job anyway. When I finished the project, the guy asked me to keep it at my place until the big day—which is in *two days.* What with my move and change of jobs, I'd completely forgotten about the book until he called me this morning. I had to tell him what had happened. He's going to be so relieved to get that ring back. Could I swing by and pick it up now?"

Sam thought fast. He didn't want to deprive Sadie of this moment—she'd been so excited to return the ring to the owner. "Actually, if you'd give me the man's number, my friend and I would like to return it ourselves. We can do it right now." Sadie would make time for this—even in the middle of her deadline crunch.

"Sure, that would be great. I'm just so glad the ring wasn't lost or stolen. Let me find his number in my phone."

Sam waited while Michael searched for the number. He could hardly wait to see the look on Sadie's face when she heard he'd located the ring's rightful owner.

"Here it is." Michael rattled off the number while Sam scrawled it on a scrap receipt. He'd just printed the last digit when realization struck. "Wait. Are you sure that's the right number?" He repeated it back to Michael.

"Yes, that's right. Is something wrong?"

Sam stared at the number, shaking his head. It couldn't be . . .

Then the dots connected. Oh, but it was. Sam's breath

released in a puff. "No, nothing's wrong at all." He was grinning to himself as he said, "Don't worry, we'll make sure he gets the ring back."

Sadie typed the last words of the chapter and leaped from her deck chair. "I did it! Rio, I got the pages done!" Her squeal rivaled the piercing cries of the seagulls overhead.

Now she just had to print it off. Tomorrow she'd read through it, giving it a quick edit, then send it off to Erin by the end of the day. It didn't have to be perfect—it was just a first draft.

But the best part of it all was . . . it was good. She loved this story and was invested in the characters—how could she not be? Her laughter carried on the breeze.

She leaned over her laptop, found Sam's printer on the network, and clicked Print. It would take a few minutes to produce all those pages.

She pocketed her phone, its happy music keeping her company while she went inside and refreshed her water and Rio's. She should probably go next door and make sure there was enough paper in the printer. Enough ink.

She couldn't believe she'd made it this far. The first third of the book was always the hardest for her. But she honestly believed she was pulling off a romance novel. Who would've thought?

She left Rio lapping up her water and went next door. Sam's door slid open easily. He never bothered locking it and had insisted she help herself to the printer as needed. Fortunately, the machine had plenty of paper and ink, especially since she would've had to make a trip to the store otherwise.

As the pages filled with her words spit out onto the tray, gooseflesh rose on her arms. She was so proud of herself for tackling this challenge. She was *this* close to paying back that advance and getting out of debt.

The rhythmic intro of "I Gotta Feeling" began, measuring out time beat by beat. Smiling at the sound of the celebratory song, she jacked it up. When the first verse began, she couldn't help but sing along.

THIRTY-FOUR

Readers enjoy the anticipation of discovery as each of your plot threads plays out, so make sure the payoff is worthwhile.

—Romance Writing 101

When Sam arrived at the duplex, he went around the side to the deck where Sadie always worked. But when he got there she wasn't at the table. He knocked on her sliding door.

Rio came running, barking a welcome he heard through the glass and wagging her whole backside.

He slid open the door, stepped inside, and picked up the dog. "*Sadie?* Where's your mommy, huh?" He called her name again, but she didn't answer. Her car was in the drive, so she must've gone for a jog on the beach, though he couldn't imagine her doing so in this heat and humidity.

He could use a shower anyway. He set Rio down and slipped out the door. He heard music as he neared his apartment.

Frowning, he slipped inside. But the sight that met his eyes stopped him in his tracks.

Sadie danced in his dining room to an upbeat tune blaring from the phone in her pocket. She gave a little shimmy and continued the verse of "I Gotta Feeling."

He watched as she grabbed a wheeled chair and took it for a turn around the table, conga-line style.

His lips twitched.

Right leg. Left leg. She snapped her head to the side with each little kick, doing it up real good. When she'd made a complete turn around the table, she chugged down the hall toward the foyer. Hit the floor plant in her path. "I'm so sorry!"

A laugh bubbled up. He covered his mouth.

But even as his amusement mounted, something equally pleasant but more serious swelled inside him. Sadie was wonderful. She delighted him like no one else. She was spontaneous and spirited. Kind and giving. Over the weekend his entire family had fallen in love with her. How could they help it?

She made a U-turn at the front door. His heart softened as he watched her. Had he fallen for her too? If the feelings welling up inside were any indication, he was well on his way to love.

Sadie headed back toward the living room, still in fine conga form, singing at the top of her lungs. "Aaaaah!" Her hand flew to her chest. The chair skated toward him. "Sam! Oh my gosh—you scared me to death! What are you doing home so early?" She silenced the music. Cut him a sheepish look. "And, uh, how long have you been standing there exactly?"

He chuckled. "Long enough." He strode toward her, pushing the chair from his path. "May I cut in?"

She gave a mock scowl. "Very funny."

When he reached her he wrapped his arms around her and gazed into her beautiful eyes, those feelings still surging through his veins like a drug. She was breathless from her passionate promenade around his house. The memory of it made him smile.

"What? Why are you staring at me like that?"

"Because you're very cute." He kissed her nose. "I take it by the, ah, *celebration* that you got your hundred pages done."

A sweet blush filled her cheeks. "I was just printing them off."

Only now did he notice the machine's sounds. "And dancing around my house like a maniac."

She pointed at him. "A *cute* maniac."

"A very cute maniac."

She palmed his face and pressed her lips to his. "What are you doing home so early? Not that I'm complaining."

Oh, that. He'd almost forgotten. He put a few inches between them and pinned her with a look. "I got a phone call. Sadie, you're never gonna believe this."

Her eyes lit. "What? Is it about the book? Did you find the owner?"

"As a matter of fact, I did. I got a call from the former tenant of that apartment—his name's Michael."

She beamed. "Was he relieved we found his ring? Has he proposed yet? Is he coming over to get it? Oh, tell me his proposal wasn't ruined!"

He chuckled. "I will if you ever give me the chance."

She poked his shoulder.

"First of all, Michael is not the ring's owner."

Her face fell. "What?"

"He was hired to make the secret compartment in the book.

The ring's owner wanted to keep the gift out of sight and asked Michael to hold on to it for him until the big day."

"Then who's the owner?"

"That's the part you won't believe." He held Sadie's gaze for a drawn-out moment. "It's my *dad*."

Sadie frowned. "*What?* That can't be right. What would your dad be doing with an engagement ring?"

"The ring's not for an actual proposal—it's for my mom and dad's anniversary, which is—"

"Tomorrow!" Sadie's face lit with pleasure. "They were telling me at the wedding."

"My dad never got my mom an engagement ring. I guess he decided to surprise her for their thirty-fifth."

Sadie gave a wistful smile. "Oh, that's so sweet."

"We should take it to him now though. He called Michael this afternoon and found out the ring was missing. He's probably about to tear his hair out. He'll be at the shop for another hour or so, and we'd better catch him before he goes home."

"Oh, I'm so excited. I can't wait to see the look on his face. I'll run and get the book."

"Meet me at the truck."

Though Sam would've loved a shower, he didn't take time for one. Sadie met him at the truck a minute later and they headed toward the shop. Afternoon traffic had picked up, so the trip was taking a little longer than usual.

Sadie fairly vibrated with excitement as she clenched the book in her lap. "I can't believe it belongs to your dad."

"I couldn't believe it when Michael rattled off Dad's number."

"And it ended up in my library. How in the world? Are we almost there?"

He tossed her a grin. "We're five minutes closer than the last time you asked."

"I can't help it. We've waited so long and your poor dad is probably—Oh! We're here."

He pulled into the gravel lot at the back where the extra trailers were parked. "Good, it looks like we caught him alone. Mom sometimes comes in to work on the books."

Sadie tucked the book in her purse as Sam came around to help her out. As they walked toward the back of the building, he took her hand.

She surveyed the old brick building, formerly a hardware store. "So this is where you work. It's bigger than I expected."

"We hope to eventually rent and sell lawn-care equipment. Although Dad says he doesn't have the energy for that. He wants Tag and me to handle the expansion." He pulled open the door and ushered her inside. The familiar smells of gasoline and motor oil filled his nostrils.

They found his dad in the front, pacing the small lobby. Since he'd hurt his back last year, he spent more time in the office answering calls and pushing papers than he did mowing lawns.

Dad glanced over at their arrival. "Sam, Sadie. This is a nice surprise."

They greeted him, and his dad offered them coffee.

"Don't do it," Sam muttered to Sadie. "It was brewed hours ago and it wasn't that great fresh."

Dad scowled at him. "I was going to make her fresh."

"Thank you, Mr. Ford, but I don't need any more caffeine at the moment."

"Well, okay." Dad put his hands on his hips. "What brings you by? You have a problem on a job, Son?"

"No, Dad, everything's fine. Can we sit and chat for a minute?"

"Sure." His dad took a seat in the lobby, and Sam and Sadie sat opposite him.

Sam glanced at Sadie, who was about to levitate off her chair. He nudged her. "Why don't you tell my dad why we're here."

"We found your book!"

Dad's gaze toggled between them. "You what now?"

Beaming, Sadie pulled the novel from her purse and handed it over.

Dad's face lit up as he received the hardcover. "My book!" He took it and opened it up. Removed the jewelry box from the compartment and snapped open the box. Upon sight of the ring, he sank back into his chair. "Oh, thank God. I was afraid it was gone forever." His gaze sharpened on them. "How did you get this? Did Michael give it to you?"

"Nope." Sam nudged Sadie. "Go ahead, tell him how you found it."

"Your book's been on quite the journey, Mr. Ford. It seems your friend Michael stashed it in the desk of his furnished apartment. But then he had to move suddenly, and in his rush he forgot about it. The new tenant, Aaron, moved in and found the novel. He handed it off to his mom, thinking she might like to read it. But it wasn't her genre, so when she was cleaning out her late mother's bookshelves, she added it to a box of books to be donated to her dad's church library. *Your* church, incidentally."

"Moss Creek?" he asked.

"Exactly. Ms. Stapleton received the box of books, but she already had several copies of the novel in the church library, so she sold it at the church's rummage sale."

"Good grief," Mr. Ford said. "That was weeks ago. It's been missing that long?"

"It's certainly made the rounds. Some tourist probably bought the book at the rummage sale and must not have had the chance to read it because she left it in the Little Free Library I set up on the beach."

He shook his head. "Little Free Library?"

Sam stepped in. "One of those small structures that are popping up on roadsides to house books."

"I put one up beside our house on the beach-access path."

"And the book ended up there?"

Sadie laughed. "I know. Isn't it wonderful?"

"I'm sure glad I didn't know how long it was missing. I didn't realize until this afternoon, and I've been a nervous wreck thinking the ring had been stolen or was permanently lost." He gazed down at the beautiful ring. "But you found it."

"And just in time for your anniversary."

Mr. Ford's face split into a wide grin. "Just in the nick of time."

"Mom's going to love it, Dad. It's a beautiful ring." And then, because he knew Sadie was probably dying to know, he asked, "Is there a story behind that particular book? I don't remember Mom ever talking about it. It's not her favorite novel." That would be *Little Women*.

Dad stared at the cover, a pensive expression coming over his face. "There is a story, actually. Your mom was in the middle of reading this book when I asked her to marry me." He offered Sam a droll look. "And I mean she was literally reading the book in her living room when I blurted out, 'Hey, you think we should get married?' I didn't figure out until much later what a disappointment my proposal had been. I was an idiot kid, what can I say?"

Sam chuckled at the thought of his dad, young and ignorant of a woman's wishes. "Why have I never heard that story before?"

"It wasn't exactly my finest hour. To add insult to injury, I didn't get her an engagement ring. I had some money put back, but we decided to use it as a down payment on a house instead." He shook his head. "I should've gotten her one years ago, but since I didn't, I wanted to do it up right."

"Boy, did you. That ring is gorgeous, and the thought you put into it is so sweet, Mr. Ford. She's going to love that you remembered which book she was reading at the time."

"She never even grumbled about that lame proposal . . . Your ma's never been one to complain."

"That's true."

"She has no idea about the ring. We agreed to have our master bathroom renovated for our anniversary."

"She'll be so surprised," Sadie said.

"And thanks to you kids, she'll be getting the proposal she deserved the first time—even if it has been thirty-five years in coming."

Sadie palmed her heart. "She'll be so touched by your thoughtfulness."

Sam suspected Sadie was exactly right.

They headed out shortly after. Not even the drizzle that started on the way home could dampen Sadie's spirits. She couldn't stop talking about his dad's romantic streak and making Sam promise to tell her how the anniversary surprise went over.

He was flying high himself. What a great day. The ring had

been returned—to his dad of all people—and Sadie was so happy to have solved the mystery. He enjoyed every mile of her bright chatter on the way home. The rain picked up, the wipers keeping time to the music on the radio. A boom of thunder sounded, followed by a flash of lightning.

A while later he pulled into the drive. "Why don't you come over for supper? I need a shower first, but I have steaks I can grill out under the overhang."

"I'm going to grab a shower too." She unbuckled her seat belt. "But I should rescue Rio first. She's probably hiding from the storm under my bed."

"Bring her with you."

Sadie exited the truck and darted through the rain. But before she could reach her stoop, he caught her around the waist, suddenly loath to part ways even for a few minutes.

She shrieked. "I'm getting soaked!"

He laughed. "So what? You're about to get in the shower."

"Good point."

He turned her in his arms and gazed down at her. Her hair already hung in wet strands around her face. Water trickled like tears down her temples, making her makeup run.

And she'd never looked more beautiful.

He brushed a gentle kiss across her wet lips, savoring her soft, compliant mouth. Her arms came around his waist, and she pressed herself to him. When her lips parted on a breath, he deepened the kiss.

The storm carried on inside him, the feelings swelling like an ocean wave. He wanted to hold on to her like this forever. The thought surprised him. Delighted him. He couldn't think of anyone he'd rather be with.

When they parted, their breaths mingled between them. "Don't be too long," he said.

"I won't."

He watched her scurry through the rain and dash up the steps. She tossed a smile over her shoulder before disappearing inside.

He headed up the steps and into his own apartment. As he closed the door the storm quieted. He pulled off his wet shoes and grabbed a hand towel from the half bath. He was still wearing a dopey grin as he passed through the living room on his way to the stairs.

His eyes caught on the stack of paper sitting in the printer's tray. Sadie's manuscript. In all her excitement about returning the ring, she'd forgotten about it. He headed that way and gathered the pages, tapping their edges on the table to line them up for her.

And since her story was right there in his hands, he couldn't stop himself from taking a peek. The first page drew him right in, the taut writing pulling him along. He was a few pages in when he realized the heroine's problem was somewhat autobiographical—she had to write a romance novel but struggled with the concept because she'd never been in love. Surely that wasn't true of Sadie. She'd mentioned previous relationships. Not that they'd talked specifically about love. He'd just assumed.

He read on, beginning to skim now. There was an offer of a beach cottage. A steady diet of romance novels. A stumble down the front porch steps, and a grumpy neighbor living next door for the summer.

Him.

He was uncertain if he should be flattered or insulted. He

continued skimming, his heart on high alert, vibrating in his chest like a tuning fork. There were differences in the manuscript. It wasn't set on Tucker Island but on some Caribbean beach. The characters' conversations weren't recitations of Sadie's and his. The hero seemed gruffer than he'd presented himself to be. The heroine was an English teacher, and her physical attributes differed from Sadie's.

But the similarities were obvious. The hero had Sam's appearance and some of his mannerisms. There was a Little Free Library and a book with a hidden compartment—including an engagement ring. The couple in the novel made the same bargain. Skipping ahead, he found that the couple's relationship developed as they searched for the novel's owner.

The heroine's struggle to write a romance novel was all too familiar. The protagonist was hoping the upcoming wedding would bring the much-needed inspiration she was desperate for.

Just as desperate as Sadie had been.

For the first time since he'd picked up the manuscript, his gaze wandered away from the words on the page. Darted unseeing around the room. The unsettled feeling inside him grew stronger as warnings wailed in his head.

They'd talked about this book. He'd offered to be a sounding board. She'd had plenty of opportunity to tell him she was basically writing their story. That she'd neglected to mention this did nothing to assuage his suspicions. Did nothing to quiet his qualms. He wished he could read the entire manuscript now because he needed to know more. He needed to see where this story was heading.

He needed to know what happened at the wedding from the heroine's point of view.

What inspired that first kiss? Did the heroine enter the relationship with the hidden agenda of advancing her career?

Had Sadie? The thought was like a fist tightening around his heart.

THIRTY-FIVE

Everybody wants to be kind and caring, but you must not go easy on your protagonist.

—*Romance Writing 101*

After her shower Sadie took the time to blow-dry her hair and salvage her makeup. Not an easy task with that perma-smile etched on her face. She basked in the wonder of returning Mr. Ford's anniversary gift. Not to mention that passionate kiss in the rain—she'd have to write that into her novel. *Whew!* Who knew thunderstorms could be so sexy?

When she finished touching up her face, a peal of thunder rattled the windows. She gathered a quivering Rio in her arms. "It's okay, baby. Mommy will protect you from the mean ol' storm. Wanna go next door and see Sam? You do? Well, let's go!"

On her way out she grabbed the plate of cookies from the stove top. She wished she had more to contribute to dinner, but she'd been too busy this week to get groceries. Oh well, she'd make him dinner tomorrow night. Something nice, maybe spaghetti carbonara or seared scallops with a nice lemon herb sauce. She'd ask him what he'd like.

Hoping to stay dry she slipped out the back and dashed for Sam's door under the overhang. He had yet to touch the grill, but then, she hadn't been gone that long.

Holding both Rio and the cookies, she struggled to slide open the door. She slipped inside and pushed it closed. "Oh man, it's a downpour out there. I brought cookies. I would've brought a side dish but—"

She stopped at the strange expression on Sam's face. He stood in the dining room, still in his wet work clothes, a hand towel thrown over his shoulder. "Why haven't you—?"

She noticed the sheaf of papers in his hand. It took a second to recognize those pages. And realize what he'd been doing the past thirty minutes or so. Her heart gave an unsettling wobble. "Oh, I left my manuscript . . ."

There was more she should say. She just couldn't figure out what that should be. The foreboding expression on his face stole the words from her mind before they could find their way to her tongue.

He set the pages on the table. "Your story seems very familiar." His deadened tone did nothing to allay her fears.

"Yes, I know, I . . ." She thought her way through the story, trying to see it from Sam's point of view. The similarities were obvious despite her efforts to deviate from real life as much as possible.

He waited for her to continue, still watching her but detached somehow. There might as well have been a cement wall between them.

"I was desperate for an idea—you know that. And then I had

the thought of using the book with the secret compartment and it all just started clicking."

"Because most of it actually happened."

She winced. "Yes, that's true. And I should've told you what I was doing, I see that now."

"Yes, you should've. Because now I'm wondering how much of *this*"—he waved his hand between them—"is real and how much is fiction."

"No, Sam." She took a few steps closer.

Eyes wary, Sam stiffened.

"It's not—I meant everything I've said and done. I care about you very much."

"Have you ever been in love? Or are you like your heroine? Is that why you were so nervous about writing this book?"

Clearly not the time to profess her love for him—he might not even believe her at this point. Anyway, he was talking about earlier on, about her fears of writing an emotion with which she'd had no experience. "Yes, that's why I was afraid to write it."

Something flickered in his eyes. "So I have to know . . . when we talked about giving this relationship a try, did this story factor into your decision?"

She opened her mouth, an emphatic denial on her tongue. But wait. She had considered that the relationship would be an inspiration. She specifically remembered thinking in terms of *research*. She grimaced.

His expression closed as he looked away. "Right."

"That was just a small part of—that wasn't the main factor at all, Sam. I was going to tell you about the similarities in the story, but—"

"Similarities? It's practically autobiographical."

Rio wriggled in her arms and Sadie loosened her grip. "Yes, you're right. To be perfectly honest—"

"That would be refreshing."

"—it was earlier in our relationship, and I didn't know how you'd feel about it, and I was getting stressed, and I guess I figured it was easier to ask forgiveness than permission." She squeezed her eyes in a wince. "That sounds so awful. It was wrong. I should've been up front with you about it. I should've asked if you were comfortable with the idea."

He crossed his arms. Somehow that barrier seemed bigger and thicker than the cement wall she'd imagined before. "It's not that you used our story for your book. I wouldn't have minded that—you were desperate for an idea and I would've been happy to help. What bothers me is that you didn't tell me what you were doing. You *hid* it from me and now I feel used. Now I wonder about your motives."

Her eyes burned. This was bad. Swallowed-by-a-big-fish bad. She was getting the terrible feeling she couldn't talk her way out of this one. "I totally get where you're coming from. You're right. I should've asked you before I ever started writing that proposal."

He shifted. Scratched his neck. "I told you about my last relationship, Sadie. You knew that trusting someone again would be difficult for me."

Guilt pinched her chest. "I know. And I'm so sorry, Sam. I didn't mean to break your trust, but I see now that I have."

He paced away from her, palming his neck in that familiar way while Sadie searched for something to say. Something that would fix this. Something that would ease the pain she'd caused.

He stopped by the sofa and turned. Hurt flickered through the *No Vacancy* sign shuttering his eyes. "I don't think this is going to work for me, Sadie. Maybe if I wasn't coming off a previous betrayal . . . but I am. And I can't be with someone I can't trust."

Ouch. She absorbed his words. Pushed past the pain. Maybe he just needed a little time. Maybe a little distance would help him believe she had real feelings for him. She'd just made a stupid, selfish decision.

But the pain in his eyes was etched on her heart, and she had a feeling she'd never be able to eradicate it. She blinked back tears. "I'm sorry, Sam. I never meant to hurt you."

THIRTY-SIX

Fiction should be a visceral experience. Whatever your protagonist is feeling, your reader should be feeling it too.

—*Romance Writing 101*

The last time Sam had felt this way he'd been sick with the flu. Then in one terrible, enlightening moment, he'd been sick at heart. The image of his cousin and Amanda on that couch was permanently burned onto his brain. That and the feeling it had evoked—that horrible exposed, sucker-punched feeling. The gaping hole inside that ached somehow, despite its emptiness.

He rode the mower across one of his larger properties, wishing the task didn't offer so much thinking time. The late-afternoon sun beat down relentlessly on his skin. He shoved his sunglasses into place, trying to shake from his mind that stunned look on Sadie's face last night.

After he'd broken up with her, she'd slipped quietly from his apartment. For someone so adept with words, he would've expected her to make a lengthy case for herself. He was relieved she didn't, as he wasn't in a headspace to hear it.

This morning he wondered why she hadn't fought harder. It wouldn't have made a difference, except maybe to assure him that her affection had been genuine. As it was, he wasn't so sure.

He only knew that his feelings for her were very real—confirmed by the misery he now experienced. He was so stupid. She had kept her story a secret and he was oblivious. Amanda and Tag had been falling in love right under his nose and he had no idea. Was he that clueless? Was he missing some observant gene? He should probably stay far away from women. Not only could he not trust them—he couldn't even trust himself right now.

After Amanda's betrayal, that awful feeling had hung around for months, hurting him, haunting him, and he didn't welcome it back now. He wanted to eradicate it. He wanted to uproot Sadie from his heart, his life, so he could feel normal again.

But in an hour or so he'd go home, and she'd be out on the deck working or getting ready to fix supper. He certainly couldn't live next door to her, share a deck with her, for six more weeks.

And there was no reason he had to.

He would call Mrs. Miller on the way home and try to bow out of his rental agreement. Even if he couldn't do so, he would still return to his apartment. Whatever it might cost was worth it for his mental health's sake.

His chest tightened at the thought of saying goodbye to Sadie. He'd come to anticipate being with her at the end of each day. To anticipate seeing her sparkling brown eyes, hearing her bright chatter, receiving her passionate kisses.

He shook the thoughts away. That was over. Seeing Sadie now would only torture him. And all his original reasons for moving to the island had evaporated. He'd run away from his pain only to find it again, thanks to someone else. His plan to escape had blown up in his face. And somehow the loss felt even worse this time around.

Sadie didn't like her story anymore. She flipped over the last page and weighted the stack with a conch shell. It probably wasn't the story itself, only the feeling of loss it now dredged up. But it was impossible to separate the two.

If it was bad, Erin would let her know. Right now Sadie didn't even care. She couldn't think past the ache in her chest.

The afternoon was waning and she had to get her pages turned in by end of day. She forced herself to key in the edits she'd made on the printed copy. This was much less heinous than reading the story had been, as the scenes came alive in the form of memories, taunting her. She had a king-size box of Kleenex sitting on the table for that very reason.

The edits took the better part of an hour, and she was relieved when the sun sank behind the house. The heat and humidity were intolerable today. She should've worked inside, but she'd thought the sunshine and sea breeze might cheer her. And she was in desperate need of cheer.

All day she'd prayed Sam would have a change of mind. Maybe if she found the right words, she could convince him her feelings were real. But perhaps that wasn't even the issue. It seemed his concern had been her secrecy. But surely he could see she'd just made a mistake. People were wont to do that on occasion. She wasn't perfect. Did that mean he couldn't trust her?

The thought had been like a pesky mosquito buzzing in her ears all day long.

Several people had stopped by her Little Library, and she chatted with each of them. Recommended a couple of books. Keisha called to see if she had time for coffee, and Sadie would've loved the chance to escape this stupid story. Would've loved to soak up some baby snuggles (and fresh oxytocin). Heaven knew the endorphins from her morning jog hadn't done the trick. But she hadn't had time for a coffee chat today.

It was nearing five when she finished keying in the final changes. She wrote a brief letter to Erin and attached the file, and with a tap on the touchpad it whooshed into cyberspace.

"There," she said quietly. "All done." Somehow the triumphant moment didn't feel so triumphant. She glanced at Rio, lying in the shade of a palm tree. "Want to go get some water?"

Go was all Rio needed to hear. Sadie gathered her things and Rio followed her into the apartment. After setting out a fresh bowl of water, Sadie contemplated dinner. Her appetite had been off today so she hadn't made much of an effort for breakfast and lunch. Okay, so she'd snacked on cookies all day. Who could blame her?

She could scrape together the ingredients for an omelet with the meager supplies in her refrigerator. But maybe Sam would come over to talk. Maybe he'd suggest they eat together. She would hold off awhile just in case. She needed a shower anyway since she'd been stewing in the heat all day. Also, it would prevent her from listening for Sam's truck in the drive.

She took a long shower, then changed into leggings and a

T-shirt. And since she was right next to the front window she peeked out. Sam's truck and trailer sat in the drive.

Her heart gave a hard squeeze. Would he come over to see her? Should she go over there? Maybe he needed space to figure things out. Just because her day had lasted eight decades didn't mean his had too.

She touched up her minimal makeup and blow-dried her hair while Rio napped on her bed. She ran a styling product through her hair and was ready to give up and make dinner when the doorbell rang.

Sam.

Of course he usually came to the back door, but maybe he'd knocked when she was drying her hair. She took the stairs quickly, Rio on her heels. Her thumping heart and trembling legs had little to do with the sudden activity.

In the foyer she picked up the dog and opened the door. The sight of him made her world tilt upright again. "Sam." Even she could hear the note of hope in her voice.

Rio stretched toward Sam, whining and squirming in her arms.

He reached for the dog and Sadie handed her over, taking in the way his eyes tilted down at the corners. There was no smile, no dimple. Sadie braced herself.

"Hey," he said.

"Hi."

"How did your work go today? Get your pages turned in?"

"Yes, just a little bit ago." An awkward pause had her shifting in the doorway. "You, uh, want to come in? I don't have much in the way of food, but I could whip up a couple—"

"That's okay. I just wanted to let you know that I, ah, decided to move back to my apartment in Bluffton. Bills are piling up, you know, and at this point there's no reason for me to stay here."

Pain unfurled in her chest. Adrenaline rushed through her veins, but she didn't want to fight or take flight. She wanted to fling herself into his arms. But he didn't want her there. "I'm really sorry about what I did, Sam. The last thing I ever wanted to do was hurt you."

He nodded slowly, the corners of his lips lifting in something that wasn't quite a smile. "I know that."

She wanted to beg him to stay, but that was stupid. What else was there to say? This had always been a short-term relationship at best, despite the love she'd come to feel for him. She'd always known it would come to an end. She just hadn't expected it to happen like this.

Or for it to feel so awful.

"Maybe this is for the best anyway. I know how much you love the city, and my life is here."

He'd only echoed her own thoughts. But if it was really for the best, why did it hurt so much? Why did it feel as if he were ripping her heart from her chest?

"Anyway . . . I'm going to load up my stuff and then I'll be going. I just wanted to come by and"—he scratched his neck—"tell you I was leaving, I guess."

He was leaving *now*? Her thoughts scrambled for purchase. *Don't leave. Not yet.* "I—I appreciate that."

He kissed Rio on the head and handed her back. "Good luck on your book, Sadie. I hope your publisher loves it."

"Thank you."

He gave her a wan smile and then he was gone, taking the

steps, returning to the apartment that, in a matter of minutes, wouldn't be his anymore.

With nothing else left to do, she took Rio inside and closed the door, her legs wobbling like stilts. "Well . . . I guess he's made up his mind."

Not only was he finished with her, but just to make sure their relationship was good and over, he was leaving. She blinked against the sting in her eyes. A lump the size of Texas formed in her throat.

"*No.* No, we're not going to do that. We're going to pull up our big-girl pants and . . . and make dinner." Never mind that the thought of food made her stomach roil. "Or go for a walk on the beach." The thought of being around other people was repelling.

But after hearing her favorite word, Rio squirmed to get down.

"Fine, we'll go for a walk."

That would occupy her mind at least. Keep her from staring out the window like a stalker while Sam loaded up his truck. She leashed the dog and headed out back. The temperature had cooled considerably as the sun sank low in the sky. They headed down to the shoreline and turned south. But all the things that usually cheered her—the scampering sandpipers, the ripple of the waves, and the friendly passersby—did nothing for her gloomy mood.

Sam was leaving and she'd never see him again. Sadie rejected the thought. It was silly, since she'd known it would end when she returned to New York. She just hadn't expected to get so attached to Sam so quickly.

Five minutes later her thoughts were so maudlin she cut

the walk short and headed back to the house. Once inside she couldn't resist a peek out the sidelight. He was still here, and she couldn't just sit around waiting for the sound of his engine.

Needing to talk to someone, she dialed Caroline's number. She hadn't exactly confided in her bestie about her relationship with Sam since it had only been temporary at best. But the phone rang until it kicked over to voice mail. Sadie hung up as tears threatened again.

"Nope. We're not feeling sorry for ourselves."

Rio didn't even look up from where she lay chewing on Mr. Mouse.

Sadie's stomach released a deep rumble. As much as she didn't feel like eating, she needed some real food in her stomach. Plus cooking would keep her away from the sidelight. She chopped an onion (legitimizing her tears), sautéed it, then whisked two eggs with a dash of milk. After adding the eggs to the onions, the mixture bubbled around the edges. The smells emanating from the skillet did nothing to stir her appetite.

Rio joined her in the kitchen, staring up from the floor with eyes that seemed sad. Her ears hung low and her tail sagged.

"I know, girl. I'm sad too. You know what we need? We need some happy music." She pulled her phone from her pocket and started her playlist. A second later the upbeat tune "Uptown Funk" began. The pulsing beat usually made her want to dance, but the rhythm seemed to have drained right out of her.

Rio whined and plopped in the middle of the kitchen floor, laying her head on Mr. Mouse.

"We're going to be okay. We have a lot of work to do over the next several weeks, and then we'll be back in New York and you can see your friends again. I'll bet Lulu misses you." Caroline regularly brought her rescue dog over for a visit. "Do you miss Lulu?"

Rio gave a deep sigh and looked away.

Sadie wasn't fooling her dog for one second with her upbeat tone. Sadness was probably oozing out her pores.

She thought of the long weeks of writing that lay ahead, the long weeks of sitting out on that empty deck, waiting for someone who'd never come home. Her chest hollowed out and she swallowed hard. "It'll go fast. You'll see."

When the omelet was done she scraped it onto a plate and set it on the island. She was just pulling out the barstool when the doorbell rang.

Rio raced for the door and Sadie wasn't far behind. Her heart threatened to burst from the confines of her rib cage. She pressed her palm there. *Rein it in. You're gonna scare him off for good.* But she didn't slow her steps and paused only to grab Rio before twisting the handle.

"Surprise!"

Sadie blinked at the woman standing on her porch as her stomach bottomed out in disappointment. "Caroline. I just called you."

"I know. But I wanted to surprise you."

"And you did." She forced a happy tone. "What are you doing here?"

"I have an unexpected three-day weekend and thought I'd make a quick trip to visit my best friend."

"That's great." Sadie surveyed her side of the drive, empty but for her own car. "How'd you get here?"

"I flew and then Ubered. Are you going to let me in or what?" She laughed.

"Of course. Come in." Sadie moved aside for her friend and peeked out in time to see Sam striding back toward his apartment. His truck's passenger door stood open.

She closed her door and set Rio down.

"This place is so nice." Caroline spun around, taking it all in. Then she headed for the back and stared out the door toward the ocean. "Wow, the pictures didn't do it justice. My mom's been holding out on me. Speaking of holding out"—she pointed a finger at Sadie—"your *neighbor*."

"Wh-what do you mean?"

"You said he was curmudgeonly and hairy. I was picturing an ogre."

Sadie couldn't even dredge up a smile. "Oh, that. Yeah, he's actually very nice. We, um, we dated for a little while. But that's over now."

Caroline gave her a wry grin. "Let me guess, you broke up with him. Does he root for the Mets? Have a complicated coffee order? Did he do something mean to you in a dream?"

He hadn't done anything at all. It was all Sadie's fault, and somehow that made it so much worse. Her face crumpled as tears welled up in her eyes.

Caroline's expression wilted. "Hey, hey, I was just kidding."

"I ruined it, Caroline. I messed everything up."

The woman's arms came around her. She patted her back and made soft crooning noises while Sadie completely lost it. Caroline led her to the couch.

"Come on, honey, sit down. Tell me all about it."

So Sadie did just that, starting at the beginning with the trade they'd made and her decision to use their story for the plot of her novel. She told her friend about his previous relationship with Amanda and the betrayal that had followed. She continued the story right up through yesterday when he'd read her pages and broken up with her.

Caroline listened to the whole thing without interrupting, without passing judgment. At one point she pulled a tissue from the nearby box and pressed it into Sadie's hand.

Sadie swallowed against the lump in her throat. "And now he's moving back to his apartment . . . to get away from me."

"Why didn't you tell me you were dating Sam?"

"I didn't see the point. It was always destined to be a dead-end relationship."

Her friend's gaze drifted over Sadie's face, no doubt seeing splotchy cheeks and smudged makeup. She covered Sadie's hand. "Oh, honey . . . you're in love with him."

Sadie pulled her hand away and sent her friend a mock glare. "Why didn't you tell me it was this awful?"

"It's not . . . when it's right."

Sadie should've known better than to lose her heart to Sam.

"This just happened yesterday?" Caroline asked. "Are you sure it's really over?"

"Did you not see him loading his things into his truck?"

"Still . . . he must have feelings for you. That doesn't just go away overnight."

"I broke his trust and that was already in short supply. I should've been honest with him from the first." Enough of this. Sadie swiped the tissue across her face and blew her nose. "I'll be okay. It had to end eventually. Probably better that it happened now than later. I would've only grown to care for him more." Was that even possible?

Caro's eyes softened as she wrapped her arm around Sadie.

"There's nothing wrong with falling for someone, you know. When it's right it's the most wonderful thing in the world."

Sadie wasn't too sure about that. "Well, obviously this wasn't right. I live in New York and Sam's life is here. It's fine. This is just the way it was meant to be."

And maybe this was the way Sadie was meant to be all along—alone.

THIRTY-SEVEN

Your protagonist should slowly progress toward her goal—two steps forward, one step back.

—*Romance Writing 101*

It was a true testament to Sadie's misery that even the email from her editor barely lifted her spirits. Surprisingly, it came on Saturday afternoon soon after she and Caroline returned from PJ's Clam Shack.

Sadie had shown her friend the island's sights all day. Caroline deserved a refreshing weekend away from the city. Besides, Sadie preferred to stay busy. She'd done a pretty good job pasting on a smile and forcing enthusiasm about the island's fort and pretty pastel shops in town. They'd stopped by Island Art where they'd each found a unique souvenir.

Over dinner Sadie wondered if Mr. Ford was even now presenting his wife with that beautiful ring. Wondered if the woman would tear up as he slid it on her finger. She almost expressed her thoughts to Caroline, but just then their meal arrived. Besides, she'd talked enough about Sam today. She didn't want to put a complete damper on the weekend.

As soon as they got home they headed for the deck to enjoy the mild evening. Rio's nose led her around the backyard while Caroline headed to the Little Library to scope out the books.

Sadie glanced at Sam's empty side of the deck. At their table, front and center. She wished she could evict him from her brain—and her heart. If only such a thing were possible.

A minute later Caroline headed up the steps, two books in hand. "I didn't have a book to leave—don't tell the librarian."

"What did you choose?"

"A Nancy Naigle beach read and a Francine Rivers novel. Plenty of reading material to keep me busy on my flights back."

"Those must be new—I haven't read them yet." Sadie scanned the deck and, making a decision, approached the table. "Can you give me a hand with this?"

"Sure." Caroline set the books down and followed her lead, grabbing the other side of the table and moving it to Sadie's side of the deck.

"Help me with these planters. We're going to line them up across the center."

The big trees were much easier to move with her friend's help. When the plants were placed, Sadie headed toward the table and Caroline sank into the chair next to her.

She could feel her friend's unasked question. "That's the way they were when I got here."

"I didn't say anything."

"I know, it's just . . . he's gone now so there's no reason to have an open deck. Besides, your mom might rent the other side out to someone else, and I don't want to share space with a stranger. I have a book to write."

"Makes perfect sense." When Rio approached, Caroline scooped the pooch into her arms and rubbed her head.

Sadie pulled her phone from her pocket where she'd left it most of the day. She had a couple of texts and several emails—none of them from Sam. But what had she expected?

But her heart jolted when she saw one of the emails. She opened it and quickly scanned its contents. When she finished reading she smiled at Caroline. "I just got an email from Erin. She read the first hundred pages and said she *absolutely loves* it."

Caroline beamed. "Sadie. That's great news. I knew you could do it. Didn't I tell you that you could write a romance novel? You should probably tell me I was right—you know I'll keep going until you do."

"Fine, you were right. Do you want a trophy?"

"A cookie will do. I saw your stash in the freezer."

"We should definitely thaw those for later." Sadie glanced back at Erin's email and blew out a breath. "Now I just have to pull off the rest of the story."

"No problem for a pro like you."

She read the message a second time. Her editor had a couple of minor suggestions for character development. Good ideas. Sadie was eager to incorporate them. Except . . .

Working on this story would be pure torture because, let's face it, her characters were actually Sam and her. And since the real relationship had come to a depressing conclusion, the happy ending of her story would have to be purely fictional. The writing of it was sure to feel bittersweet. Not to mention for the next six weeks she would be immersed in their doomed relationship.

Out here on this lonely deck where Sam wouldn't be slipping through the door at any moment.

The thought opened up that gaping wound inside. She didn't want to sit out here alone for weeks on end. Writing about their relationship would be hard enough. She didn't want to do it in the place where they'd spent so much time together.

"I can practically hear you thinking over there. What's wrong?"

Sadie's gaze snapped to Caroline. "I think I want to go home."

"Now?"

"No." She put her hand on Caroline's arm. "You came all the way out here, and you deserve a relaxing weekend. But when you fly out Monday, I'm going to head back to the city too."

Her eyes sharpened on Sadie. "Are you sure that's what you want?"

Sadie's gaze drifted around the deck. It had seemed like such a wonderful oasis when Sam was here to share it with her. Now it just felt sad and desolate. "I'm sure. I'll write the book at home."

"What about all the distractions? I assure you the construction next door is ongoing."

As she thought of the ghostly distractions around here, her eyes stung with tears. "The ones here are so much worse."

Caroline reached across the table and squeezed her hand. "I'm sorry this is so hard. I promise it'll get better. And you know what? You don't have to drive home alone. I'll go with you."

"But you bought a plane ticket."

"So what? I'd rather keep you company. Besides, what's better than a road trip with your best friend?"

"I'm not sure I'm the best company right now."

"All the more reason for me to come along."

THIRTY-EIGHT

Just as in real life, the old adage "No pain, no gain" applies to your protagonist. If she is to learn something vital about herself, suffering will likely be involved.

—*Romance Writing 101*

Caroline had been right: the construction next door to Sadie's apartment was still in full swing. But since she didn't arrive home until almost nine o'clock, it was at least shut down for the night. Just as she had the thought, a jet streaked by, making the windows rattle.

At least Julie was out—likely at work. Sadie didn't feel like answering questions about her trip or explaining why she'd decided to return early. The text Sadie had sent her yesterday was purposefully vague.

While Rio gave the apartment a thorough sniffing, Sadie dragged her suitcases into her room and collapsed onto the bed. It had been a long day in the car. They started before daybreak and stopped as few times as Rio's bladder would allow. She and Caroline were both eager to get home.

The rest of the weekend on the island had passed quickly. Yesterday they attended a church service on the beach and followed it up with a consume-the-groceries lunch. Sadie spent the afternoon cleaning the apartment and doing laundry. She shoved Caroline out the back door with a beach towel and book and strict orders not to return for at least three hours. When Sadie finished cleaning she straightened the books in the Little Library one last time and said a quiet goodbye.

Keisha had found out Caroline was in town and invited them over for dinner. Her husband was working and she seemed eager for adult conversation. Chatter, good food, and baby snuggles ensued. It was as if the three of them had been friends for years. They didn't leave until after ten. Sadie would sorely miss Keisha and baby Marcel. And the sound of the waves crashing the shoreline. She'd miss the glitter of the sun on the sea's surface, the briny breezes, and the feel of sand between her toes.

And Sam. She'd miss Sam.

Tears swelled and burned her eyes. She blinked them back and sat up in bed. "No, you're not going to do this. You're not going to lie here and feel sorry for yourself. You have things to do. You have a book to write."

But there was one order of business she needed to clear off her desk. She still needed to tell Hayley she'd left the island. She'd been putting it off, not wanting to think of Sam, much less talk about him with his sister. He'd surely told her about the breakup by now.

Still, she owed the girl a brief explanation at least—they'd talked about doing a back-to-school shopping spree. Plus she could find out how Mr. Ford's anniversary surprise had gone over with his wife.

Sadie pulled her phone from her pocket and tapped on Hayley's name.

The girl answered on the second ring. "Hey, Sadie. I just got home from my softball game. We won!"

"Yay. Did you get to pitch?"

"Just two innings, but I only allowed one on base."

"Wow, that's great."

"The batter only got a single and she never scored. We're second in our league now because we won Saturday, too, and Coach says she's starting me on Thursday. I've never started a game before."

"Oh, that's great news. I'm so happy for you."

"Mom and Dad were there—they always come to my games. Mom was flashing her new ring around like it was ten carats."

"I take it your dad's big surprise went over well?"

"It must've. She got all teary when she told me about it, and now they can't keep their hands off each other. It's disgusting."

Sadie chuckled. "You have to admit, it was very romantic of your dad."

"Now, see, you can't use *romantic* and *dad* in the same sentence. It's just wrong. Besides, did you hear how he proposed to her all those years ago? Lame."

"Yeah, it was pretty bad."

"I hope I've got better game than that with boys. Speaking of game, maybe you and Sam can come watch me pitch Thursday. The game's not far from the island."

So Sam hadn't mentioned the breakup. Sadie winced. "That's actually what I was calling about. I'm not on the island anymore.

I'm back in New York. I left this morning and it kind of happened suddenly so I didn't have a chance to call you."

"When are you coming back? Maybe you guys can make next week's game."

"Well, that's the thing. I guess Sam didn't tell you . . . We broke up."

"*What?* No, when did that happen?"

That moment came back just then—when she'd walked into his apartment and found him holding her manuscript. She'd never forget that awful detached look he'd given her. "Thursday night."

She huffed. "He was at my game Saturday and never said a word."

"He probably didn't want to distract you from the game or bring you down after your win."

"What happened between you? Did he do something stupid? Because guys do that sometimes. It doesn't mean they're no good. Sam's all right . . . for a big dork."

"He didn't do anything stupid. It just . . ." Sadie couldn't bear to go over the details. Once had been enough. "It didn't work out, that's all. It's fine, really, it is. Sam moved back to his apartment, and I decided to come back home and finish my book here. Then, of course, I'll have to go back to work the third week of August. It just seemed like the best thing to do under the circumstances."

"But you and Sam were so great together," she all but whined. "He really likes you."

Sadie's eyes filled with tears. She worked to keep her voice level. "I like him too, honey. But these things can be complicated. My life is in New York and his is there. I'm afraid it just wasn't meant to be."

"I was hoping you'd move here. Who am I going to go shopping with now? My mom has terrible taste and my friends don't care about clothes."

"Maybe you can come visit me sometime. New York is a shopper's paradise. And you can call anytime. I love chatting with you."

Hayley's mood was noticeably lower as they talked for a few more minutes, then they ended the call. Would that be the last time she heard from the girl? She hoped not. On the other hand, having a window into Sam's life might not be the ideal way to get over him.

Sam clapped with the rest of the crowd gathered at Sully's Sports Bar. The Braves were down by only one run now in the sixth inning after the Red Sox had carried a convincing lead the entire game.

"Nice hit," Tag said from across the table.

"Hopefully Harris will bring him in."

It was his first time out with Tag since they'd officially made peace. Once Sam had gotten past the requisite honeymoon inquiry, their conversation headed back into comfortable territory. Between plays they talked about the business, the forthcoming expansion, and the upcoming college football season. Sam had briefly touched on his breakup with Sadie and only after Tag asked. His cousin seemed to understand his need to change the subject.

They'd ordered forty wings with three different sauces. All that was left now was a basket of bones and sticky napkins.

Sam leaned back in his chair. He'd had a busy weekend. He worked all day Saturday, then attended his sister's softball game since his parents were celebrating their anniversary. Afterward he took her to the Dairy Bar with the team to celebrate their win. Since there was a Braves game on later that night, he'd watched it at the bar around the corner from his place.

Sunday he'd gone to church, then out to eat with a friend he hadn't touched base with in a while. Then he headed over to the office to do some paperwork. On the way home he stopped for groceries but ended up having pizza at one of his cousins' houses.

In short, Sam seemed to be avoiding his apartment. Strange that he'd run to the island to find solitude and now he was trying to avoid it.

He loved Sadie. He'd known he was falling for her Thursday when he'd walked in on her one-woman conga line. But losing her had crystallized his feelings. Even now, knowing she'd misled him, he still ached for her.

Even though she'd as much as admitted she'd pursued the relationship for the sake of her novel. Sure, she'd been desperate to come up with an idea for her story, but that did nothing to ease his pain.

Stop feeling sorry for yourself, idiot. It's done and over. Move on.

The whole place exploded in cheers. Sam blinked at the screen, orienting himself. The Braves' base runner crossed home, tying the score. A beat late Sam joined the fans in cheering. High-fived Tag.

As they headed into the seventh-inning stretch, his phone vibrated in his pocket. Hayley. He'd ignored her call an hour ago.

"Hayley's calling," he told Tag. "I should take it."

Tag gave a distracted nod as Sam headed outside where he could hear. He answered as he exited the building. "Hey, Meatball, how's it going?"

"What did you do?" Hayley said by way of greeting.

"Well, hello to you too."

"What happened with you and Sadie? She was perfect for you—even I could see that."

He really didn't have it in him to review this with Hayley. Not that it was her business anyway. "It just . . . didn't work out, that's all."

Hayley gave a huff and he imagined her eyes rolling back in her head. "That's exactly what she said."

"Because that's what happened," he said, then curiosity got the best of him. "What else did she say?"

"Wouldn't you like to know. Why don't you call her and apologize and then you won't have to interrogate me."

"It's complicated." Because Sadie hadn't wanted him to begin with. And that bothered him more than he could say. Made that wound in his gut open. "Just let it go. These things happen sometimes."

"They don't have to happen. You could actually work out your problems instead of just giving up."

"Some things can't be worked out, Hayley."

"They can if you try. If you compromise. If you care about each other enough, and I can tell you do."

Maybe *he* did. He paced the strip of sidewalk in front of the restaurant, wondering what else Sadie had told her but not desperate enough to beg. Probably best if he didn't know anyway. It would only give him reasons to keep thinking about her—and he really had to stop this nonsense.

"You blew it, didn't you? You broke up with her and she was just too kind to say anything bad about you."

Nice of his sister to take his side. "You don't know what you're talking about. You don't know anything about this."

"I know she's sitting in New York, and you're probably sitting around your apartment sulking over something you could fix if you really wanted to."

Sam stopped in his tracks. His heart stuttered. "She went back to New York?"

"Yes, she went back to New York because you moved back to your apartment. What did you expect her to do?"

She was *gone*. Miles away. States away. And now he couldn't imagine her out on the deck typing away. Or jogging on the beach, the wind ruffling her hair. He couldn't picture her dancing around her kitchen or nuzzling Rio or watching a movie with her bare feet propped on the coffee table, toenails painted purple.

Good. He shouldn't be picturing her at all. She sure wasn't picturing him.

"You're an idiot, you know that?" Hayley barked, then hung up.

Sam frowned at the phone. Teenagers. What did they know? Feeling lower than he had all weekend, he pocketed his phone and rejoined the rowdy fans for the seventh inning.

THIRTY-NINE

> Everything that happens in your story should push your protagonist toward her *epiphany*, a moment when she comes to grips with a truth about herself or the world around her.
>
> —*Romance Writing 101*

Sadie was beating her head on the back of her chair when an incoming call vibrated her phone. Caroline. Willing to reach for any distraction, Sadie answered the phone with a disheartened hello.

"Good grief, you sound terrible. Meet me at the coffee shop. I'm between jobs."

"I can't. I'm almost two weeks behind schedule and I'm stuck."

"Come on, you have got to get out of that dingy apartment for a few hours. You've been chained to that desk for four straight weeks. A little daylight and human contact might inspire you."

"My hair's dirty and I'm still in pajamas."

"It's three o'clock! And you're only proving my point. Throw your hair up in a bun and put on some real clothes. Better yet—take a quick shower. Thirty minutes. I'm not accepting no for an answer."

And just like that Caroline hung up.

Sadie sighed. "Fine." So she was a little depressed. And stressed. Who could blame her? The deadline was creeping up on her, and she had no idea how to work this story out. It was so much easier with westerns—the protagonist fought the antagonist and won. Easy-peasy. Maybe a little distance from the story would help. Sitting here staring out at the construction site sure wasn't doing any good.

Thirty minutes later Sadie neared the coffee shop. She'd put her damp hair up in a bun, and she was feeling a little better. The sun was even trying to peek out. Somewhere between South Carolina and Queens, she seemed to have lost her optimism. She needed to stop thinking about Sam and her story for two seconds and just enjoy the day. Enjoy her time with Caroline. Enjoy all the lovely people around her.

She reached the door at the same time as two male teenagers. She gave them a wide smile and opened it for them. "After you, gentlemen."

They barely glanced her way as they slipped inside and made a beeline for the barista.

Okay . . . Sadie swept her gaze over the interior, searching for her friend. But Caroline hadn't arrived yet, so she got in line behind the teens. When it was her turn she placed her and Caroline's drink orders.

"Looks like it's trying to sun up out there," Sadie said to the thirtysomething woman ringing up her order. "At least it's not raining, huh? It was so dreary yesterday."

"That'll be nine seventy."

Sadie used her phone to pay, making sure to leave a nice tip. "Long day? I get it. I've been typing so hard my fingers have calluses. I'm writing a novel."

"Want your receipt?"

"Um, no, that's okay."

She headed toward the pickup counter. She was starting to miss more than Sam and the beach. She hadn't had a decent stranger-chat since she'd come home. Had people in her neighborhood always been so unfriendly? Didn't anyone around here have the time or inclination to shoot the breeze? She barely had to nod her head on Tucker Island and soon they were talking about the weather, books, or the economy.

"Well, lookee there." Caroline came up beside Sadie and squeezed her shoulders. "You can come out in the daylight."

"I'm not a vampire."

"I was starting to wonder. I haven't seen you in two weeks."

"I haven't seen anyone except my characters, and they're miserable company right now. I ordered you a lavender tea with a dash of cream."

"Perfect, thank you. I assume you got yourself something with plenty of caffeine."

"I'll need it if I have any hope of finishing this story on time."

When their order came up they took their drinks and settled at a table in the back corner.

"It has to be hard," Caroline said, "drafting a story about characters who are essentially you and Sam. I'd ask if the writing has been therapeutic or just heart-wrenching, but judging by your expression I think I can guess."

Sadie took a sip of her Americano. "If this is what therapy feels like, count me out. So far it's only made me miss him more. He was so kind and generous and loving. He's everything I ever wanted in a man, Caro."

"I'm sorry, honey. I wish I could make it better."

"Me too." Her characters were now broken up, and Sadie didn't know how she was going to put it all back together. It was a romance novel—a happily ever after was a requirement. Sadly, that was not the case in real life.

She took another drink, hoping to dislodge the lump swelling in her throat. Her chest ached all the time. And if she wasn't actually crying, she felt like it.

She turned a beseeching look on Caroline. "It hurts so much. I've never experienced anything like this. What if it never gets better? Because it doesn't feel like it will. What if I just have to feel like this the rest of my life?" She blinked back tears.

Caroline covered her hand. "Oh, honey, you won't. I know it hurts, but I promise it will get better. Remember how much I loved Eric Dugan in college? Two years together. When we broke up I thought I would shatter."

"I remember." Her friend had fallen apart for a while. Missed some classes, bombed a test or two. "How long was it until you started feeling better?"

"I don't know. It happened gradually. It sure didn't help that we shared a class that semester. But the bottom line is, you will start feeling better. And someday you'll meet your own Carlos, and you'll be grateful it worked out this way."

She found that hard to believe. At the moment it was taking everything she had not to dissolve into a puddle of tears. She swallowed hard. "Can we talk about something else? I'm so tired of wallowing in misery. Tired of *thinking*."

"Of course. What do you want to talk about? My adorable doggie, my mother's new career opportunity, or your plans for the upcoming school year? See how I made it multiple choice for you?"

"Very kind. What's going on with your mom?"

"Well, you know she was thinking of retiring and eventually moving to Tucker Island, but the owner of the realty office where she works offered to sell her the company."

"Oh, wow, that's huge."

"She has the funds to buy her out, and it seems to have reignited her enthusiasm in her career."

"She's awfully young to retire. You think she's going to buy it?"

"I think she might. I have to admit, I don't love the idea of her moving to South Carolina."

"You've always been so close."

"I'd be happy to keep her here for another ten years or so. How are your parents doing, by the way?"

"They're still separated but Mom's been seeing a therapist, so that's good."

"Oh, that's great. That's new, isn't it?"

"It is. She's always been resistant before, but I think she's finally tired of the roller-coaster ride. I know Dad is. He's thinking about going to counseling with her, so that's something."

"That would be great for both of them. Maybe they can finally build a healthier relationship."

"That's the hope. Better late than never." How ironic that her parents were finally getting their relationship on track just as Sadie's had fallen apart. Maybe love was more complicated than she'd imagined. Maybe it involved more effort than she'd ever realized.

They paused as a car went by, its bass thumping loudly.

Caroline sipped her tea. "Wanna brainstorm your story a little? I'm no writer, but I've read my share of romances."

"It couldn't hurt, I guess. My hero and heroine are in love but have broken up because her life is in the city—Chicago—and his is on St. Lucia. I can't decide how to resolve the geographical problem."

"She should definitely move to St. Lucia."

Sadie gave her a droll grin. "It's not that simple. The city is her dream—it's who she is. I can't make her give up a part of herself for some man. That's so 1950s."

"You make a good point. And why can't your hero just move to the city to be with his one and only?"

"He owns a boat-charter business on the island, one he's built from the ground up."

"I guess they are in a tricky spot. But there has to be compromise with any relationship. If they're going to be together, someone has to make the sacrifice."

"But does it have to be the heroine?"

"Not necessarily. If Carlos had a big opportunity in another state and it meant a lot to him, I'd move for him—and I know he'd do the same for me. So maybe your hero and heroine are both willing to move." Caroline paused, tilted her head. Her gaze sharpened on Sadie's. "Are we still talking about your characters?"

Sadie blinked. She'd thought they were. "That point is moot. Sam and I never even got around to discussing where we might live. I never even told him I—"

"That you love him?" Caroline asked softly.

"I never told him and he certainly never told me."

"Well, just for the record, you did a lot of dreaming in college about living in the Big Apple . . . but from what I can see, you don't love city life all that much."

"What? What are you talking about? I love the city. The energy, the excitement, the opportunities."

"Those are clichés. And anyway, you never talk about those things."

Sadie frowned. "Yes, I do."

"No, you don't. You talk about the noisy traffic and the difficulty getting around town. You talk about the outrageous expense of rent and the lack of space for children to play. And you're an optimist! Sometimes I wonder why you were so stoked to settle here after college. Not that I'm complaining—I love having you close by."

She wanted to refute what Caroline said. But she stopped herself. Was that true? She did hate paying so much for a tiny apartment she had to share. As far as opportunities went, her job hardly paid enough to keep her in chocolate chip cookies. She'd had to supplement it with her writing—obituaries and now books. And yes, the traffic was a pain in the patootie.

She thought back to her recent conversation with her mother. While Sadie had been growing up, Mom talked about Manhattan as if it were heaven on earth. But their recent chat had set her straight. Her mom was simply nostalgic about that time of her life.

She'd thought her mother had given up her dream. Had Sadie taken up that aspiration for herself as some sort of lame proxy? Was she living out someone else's dream? "My mom talked about Manhattan with such reverence. I guess maybe I started . . ."

"Viewing it through rose-colored glasses?"

"Something like that."

"I kind of thought that when we talked about it in college. I mean, I love NYC, don't get me wrong. It's home. But even I can see the drawbacks. And you never really struck me as a city person."

Sadie gaped at Caroline. "Really?"

"You always reminisced about your grandpa's ranch like it was the best place on earth. And you're awfully frugal—I see how much it pains you to pay so much for rent. Plus you like to strike up conversations with random strangers. Whenever you do that here, people think you're a freak."

Sadie gave a wry chuckle. "I'm more like a southerner in that way, I guess. I had so many conversations down there with random people, you wouldn't believe it." She smiled just thinking of Nick and Anna, Jared and Roscoe, and Keisha, whose friendship had grown from a random conversation about books. "There's a laid-back vibe down there. People aren't in such a rush. And the beach is so nice. It's quiet and peaceful in the morning, but it comes alive as the sun gets higher in the sky, and then there are people walking and sunbathing and—"

"I was there, remember? I totally get the appeal." Caroline tilted her head as she gazed at Sadie. "You'll never get those things in New York, you know. And you won't find Sam here either."

Sadie straightened in her seat. Pointed a finger at her friend. "*Don't.* Don't do that. He broke up with me. This was his choice."

"Maybe he made a rash decision. Maybe he didn't realize you love him. Maybe there's a reason you can't forget him."

Hope dangled a rope down the deep canyon into which she'd fallen. But fear kept her from grabbing hold. Her adrenaline spiked, making her want to flee instead. "That's a lot of maybes. When he found out about my story, Sam couldn't get out of there fast enough. And what, are you trying to get rid of me? You're making me feel unwanted."

"You know better than that. I just want what's best for you."

If only Sadie could figure out what that was.

Today was the day. Sadie's tight shoulder muscles complained as she sat down to her desk after only six hours of sleep. She'd done nothing but work, eat, and sleep since she'd met with Caroline six days ago. The conversation had loosened something in her. She'd figured out how to make the logistics work for her couple. It seemed so obvious now.

She had to write her heroine's epiphany, then the couple's happily ever after, because she had to finish this manuscript *today.* With school starting Monday there would be no time for rewrites. She'd already let Erin know she'd be receiving a first draft, and she seemed okay with that.

Sadie took three deep breaths. Stress was not her friend. Outside her bedroom window the day was gloomy and overcast, but no rain had fallen yet. She missed the sunny beach and all its delightful smells and sounds.

Enough of that. The clock is ticking.

She glanced back at the screen where a new chapter would begin. She'd somehow made it all the way through the story, from the wedding to the breakup. Her heroine was officially as miserable as Sadie was. At least she'd been able to write the character's pain with total clarity. Because now Sadie not only knew how it felt to fall in love—she also knew what it felt like to lose that love.

The cursor blinked on the blank page. Her heroine needed an epiphany, and Sadie had no idea what it would look like. Stalling for time, and perhaps avoiding the building anxiety, she opened her Facebook newsfeed and scrolled. Maybe she'd find some insight. It was a lie she told herself sometimes.

When she'd been on the island, she friended Sam on social media, so now she saw his occasional posts. A photo of him eating out someplace with Tag. A picture of Hayley pitching a game, the two of them afterward. She searched his face in the photos and read every word he wrote several times as if this made her a part of his life and not a stalker.

Pathetic. She should probably hide his posts and stop tormenting herself. But then she'd never know what he was doing or who he was hanging out with, and somehow that seemed even worse than knowing.

She glanced at the time. She was losing minutes and stalling wasn't putting words on the page. She opened her document again, feeling lost. Sometimes if she just started typing, the words came. She placed her fingers on the keyboard and began the chapter.

After a couple of faulty starts, the words finally began to flow. Her heroine had reached the end of her rope just as Sadie had. She had inner issues to deal with just as Sadie did. Things that kept her single and searching even though deep down she wanted to love and be loved—didn't everybody? Sadie followed the thought on the page, digging deeper, fingers flying. Page after page.

Yes, this was it. Her soul let loose a sigh of relief. This was right for the story.

Her heroine desperately wanted love, but she didn't want to end up like her parents, married and miserable. So she pushed men away. She found fault with each potential suitor. She ended things before they could even begin. She ran away. She sabotaged relationships—including the one she'd had with the hero.

Sadie's fingers stopped cold on the keyboard. Her gaze flew back to the last paragraph. A shiver lifted the hairs on her arms.

That was *her.*

Sadie found fault with every man she'd dated.

Sadie ended things before they'd even begun.

Sadie sabotaged relationships.

Her breath felt caught in her chest. How had she not seen this before? She'd been attracted to Sam right away and she'd bonded with him soon after. But she held him at a distance. Even after realizing she loved him at the wedding, she wanted to run away from the feelings. But Amanda's words had left her shaken. Her admiration for Sam grew by leaps during that conversation. And then she kissed him impulsively.

And what a kiss it was.

Even then she would've run from her feelings. It was only this darned book that made her push through in spite of her fear.

Her desperation drove her toward a story solution—and a real relationship with Sam.

She could now see all the ways fear had driven her behavior.

She'd withheld from Sam that she was borrowing their real-life story for her book. Sabotage. And when he'd broken up with her, she hardly tried to convince him to give her another chance. Not because they lived in separate states—but because she was so afraid to give her heart away. She'd run away.

Far, far away.

Because what if the relationship turned out like her parents'? What if she had to live with that uncertainty again? Sadie's heart thumped like a bass drum in her chest. Her heroine wasn't the only one who'd just had an epiphany.

Rather than stop and sort out her thoughts, she used the momentum to carry her through. She didn't pause until lunchtime when she finished the happily-ever-after chapter. Only the epilogue to go now, and she needed to get it just right. She gulped down a sandwich and went back to work.

She wrote feverishly through the afternoon, losing track of time as the ending played out on the page. She'd already tied up the loose threads of the subplots, but she included newsy details of life several months out from the previous chapter.

Throughout the afternoon an idea formed in the back of her mind. It grew stronger and stronger, pushing her toward *the end.* Rather than envisioning Erin's opinion of the story, she began to imagine Sam's. Because, yes, she wanted him to read it. She wanted him to see what she'd only just discovered about herself. She wanted him to know that she loved him.

More than that—she wanted to tell him in person. Before,

she'd been too afraid to fight for their relationship. Truth be told, she was still scared to death. Her trembling fingers made that clear enough. But this time she was going to push through the feeling.

Because Sam was worth it.

FORTY

Readers will often see your characters' flaws and mistakes long before your characters do.

—*Romance Writing 101*

It was after seven when Sam arrived at his parents' house to hang a mirror for his mom. Dad tended to procrastinate on such endeavors, and his mom wanted it on the wall sometime this decade.

He parked in the drive and entered through the garage door. Looked like Hayley was the only one home. "It's just me," he called.

"What are you doing here?" Hayley asked from somewhere upstairs.

"Hanging a mirror for Mom."

"Have fun with that. I'm going out." His sister trotted down the stairs, a backpack hanging from one shoulder.

"Where are you headed?"

"I'm staying all night with Tara. We're going to start filling out college apps."

He set his toolbox down on the coffee table. "Really? I didn't know you'd made any decisions. Where are you applying?"

"I'm going to start with Pace University, then I'll probably apply at U of SC and Coastal Carolina. They're closer to home and I think I can get a soccer scholarship at CC."

"Isn't Pace in New York?"

"Yeah, Sadie really liked it and she said they did a good job of preparing her to be a teacher."

He blinked. "You're still talking to Sadie?"

"Duh, why wouldn't I? She's awesome." Hayley gathered her purse and backpack and headed toward the door. "See you later."

"Bye."

The door slammed and Sam was left alone with his thoughts. He took his toolbox to the end of the hall where his mom had propped the mirror. She'd marked the appropriate spot on the wall, and he was glad to see the mirror had come with hardware.

He began measuring for placement, thinking about what Hayley had said about keeping in touch with Sadie. It had been a long six weeks since he'd last seen her. He couldn't help but wonder how her book was going. How Rio was doing. And, of course, if she missed him as much as he missed her.

Thoughts of her were eating a hole in his gut. The end of their relationship seemed unresolved somehow. After Amanda's betrayal he'd been left feeling shock and anger. Those feelings eventually faded as hurt and confusion took their place.

But the end of his relationship with Sadie had left him unsettled. And yes, heartbroken. The latter was self-explanatory. The former, not so much.

The garage door opened and a moment later his mom spotted him. "Hi, honey."

"Hey, Mom. How was your day?"

"It was good. I was at the store paying bills. Your dad's stopping for takeout from Franks on his way home. Want me to add your order to ours?"

"That's okay. I have leftovers at the apartment."

She leaned against a doorframe as he marked the wall. "I know I asked you to hang my mirror, but I didn't mean for you to give up your Friday night. You're young and free. You should be out with your friends or something."

"Nah, I'd rather score brownie points with my mom."

She gave him an affectionate smile. "As if you need any."

She kept him company while he worked to hang the mirror. They talked about the business and family, Hayley's choice of colleges. Mom had eaten lunch with Aunt Betty earlier in the day, so she caught him up on news from that side of the family.

At one point he caught sight of her sparkling ring, and of course that made him think of Sadie again. Maybe he was feeling unsettled about their breakup because he'd responded so hastily to her lie by omission. The realization came out of left field and left him feeling even more troubled.

He had overreacted. He hadn't given Sadie the chance to explain. He refused to even consider that she could've had feelings for him *and* also could've been hoping for novel inspiration. Why couldn't both of those things be true?

"Did I lose you somewhere?"

"What? Sorry. I was distracted." And not by the drywall anchor. He placed it and screwed it into the drywall.

"It wasn't really important. But, honey . . . do you want to talk about it?"

"Talk about what?"

She pierced him with a droll look mothers everywhere seemed to have down pat.

Fine, so he was still hung up on Sadie. He hadn't told his parents any more about their breakup than he'd told Hayley.

Not for the first time he wondered how his parents had maintained a solid relationship for so many years. For starters, his mother was a patient woman, as confirmed by her response to his dad's awkward proposal all those years ago. She wasn't perfect either, of course.

"How do you and Dad do it? You must fail each other from time to time. How do you keep that from sinking your relationship?"

"Oh, sweetie, of course we fail each other. Whenever that happens, we each have a responsibility to the other. The one at fault should own up to it. And the one who was wronged should give the other grace."

"You make it sound so simple."

She laughed. "Oh, it's not easy at all. Sometimes I get frustrated when your dad doesn't understand what he did wrong. And sometimes I struggle to give grace when my feelings are hurt. We don't always get it right. But we keep trying." Her gaze sharpened on his face. "What's bothering you? Are you wondering what went wrong with you and Sadie?"

He pressed his lips together. He was starting to figure out exactly what went wrong, and it tweaked his conscience. "I guess after everything that went down with Amanda, I'm having trouble trusting again. Sadie and I broke up because . . . well, she neglected to tell me something. At the time it seemed like a deal breaker. But now I'm wondering if my trust issues got in the way. I think I might've responded poorly."

"Hmm . . ."

"How do you know if you can trust someone?"

"Well, only time can tell you that. Trust is earned when our actions line up with our words. That doesn't mean mistakes aren't made sometimes though."

He placed the second anchor and screwed it in. Sadie had proven herself to be a person of her word. She'd followed through numerous times in their brief relationship. He'd never seen any reason to distrust her—except in that one instance.

His mom cleared her throat. "You know what impressed me most about Sadie? And I didn't even discover it until after you'd broken up."

"What's that?"

She gazed at her new ring, letting the light catch and reflect on the walls around them. "When she found an expensive diamond ring inside a book, she didn't take it to a pawn shop and cash out. She went to a great deal of trouble to track down the owner—someone she'd thought was a stranger."

It was true. He'd had the same thought a time or two. He picked up the mirror and hung it on the wall, then stepped back.

In the mirror his mom gave him a little smile. "That doesn't strike me as something an untrustworthy person would do."

A while later Sam thought about Mom's words on the short drive home. When he got there he heated up leftover pizza and sat down to watch the rest of the Braves game. It wasn't until the first commercial that he checked his phone. No new texts but several emails had come in. Some junk mail and . . .

An email from Sadie with an attached document.

FORTY-ONE

If the romantic relationship in your story does not end happily, then it's not a romance novel.

—*Romance Writing 101*

Sadie's insides were as tangled as a knotted skein of yarn. She clenched the straps of her purse as she navigated the short terminal of the Tucker Island Airport. Her first flight had left LaGuardia at seven this morning, she'd had a layover at Charleston, and now it was after two o'clock. It had been a long day of waiting and wondering.

Because really, she had no assurance that Sam would be happy to see her. For the millionth time since she'd sent him her manuscript last night, she checked her phone for a text or email.

Nothing.

Her stomach sank like a cement block. Well, what had she expected? It would probably take him days to read the story—if he chose to read it at all. And even then, just because she'd had a change of heart didn't mean he would.

Strangely, the thought of losing him for good was now worse than the fear that they could become her parents.

She whispered a prayer for guidance as she turned toward baggage claim and transportation with the small group that had just deplaned. The others seemed excited to have arrived on the island. A young family, clearly here on vacation and in high spirits. An older couple, likely returning home. As for herself, she was a nervous wreck. She'd hardly eaten, unable to stand the thought of food. The tension grew worse as she neared the exit.

She hitched her duffel bag higher on her shoulder. She'd left Rio in Caroline's capable hands, and her return flight was scheduled for tomorrow since she had to be at school Monday. She'd flinched at the cost of the last-minute ticket. But the price of staying home, of doing nothing, seemed so much higher. This was something she had to do in person—no matter the outcome. Her breath felt trapped in her lungs at the thought of baring her soul.

She'd tossed and turned all night in anticipation of seeing him again. Funny, now that the manuscript was finished, her biggest concern wasn't fear of being rejected by Erin and the publishing team.

It was fear of being rejected by Sam.

Tears swam in her eyes. She shook off the negative thought and pushed through the exit door, following a group of travelers. The August heat smacked her in the face. She could feel her careful curls wilting by the second—not to mention her makeup.

She paused, closed her eyes, and drew in a deep breath of air, letting the salt-scented fragrance soothe her. The warm breeze also carried a hint of some sweet-smelling flower that reminded her of the island. The calming effect on her senses slowed her raging pulse.

Okay. One thing at a time. She opened her eyes. She'd have to Uber to Sam's apartment. At LaGuardia there was a line of cabs, but this was hardly LaGuardia.

The sight of a taxi pulling around the drive made her smile. Wonderful. She wouldn't have to wait after all. As it pulled to a stop she approached the vehicle.

When she opened the back door, it fell open so quickly she stumbled backward over the curb. She got her footing and gaped at the person rising from the cab.

"Sam."

His brow furrowed. *"Sadie?"*

She blinked up at him, transfixed.

His lion eyes widened as he took her in. His black hair ruffled in the warm wind. His beard had grown out a bit, making him appear as he had the first time she'd seen him. He looked a little tired but a lot wonderful to her starving eyes.

He'd just arrived at the airport, which begged the question . . . "Are you going somewhere?"

"I was coming to see you."

Her breath released in one relieved puff. "You were?"

"What are you doing here?"

Their gazes tangled. "Coming to see *you.*"

The muscles around his eyes relaxed as his lips tipped up at the corners. "Well."

"I sent my manuscript to you last night, the minute I finished it, but I needed to see you in person." She gazed at him, her heart filling with warmth. "I can't believe you were coming to see me."

"Sadie . . ." He dropped his bag and took her hands. "I read your story. I couldn't stop reading it. I was up all night and I booked a flight this morning. I have questions. But first I have to apologize . . ."

"No, Sam—"

"Let me finish. I reacted rashly when I found out you'd used our story. That was a mistake and I'm sorry for it."

She shook her head. "I shouldn't have used our story without asking."

"And I should've shown you a little grace. I guess I wasn't ready to trust again after Amanda. But you weren't the one who betrayed me with my cousin. I should've given you the benefit of the doubt. I should've heard you out instead of filling in the gaps myself."

She squeezed his hands. "It was my fault, not yours. I should've explained myself. I didn't do it then, but I'm going to do it now." She paused to gather her courage, staring him in the eyes. "I love you, Sam. I realized it way back at the wedding and I can't seem to stop—"

He brushed her mouth with his in a kiss that quickly swept her away. Sadie lost all train of thought. She only cared about the feel of his lips on hers. The feel of his arms slipping around her waist. The feel of his hands gathering her close.

Don't stop.

Her heart heaved a sigh as she sank into his embrace. Oh, how she'd missed him. She'd never thought to find herself in his arms again. The smell of him, the taste of him teased her with tantalizing familiarity.

When at last he drew away, his eyes opened lazily and fixed on her. "I love you too—in case that wasn't obvious enough."

She filled with joy as she swept his lips with her own, unable to contain a smile.

"Hey, buddy," the cabbie called. "You ever gonna shut my door?"

Sam drew back, taking stock of his surroundings. "Oh, sorry." He gave the door a push and joined her on the curb.

"You said you had questions."

"You made me forget them all."

She thought of him reading her manuscript all night and focused in on his tired eyes. "You must be exhausted."

"I've been too nervous about seeing you to feel tired."

"I was nervous about seeing you too."

He palmed her cheek, staring deeply into her eyes. "The end of your story . . . was it the same for you as it was for your heroine? Your fear of us becoming like your parents?"

"It was exactly like that. And I didn't even realize I was doing it until I wrote that scene. It seems I've been running away all my life."

"I know what that feels like. I ran to the island, remember? I'm sorry about your childhood, Sadie. It must've been hard growing up that way."

"I never knew what to expect. The foundation of our family was unstable, and it terrifies me to think of ever living that way again."

He brushed his thumb across her cheek. "And yet you came to see me anyway. Came to tell me you love me. You're very brave, Sadie."

A wry laugh escaped. "I was scared to death."

"That's what makes you so brave."

Her soul stirred at the truth in his words. But honesty compelled her to add, "I'm still afraid."

"So am I, honey. Trusting again is hard for me." He cupped

her chin, his gaze skating over her features. "But you are so worth it, sweetheart."

Her heart turned over in her chest. "I missed you so much, Sam." She never wanted to be without him again. But she would have to leave tomorrow. "What are we going to do?"

"We'll figure it out, one step at a time. For now, how about I show you my apartment? Then I can take you out and we can celebrate." He glanced toward the circle drive, then gave her a sheepish look. "I wasn't thinking before. We should've had the cabdriver take us back."

She chuckled. "I wasn't thinking either."

"How long can you stay?"

"My return flight is tomorrow. I have school on Monday." A smile played on her lips. "Besides, I was afraid you might send me straight back home."

He clutched her tighter. "Not a chance. I'm not letting you get away that easily." Just to make his point, he brushed his lips across hers. Once. Twice. Then Sadie lost all track of time and place once again as he swept her up in his embrace.

EPILOGUE

A romance reader waits the length of a novel for that happily ever after. An epilogue allows her to bask in the couple's bliss for just a moment longer.

—*Romance Writing 101*

The briny air filled Sadie's lungs as she stepped out of Sam's truck and into the night. They'd just had the most wonderful dinner out, and it was a perfect summer evening for sitting under the night sky. As if by silent agreement they walked around the beach house to the deck. The stars twinkled from a black canvas, and a half-moon's reflection glimmered on the ocean's surface.

She glanced at him, taking in his carefully cropped beard and crisp white shirt that glowed in the moonlight. "Dinner was delicious. And you look so handsome in your suit."

His gaze swept over her from head to toe and back. "I can't keep my eyes off you tonight. That dress . . ."

"I'm glad you like it." She didn't mention that Hayley had been the first to spot the red dress. Its halter-style top drew attention to Sadie's newly bronzed shoulders, and the wispy fabric of the short skirt flirted with her legs as she moved.

He took her hand. "Careful in those heels."

"You know me too well."

"I was just telling someone about the first time we met."

"You mean my klutzy trip down your stoop?"

"It was adorable. I think I fell in love with you that instant—I just didn't know it yet."

She laughed. "Well, you sure didn't show it. I thought you took me for a clumsy chatterbox."

"You talk a lot when you're nervous." His mouth eased into a sly grin. "And you must've been very nervous."

"You were so handsome and rugged and broody." She shivered in remembrance.

"Broody?"

"Well, you were."

He squeezed her hand, chuckling.

It felt so good to be with him again. They'd dated long distance through the entire school year, getting to know each other better via FaceTime and long-weekend visits. Sadie had spent her entire Christmas break on the island. Sam had come to New York during her spring break.

They discussed their future often. While Sam was willing to give up his place in the family business, she wouldn't let him do that. She'd come to realize the city wasn't her dream after all.

In fact, her returns to the island had felt very much like coming home.

And thanks to Mrs. Miller's generosity, Sadie had been able to come here for the summer—or at least part of it. After buying the real estate company she'd spent years working for, Mrs. Miller had decided to put retirement on hold. She'd recently put the beach duplex on the market. Sadie happily agreed to keep it in tip-top shape for showings. Although since she'd arrived June third, there'd been only two.

Sadie's parents had loved the island—they'd visited two weeks ago. They were still in counseling and seemed to be doing well. They were determined to work on their issues. Sadie was hopeful they were on their way to a better relationship. The three of them had an honest discussion about Sadie's childhood. Her parents felt terrible about the instability they'd put her through and apologized for hurting her. It had been a tearful but healing night.

Later that week the Fords had them all over to dinner one evening, and the families got along well. Her parents adored Sam, as she'd known they would.

Now Sadie and Sam reached the backyard, and out of habit she headed straight for the Little Library. She would let Rio out after she checked on her books. She'd had precious little time to maintain it recently as she'd been busy writing her second romance novel.

Because, yes, her first book had actually been quite a hit. It hadn't made a big bestseller list or scored a national TV interview, but she'd enjoyed a very successful launch. In only one month the book had earned out, and Rosewood House had already offered her a four-book contract. She had at least a few more romance novels in her.

Sam was right at her side as she opened the door of the library. Though the beach path was lit, the inside of the box remained dark.

"Need a little help?" He shone his phone flashlight, illuminating the full shelves.

"Thanks. I need to put another one of my books in here. I added one the other day but somebody already—Oh. They must've brought it back." Sulking, Sadie pulled it from the top shelf. "Hopefully they didn't hate it."

"I'm sure that's not the case."

"The binding hasn't even been creased. It looks like they didn't even—Huh." She frowned. The cover wasn't lying flat, as if there was something inside. Sadie flipped it open and found—

A ring.

An engagement ring tied somehow to the title page with a white ribbon. She sucked in a breath. Her heart pounded in her chest. She glanced up to find Sam . . .

Kneeling beside her.

Her hand flew to her mouth. "Oh my gosh."

"The last ring you found in that library took us on a journey that led us right here. And I hope this ring will lead us on an even longer journey that takes you everyplace you want to go."

Her eyes filled with tears. She couldn't so much as breathe past the feelings swelling inside.

"Sadie Goodwin . . . I love you more than I ever thought I could love a woman. I've loved you from near and loved you from afar, but I'm ready to have you by my side every day for the rest of my life. I hope you want that too. Will you marry me?"

Sadie dropped down to her knees—mostly because her legs failed. "Oh, Sam, I love you so much. *Yes.* Yes to all that and so much more."

He took her mouth in a kiss that stole the rest of her breath. His arms tightened around her and she threaded her fingers into his lovely hair. This man. She would move across the world to be with him. And even better—she knew he would do the same for her.

It was minutes before they came up for air. As they gazed into each other's eyes, Sadie soaked up his love for her. His was a steady kind of love. He'd proven that over and over during their months together and apart. They'd failed each other a time or two. And they'd talked it out and come to a resolution.

They were not her parents.

She thought of what had just happened and blinked. It still seemed surreal. Her lips ticked up. "I can't believe you proposed with my book. How perfect—how thoughtful."

The ring. She searched for the book, which had fallen to the ground at some point. She grabbed it and opened to the page. She couldn't wait to get that ring on her finger. Her fingers trembled as she worked the ribbon.

"Here, let me." He helped her untie the meticulous knot. "I couldn't bring myself to mutilate your beautiful book."

"What if someone had taken it while we were at the restaurant?"

"I had my mom and dad slip it inside the box when we were leaving the restaurant. They were thrilled to have a role in our big night."

By the time he pulled the ring from the ribbon, they were

sitting side by side on the grass. He held the twinkling marquise diamond set on a silver band and she lifted her hand. It slid easily onto her finger.

She waggled it this way and that under the moonlight. Then she beamed up at him. "It's beautiful. Perfect. I couldn't have chosen better myself."

"I'm glad you like it. But there's one more thing . . ."

She pressed a palm to her chest, releasing a huff. "My heart's already about to leap right out. I don't think I can stand any more."

"Do you think you could stand to live here?"

"Of course. We've already talked about this. I'm happy to move here to be with you. I can find a job at a local school and write during the summers, just like I do in New York."

He kissed her hand, his eyes twinkling in the dark. "No, love, I mean *here*." He glanced up at the house.

She let her gaze follow his, then darted it back to his face. Did he . . . ? Was he saying . . . ?

"I asked Mrs. Miller if she'd put the showings on hold. I'd like for us to buy it. We can rent out the other side and nearly cover the mortgage with rent alone."

She couldn't imagine anything more perfect. She threw herself into his arms. "Oh, Sam, I love that idea. Yes, let's do it." She drew away enough to glance back at the house, then turned and faced him again, beaming. "I love that we'll be living where we first met. Where we fell in love. It just feels so right."

He gave her a lazy grin, affection glittering in his eyes. "Know what else feels right?"

"What's that?"

"You." He slowly brushed her mouth with his. "Us." He kissed her again. "Forever," he said against her lips.

Oh, she did like the way he thought. She couldn't seem to tear her mouth from his for long enough to say it. But that was okay. There would be plenty of time for conversation later.

ACKNOWLEDGMENTS

Bringing a book to market takes a lot of effort from many different people. I'm so incredibly blessed to partner with the fabulous team at HarperCollins Christian Fiction, led by publisher Amanda Bostic: Patrick Aprea, Kimberly Carlton, Caitlin Halstead, Jodi Hughes, Margaret Kercher, Becky Monds, Kerri Potts, Nekasha Pratt, Anna Sudberry, Savannah Summers, Taylor Ward, and Laura Wheeler.

Not to mention all the wonderful sales reps and amazing people in the rights department—special shout-out to Robert Downs!

Thanks especially to my editor, Kimberly Carlton. Your incredible insight and inspiration helped me take the story deeper, and for that I am so grateful! Thanks also to my line editor, Julee Schwarzburg, whose attention to detail makes me look like a better writer than I really am.

I would be remiss if I didn't mention my writer friend Janine Rosche. When brainstorming this story I knew I wanted Sadie to find *something* inside a book that would lead her on a quest. The ring in the hidden compartment was Janine's suggestion. Thank you, Janine, for that inspired idea!

Author Colleen Coble is my first reader and sister of my heart. Thank you, friend! This writing journey has been ever so much more fun because of you.

I'm grateful to my agent, Karen Solem, who's able to somehow make sense of the legal garble of contracts and, even more amazing, help me understand it.

To my husband, Kevin, who has supported my dreams in every way possible—I'm so grateful! To all our kiddos: Chad, Trevor and Babette, and Justin and Hannah, who have favored us with two beautiful granddaughters. Every stage of parenthood has been a grand adventure, and I look forward to all the wonderful memories we have yet to make!

A hearty thank you to all the booksellers who make room on their shelves for my books—I'm deeply indebted! And to all the book bloggers and reviewers, whose passion for fiction is contagious—thank you!

Lastly, thank you, friends, for letting me share this story with you! I wouldn't be doing this without you. Your notes, posts, and reviews keep me going on the days when writing doesn't flow so easily. I appreciate your support more than you know.

I enjoy connecting with friends on my Facebook page: www.facebook.com/authordenisehunter. Please pop over and say hello. Visit my website at www.DeniseHunterBooks.com or just drop me a note at Deniseahunter@comcast.net. I'd love to hear from you!

DISCUSSION QUESTIONS

1. Who was your favorite character and why?
2. If you were asked to write an autobiographical romance novel, what would you title it?
3. Sadie dreamed of being a novelist. Do you have a dream that you're pursuing? Discuss.
4. How did you feel about the epigraphs that opened each chapter? Did you learn anything about writing romance novels? If so, what?
5. Did you feel it was wrong of Sadie to withhold her story's plot from Sam? Why or why not?
6. Sometimes children misconstrue things that happened in their childhood the way Sadie did. Did that happen to you? What resulted from that misunderstanding?
7. Discuss how fear of finding herself in a marriage like her parents' caused Sadie to make poor decisions.
8. Do you think Sam should have forgiven his cousin and Amanda sooner? Discuss.
9. The betrayal in Sam's past affected his ability to trust

others. Has that ever happened to you? What was the result?

10. Sam ran from his reality and Sadie ran from her feelings. Have you ever run from anything? How did that work out?

From the Publisher

GREAT BOOKS

ARE EVEN BETTER WHEN THEY'RE SHARED!

Help other readers find this one:

- Post a review at your favorite online bookseller
- Post a picture on a social media account and share why you enjoyed it
- Send a note to a friend who would also love it—or better yet, give them a copy

Thanks for reading!

The Riverbend Romance Novels

Don't miss the Riverbend Gap romance series from Denise Hunter!

Available in print, e-book, and audio

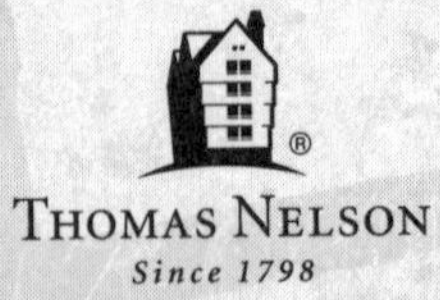

ABOUT THE AUTHOR

Photo by Amber Zimmerman

Denise Hunter is the internationally published, bestselling author of more than forty books, three of which have been adapted into original Hallmark Channel movies. She has won the Holt Medallion Award, the Reader's Choice Award, the Carol Award, the Foreword Book of the Year Award, and is a RITA finalist. When Denise isn't orchestrating love lives on the written page, she enjoys traveling with her family, drinking chai lattes, and playing drums. Denise makes her home in Indiana, where she and her husband raised three boys and are now enjoying an empty nest and two beautiful granddaughters.

DeniseHunterBooks.com
Facebook: @AuthorDeniseHunter
Twitter: @DeniseAHunter
Instagram: @deniseahunter